RANKIN INLET

A NOVEL

RANKIN INLET

A NOVEL

Mara Feeney

GP

GABY PRESS
FIDDLETOWN, CA

Published by Gaby Press, Fiddletown, California
For additional copies visit www.gabypress.com

The front cover art, painted on plywood in the early 1960s by Nauya, is used with permission of the owner, Jean Williamson of Saskatoon, Saskatchewan, as well as Nauya's relatives living in Rankin Inlet, Nunavut. The back cover photograph was taken in Rankin Inlet in 1993 by Sally Luttmer of Calgary, Alberta. Interior line drawings were created by Marilyn Duffey of San Francisco, California. The author photograph on the back cover was taken by Shawn Clark of Colorado Springs, Colorado. Book cover and interior were designed by Nancy Webb Graphic Design, Oakland, California.

This is a work of fiction, although it draws on ethnographic research, as well as the author's experiences living and working in the Northwest Territories and visiting Nunavut. Names, characters, places, and incidents in this novel are a product of the author's imagination or are used fictitiously, and any resemblance to actual incidents, locales, or persons (living or dead) is entirely coincidental.

LCCN: 2008909265
ISBN: 978-0-9819319-5-1

Publisher's Cataloging-in-Publication Data

Feeney, Mara.

Rankin Inlet : a novel / Mara Feeney.

p. cm.

ISBN 978-0-9819319-5-1

1. Nunavut—Fiction. 2. Northwest Territories—History—20th century—Fiction. 3. Indigenous peoples—Fiction.

PS3606.E363 R36 2009
813—dc22   2008909265

Printed in the United States of America

10 9 8 7 6 5 4 3 2 1

Dedication

To all of the Nunavummiut
but particularly the Kappi family
and especially my angajuk Leonie

Turaaqtitaujuq

Tamainnut nunavummiunut
piluaviktumit Kaapikkut ilagiinut
ammalu angajumnut Leonie-mut

ᑐᕋᖅᑎᑕᐅᔪᖅ

ᑕᒪᐃᓐᓄᑦ ᓄᓇᕗᒥᐅᓄᑦ
ᐱᓗᐊᕕᒃᑐᒥᑦ ᑳᐱᒃᑯᑦ ᐃᓚᒌᓄᑦ
ᐊᒻᒪᓗ ᐊᖓᔪᒻᓄᑦ ᓕᐅᓂᒧᑦ

CONTENTS

AUTHOR'S NOTE

The language of the Inuit is so intertwined with life in the Arctic and the ways of the people who live there that I could not write this book without using some Inuktitut words and phrases. For those not familiar with the language, the look of all those q's and vowels can be daunting.

The first time an Inuktitut word appears, it is shown in italics. My advice to the reader is to try to read through the paragraphs without getting stuck on words that may seem very foreign. Hopefully, their meanings can be guessed from the context, but a glossary of Inuktitut words is also provided at the end of the book.

I have tried to use spellings for Inuktitut words that are consistent with ICI Standardized Orthography. This means the only vowels used in Inuktitut words are u, i and a. For English language speakers, 'u' is pronounced like 'oo' and 'i' is pronounced like a long 'e.' Thus, the word *iglu* is pronounced "eegloo." The 'a' is pronounced like a short 'a' in English (as in the word 'apple'), and a double vowel would be held a bit longer. Thus, the common Inukitut words for mother and father—*anaana* and *ataata*—would be pronounced "anahna" and "atahta."

Many thanks to Leonie Kappi, Mick Mallon, Alexina Kublu, and Shirley Tagalik for their help with Inuktitut dialects, spelling, and translation issues.

PART I

KEEWATIN

ALISON 1
Liverpool, England
March 15, 1970

I feel daft—a grown woman writing to her damn diary, like a schoolgirl.

I kept a diary when I was a teen, but it was mostly besotted rubbish—lovesick daydreams about dating a Herman's Hermit.

But soon I will be moving far, far away from here, to a place where I don't know a soul. I fear I may go mad without someone to talk to, living all by myself in an Eskimo village in the frozen north. I think I shall need this diary. I hope it will be more than a place for depressed musings, perhaps the record of a Grand Adventure, as many Brits and Scots have had before me—the ones with dim futures at home who signed on as traders or missionaries to explore the Arctic.

Canada needs nurse-midwives to work in the remote communities, so you'd think they would teach midwifery in their own nursing schools, but they don't. Instead, they come to Europe to recruit trained midwives. They made me an offer I could not refuse, with terms much better than anything a new graduate can expect here nowadays. It includes generous pay, with an annual "isolation" bonus. Even my room and board is covered. I've signed on for two years, and then, who knows? Perhaps I will take all the money I will have saved by then and travel on to New Zealand or Australia, or somewhere warm like that, where I might find handsome fellows who speak English.

I've come back to Liverpool to say my goodbyes, which has not been easy. I feel badly about leaving Nancy behind, but I can't go carting my little sister to the back of beyond. She wouldn't be able to stay with me at the nursing facility, and who knows what kind of schools they have in the Arctic? It was her bad luck to be born last in our family. She will have to learn to deal with Mum and Dad, just as I did. They are not cruel, just disappointing at times, and boring as sod. I told Nancy she must work hard at school, and above all else do not get pregnant like Lydia did, then perhaps she will be lucky like me and win a scholarship to go to school in London, or somewhere away from here. It would save her life.

I have always felt as if the stork dropped me down the wrong chimney, into that cramped terrace house near the city centre. I could never decide which was worse—the depressing ranks of red brick houses with the odd gap left over from the war, or the anonymous high-rise blocks the government built to re-house people and "improve" the neighbourhood.

There were already four wee children in that home on Scottie Road when I arrived, and Nancy was still to come after me. Mum was our caregiver, and she became more and more of a martyr, as Dad began drinking more heavily. Without him around much to give them a good cuffing, my brothers ran wild. My sisters were better behaved, but where has it got them. Lydia eventually married and moved to Edinburgh, Marion's gone to the nunnery, and poor Nancy is still in school, dreaming.

It is hard to believe that Liverpool was once the most prosperous city in the whole world, grown rich from trading sugar and cotton from the Indies. You'd never guess it now. It feels like a dying place. My brothers wanted to work at the docks like Dad, even though he complains about having to cross the water to Birkenhead now. But shipping has declined so much, there are no new jobs to be had. Seamus and Pete consider themselves very lucky to have found assembly work at the new Ford plant out in Halewood. So, when they are not on strike, they are building Escorts. Seamus even drives one now, though Pete is too fond of his Mini to give it up. They migrate like zombies from the plant to the pub or a football match, and then home to their flats that smell of sour milk, wet diapers, and chip fat.

That could have been my life, too, but I got away to London and saw a different sort of world altogether. I didn't realize just how clannish we were, until I had my eyes opened by what was going on in Soho and Chelsea in the 60's. You could actually feel the vibes of creativity and innovation around you. You could smell freedom and experimentation and dope in the air. There were young people from all over the world gathering there, and the world was looking to us as the leaders of trends and fashions. It was a funny mix of optimism and hedonism. At first I was startled by people my family would have branded as dodgy, but eventually I relaxed a bit, and even bought a miniskirt. I worked hard at school, but I learned to cut loose at the weekend. A bunch of us would gather to watch Ready Steady Go on Friday nights, and we'd be so excited after seeing the Beatles or the Rolling Stones or Manfred Mann play that we would have to go out dancing til the wee hours at the Bag O' Nails or the Ad Lib, if we could find someone to pay our way. Those were fun times, daring times. People like Twiggy shouted it is okay to be different and to explore new values, rather than be bound up in archaic ways of thinking.

Mixing with new people opened my mind. I realized I did not want to live in Liverpool again. And I quit being Catholic. I could not come up with a good defence of some of the cornerstones of the faith (immaculate conception, infallibility of the pope), and I got tired of others sniggering at me when I would say that you just have to have faith and believe these things. Why, they would ask, insistently, and I began to wonder myself.

Religion is just not important to me any more, and some moments I think it is all a lot of poppycock. But the announcement that I no longer consider myself Catholic was like dropping a bomb on the family. I've never seen my parents get such a cob on. Perhaps I should have kept my mouth shut about it, but that would be living a lie. I could ask for forgiveness, but I don't feel I have done anything wrong.

Mum and Dad barely speak to me now. Even my brothers and their wives give me swift pecks on the cheek—just air kisses really, no more heartfelt hugs. None of them seem able to look me straight in the eye, as if they are afraid they might glimpse the devil inside me. They have not even asked when I might be coming back. Goodbye and good riddance to you, too, then.

If only I were brave enough to sever all ties—just go and start a new life all my own. But when Nancy clung to me and cried, I broke down and promised her that I would write.

I am to be posted to a place called Rankin Inlet, Northwest Territories, an Eskimo village with a few hundred inhabitants, located on the west coast of the Hudson Bay, roughly halfway between Manitoba's northern border and the Arctic Circle. The recruiter offered me a choice: Rankin Inlet in the eastern Arctic, or a place in the western part of the Territories called Bison Passage, which is inhabited by an Indian tribe. At first I was leaning toward the west, as I thought there would be more trees there and a warmer climate. But then the fellow came clean and told me that there had not been a natural death in Bison Passage for over a decade. It is all hunting accidents and truck crashes and murders and suicides. That frightened me, so I decided to take my chances with the Eskimos and chose Rankin Inlet.

I am saying goodbye to my childhood friends and school chums, sorting out my belongings to decide what to give to Nancy and what to sell, etc. Like an astronaut, I have begun to count down the days until departure, with a mix of excitement and trepidation.

ALISON 2
Rankin Inlet, Northwest Territories
March 28, 1970

I left home last Tuesday before first light. It was a gloomy, misty morning, which helped me to think I would never miss Liverpool. I paid for a taxi to Lime Street Station, as no one offered to drive me down, and I had too much baggage for the bus. It took about three hours to reach London Euston, where I was able to take the tube to Heathrow. I caught an afternoon flight from London to Toronto, then another flight from Toronto to Winnipeg. I slept at an airport hotel there, and the next morning I boarded a small plane that flew from Winnipeg through a series of small communities tucked away among pine trees, until we finally reached a town called Churchill, an old military base and shipping port on the south shore of the Hudson Bay. The government had arranged for a hotel room and meal vouchers in the town for me, as I was to attend an orientation program there before travelling on to Rankin Inlet.

The cabbie who picked me up at the airport was a taciturn native fellow, who peeked at me in the rear-view mirror, but would answer my questions only with grunts. He dropped me off at a very plain building with a large plate glass window that was covered with some kind of reflective material, above which a painted sign creaked in the wind, announcing that I had arrived at the Polar Bear Inn. I checked in and had my evening meal, the Polar Bear special of the day, which was moose steak with peas, mashed potatoes, and gravy. I was too full to do the pudding, even though I was curious to know what a Saskatoon pie might be.

Dusk was falling and I was feeling completely thrashed after my long trip, but I decided to take a walk around the town before turning in. I have never seen a place like Churchill, Manitoba. So desolate. Streets littered with clumps of dirty snow, and the many abandoned army buildings giving it the look and feel of a ghost town. All under the shadow of an oversized port building whose cranes and chutes look like gangly arms waiting to load grain onto foreign ships in the summertime.

The town is perched right at the edge of the "tree line," where massive slabs of flat grey rock poke out of the snow everywhere you look, with runty pine and spruce trees growing out of their fissures. The stunted trees appear to lean drunkenly on one another for support. Where there is not pale grey rock there is paler grey ice—great frozen slabs of it piled along the shore of the Hudson Bay. I stood listening to the ice creaking and groaning, imagining the ancient voices of lost seamen, until I realized that my own exhaled breath was coating my eyelashes in frost.

I turned back toward the town and suddenly saw a splash of neon shining out from among a row of uniform metal Quonset huts. As I got closer, I saw that the neon letters spelled "Aurora Borealis." There was a Moosehead beer sign bolted onto the door, and I could hear a jukebox playing inside. Just then two men in their thirties came strolling along between the grey buildings, their breath sending up two parallel plumes of vapour to mark their progress. "Hello, love, are you new in town?" one of them inquired. I said I was, and I asked what exactly the Aurora Borealis was. "Well, it's the northern lights, of course," one man replied. "Don't be stupid—she means our pub here," said the other.

They told me the Aurora Borealis was a private club for the government workers who are stationed in Churchill, but they invited me in as their guest. I thought there could be no harm in having a beer, and I had many questions about this outpost that I hoped they might be able answer for me.

The fellows introduced themselves as Bruce and Gordy. Bruce worked for Social Services and Gordy worked for the Department of Public Works. I told them I was a nurse headed for Rankin Inlet. They hooted and rolled their eyes and said I was in for an adventure. They said that I was younger and better looking than most of the nurses they'd seen heading to settlements in the far north. "With that red hair, blue eyes, freckles, and that slim build of yours—they'll have to lock you up in your room at night to keep the rogues at bay," they laughed.

The men told me that Churchill is the government headquarters for administration of the Keewatin Region, which stretches from the Manitoba border to the Arctic Circle. The region includes Rankin Inlet and six other small communities with exotic names like Eskimo Point, Whale Cove, and Coral Harbour. It seemed odd to me that they would administer a big chunk of the Northwest Territories from an outside province, and I said so, but Gordy replied that no one would want to live any further north. Churchill is the limit for most people, he said—cold, and isolated, and lacking enough in the amenities of a civilized society. "They don't call it the Barrenlands or the Barren Grounds up there for nothing," Bruce added.

Then they teased me and said I must be prescient, as the Government of the Northwest Territories recently announced plans to move the regional headquarters up north to Rankin Inlet. There is no set timetable for the move, but it is expected to happen sometime in the next few years. According to the men, this announcement has destroyed the civil servants' morale. Everyone is threatening to quit their jobs and move back south. A half-stewed patron further down the bar chipped in with his two cents' worth. "The natives want autonomy—just let 'em try running things themselves," he slurred, with a tone that implied of course they would fail.

Bruce and Gordy invited me to join them at a going-away party for a fellow civil servant, a senior administrator who was one of the first to flee, but I declined. They insisted on escorting me back to my hotel, however, warning me about the perils of drunken natives and wild polar bears. I wasn't sure if they were kidding or not.

I collapsed onto the hotel bed in my travel clothes and slept like the dead until my morning wake up call. I brushed my teeth and took a glorious hot shower, then went downstairs and had the Polar Bear Inn breakfast special—a plate of greasy eggs and bacon with limp white toast and pitiful jelly that was nothing more than sugared gelatine. I felt a pang of missing Mum's homemade scones with currant jam.

At nine o'clock, a car came around and picked me up to take me to the place where I was to have my orientation. When I arrived, I was ushered into the office of a heavy man with a ruddy complexion, who was dabbing perspiration from his brow, though the room was none too warm. He shook my hand and introduced himself as Dick Smithers. Smithers apologized and told me that the person in charge of providing orientations for new nurses was out on leave due to a sudden family emergency, and the backup staff person was on maternity leave. Given the uncertainties surrounding when either of these parties might return to work, he thought it unwise to detain me in Churchill indefinitely. Besides, the government offices would be closed tomorrow in observance of Good Friday. He advised me to travel ahead to Rankin Inlet, and get my orientation on the job. He said I would not be working alone. There are two other nurses there, and both have had considerable northern experience, so they would be able to help me out more than he could. Besides, he pointed out, scheduled flights to Rankin Inlet were few and far between, and there happened to be one departing that afternoon.

I agreed to go, but asked what sort of things one would typically learn in an orientation program. He said he was no expert, but he believed it covered such topics as how to cope with the stress of working long hours of overtime and having your leave denied in times of medical emergencies. Also coping with foreign cultural beliefs about illness and healing practices, or even about seeking treatment at all. And getting used to the level of violence in remote communities. I asked what he meant by violence. He flushed and said: "Oh, you know, fights, stabbings, booze brawls, rape, murder, and so on."

Perhaps Smithers was an engineer or an architect, because he pulled out a diagram of the Rankin Inlet Nursing Station, to show me proudly that it was a state-of-the-art northern health facility, with three examination and treatment rooms, four private beds for longer term care, a community meeting room for classes or lectures, a large walk-in supply closet, living quarters with three separate bedrooms, a laundry, etc. Then he suggested I better hurry if I wanted to catch that plane to Rankin Inlet.

I stood up to go, and asked Smithers what his main bit of advice to me would be. He said every northern nurse should always think in terms of triage: try to sort out which patients we can treat right there, even if it means being a bit creative or extrapolating from what we have been taught to do, and which ones are in such dire condition that we will not be able to fix them with our limited resources. These patients we should arrange to have flown out as soon as possible for treatment in the bigger clinics and hospitals in Manitoba, keeping in mind how costly this would be to the taxpayers. With that, he wished me the best of luck and led me by the elbow to the door.

His secretary had already called a cab for me, and it was that same cheerless native driver, which made me wonder if he had the only cab in town. The fellow looked a bit more haggard, as if he had not slept or shaved since our last encounter. He drove me to the Polar Bear Inn, where I hurriedly packed my things and checked out. Then he drove me back out along the lonely road to the airport.

The day was cold and overcast, with an odd layer of white fog hovering a few meters above the ground. When I went to check in for the flight to Rankin Inlet I learned that, because of that fog, all flights were on hold. The agent explained that the northern navigational system is spotty and temperamental, so bush pilots must rely on their vision to get where they want to go.

I spent several hours sitting around the terminal, reading a Vogue magazine that I'd picked up in the Winnipeg airport, waiting for the fog to lift. There was no cafeteria of any kind in the terminal, but the agent had some thick coffee with tinned milk and a limited selection of candy bars available for purchase. It was just me, the agent, and a handful of Eskimos in the waiting room. There was a young family consisting of a mother and a father with their three young children and a wee baby. In addition, there were eight teenaged boys all wearing navy blue knit shirts, perhaps from some kind of a private school. The young men drew my attention like a magnet. I hoped my eyes were not popping out of my head, but I was very surprised to find them so attractive. Perhaps I've read too many books about spear hunters dressed from head to foot in fur clothing, because I was shocked to see these young Eskimo men wearing blue jeans and leather jackets and fringed suede vests and cowboy boots, snapping their gum in synch with the rock and roll music bouncing from their transistor radios and cassette players. They were smart and trim and sexy, and would have fit right in at any pub in Liverpool. They did not look like they were going home to live in skin tents or igloos. They had suitcases and backpacks, and bags of small appliances that clearly were going to require electricity: clock radios, coffee percolators, toaster ovens, and hair dryers. It seemed like enough stuff to set up a small department store wherever they were headed.

The two older adults would smile and nod at me in a friendly manner whenever our eyes met. They made me feel welcome and comfortable somehow, even though they could not speak a word of English. It occurred to me that I must learn to speak some of the local language, if I am ever to work with these people effectively.

The mother was wearing a beautiful embroidered white wool parka with a roomy pouch that allowed her to carry her baby on her back. She wore a colourful cord belt tied round her waist to prevent the baby's legs from slipping down. The baby had rosy red cheeks and the shiniest black eyes, filled with curiosity and awe about everything around it. The mother walked round and round the terminal, rocking the baby on her back until it finally fell asleep.

The two wee girls, with very runny noses, knelt backwards on their hard plastic chairs to get a good stare at me—as if I were the best entertainment around. They were wearing some type of long traditional dresses made from bright floral print cotton, with colourful ribbon sewn around the hems and cuffs. Like their parents, they wore hand-made sealskin boots that made a pleasant scuffing sound when they pattered around the terminal. The little boy was dressed in store-bought corduroy pants and black leather cowboy boots, but had a wool duffle parka with fur around the hood that looked home made, with hand-embroidered animals on the back and pockets. He had a terrible rattling cough, but he kept himself amused by yanking at the knobs on the cigarette vending machine.

Finally, a handsome and fit looking young man with pale green eyes and curly brown hair strolled into the terminal. His neat wool trousers and brown leather jacket were quite a contrast to the podgy freight agent's stained tweed coveralls. He spoke briefly with the agent, who then turned and announced that Wayne was a bush pilot who would be taking a charter to Rankin Inlet just as soon as the fog broke. He was taking a small load of perishable freight, like eggs and lettuce, for the Hudson Bay Company store, and he was concerned about taking off as soon as possible, before the goods froze solid in his cargo hold. He also had a dozen Easter lily plants on board, which would be useless to the store after the weekend.

Wayne's twin-engine plane had four seats plus the co-pilot seat available, so if passengers wanted to go along with him, rather than wait for the commercial flight, which might well be cancelled since it was getting so late in the day, they could do so. I jumped at the chance to ride up front, and it was decided that the Eskimo family could squeeze into the four passenger seats, with the two girls sharing a seat. The teenaged boys would have to wait and fly together at a later time.

Within half an hour, we were in the air at last, on the way to Rankin Inlet. As we flew north, I could see the puny trees grow weaker and thinner and ever more stunted, until they vanished altogether. From there on out, the land looked flat and white and endless, with lots and lots of frozen lakes and grey rock slabs dusted with ice and snow.

Wayne asked me why I was going to Rankin Inlet, and he seemed pleased to learn that I was a nurse coming to work there. He said the place needs all the help it can get. There is no doctor in the community, so if anyone gets really sick, they have to be flown out to Churchill or Thompson or Winnipeg, which of course is good for his company's business. I asked how he knew so much about the community. He told me he is originally from Saskatchewan but has been living up north for almost a year now, in a house owned by the airline company that employs him. He said Rankin Inlet is a small place, so all the outsiders get to know each other well and party together regularly, except that the nurses seem a bit standoffish and tend to stick to themselves more. (I wondered why that would be—perhaps some awkwardness having to do with confidential patient information? It might be hard to chitchat with someone whom you knew had an undescended testicle or an unsightly patch of psoriasis somewhere). He promised to get me invited to such a party in the near future. It became difficult shouting over the roar of the airplane engines, so I sat back and watched the clouds, trying to imagine the place I was going to.

Finally the plane began to circle and descend. At first I couldn't see anything but white and more white, as there was light snow blowing sideways across the windows and along the earth below, but soon I began to pick out a pattern of buildings—a couple of Quonset huts, a few large wooden warehouse buildings, two tiny churches with short steeples, and then perhaps a hundred houses whose pastel hues peeked out from behind the banked snow. We taxied up to a small metal shack bearing a painted sign that said "Welcome/Bienvenue: Rankin Inlet International Airport."

Wayne had radioed ahead to request that the Settlement Manager come meet us at the airstrip, so he could deliver me and my bag to the Nursing Station. As we were exiting the plane, three vehicles arrived in a convoy. One was the Hudson Bay Company's panel truck, with two young men intent on unloading the store freight as quickly as possible. The second was a Jeep driven by a man with a bushy beard and a navy blue parka trimmed with fox fur around the hood (this was the Settlement Manager, Ian MacKenzie). The third vehicle was a beat up old van with faded blue paint and a handwritten cardboard "Taxi" sign taped onto a window. The Eskimo family got into that one. Ian shook my hand, grabbed my bag, and gave me a brief tour of the community, which did not take long, as there are hardly any roads for a vehicle to drive on. Darkness was falling fast, so streetlights were twinkling by the time he dropped me off at the Nursing Station. He rang the bell, and when the door was answered, he pushed my bag inside, said goodbye, and hurried off.

"Thank god you've arrived," the thin, elderly woman who answered the door said to me. "Come along, we can deal with your gear later. Right now I need your help." She led me down the glossy linoleum corridor to a room that contained a hospital bed that looked as if it had been recently abandoned. She said that the native staff had not shown up for work and she needed me to change the sheets on the bed, so it would be ready for the next patient, as Easter weekend was upon us and you never knew what might happen. I thought changing bed linens an odd introduction to my nursing career in Rankin Inlet, but I did what she asked me to do.

As I worked, the woman introduced herself as Elizabeth Bauer, Head Nurse and Manager in charge of the Rankin Inlet Nursing Station. She said she has been here for almost three years, but she has worked in various communities around northern Canada for more than a decade. She cursed the staff assistant who failed to show up for work, and then went on a tirade about the natives in general. They are filthy and have no instinctual knowledge of hygiene and public health, she said. They take no precautions to prevent disease. When they become ill, they won't take their medications or follow instructions. Venereal disease, birth rates sky high, children with head lice, babies sucking on empty bottles caked with muck...

I worked on in silence. When I was done she asked me to put the sheets into a black plastic trash bag. Then she advised me to wash my hands thoroughly, commenting that the last patient to use that bed had died of hepatitis.

"What?! Why didn't you tell me that beforehand?" I gasped.

"Because I needed someone to change the sheets," she replied coolly. "Oh, come on, it's not that contagious," she added when she saw the look on my face. "Just be sure to wash your hands well."

I did. Then she led me down another corridor to a door with a "Private" sign on it that led to the nurses' living quarters, which has an open living/dining area with kitchen facilities off to the side, and several private bedrooms. She tapped on a closed door, then opened it to introduce me to Sherry Dunlop, a rather chubby woman a few years older than me who looked a bit depressed. She explained that the three of us would now constitute the entire full-time staff at the station. Sherry glanced up, said hullo, then went right back to reading her paperback novel. Friendly sort, I thought.

Nurse Bauer then showed me my room, which is equipped with a single bed, a bureau, a desk, and an upholstered chair with a floor lamp next to it. There is nothing on the walls to cheer or cover up the institutional mint green paint.

Nurse Bauer said I am to help myself to any food in the kitchen. Sometimes the staff takes their meals together, but more often everyone fixes a meal or a snack for themselves whenever they feel like it. There is a list on the Frigidaire where we are to write down anything we desire from the store, and the day staff will go over to the Bay to fetch it, or have it flown in from Churchill, if necessary.

I am to have the weekend off, as the nursing station is closed for the Easter holiday, and Nurse Bauer and Sherry had divided emergency call duty between them, as they had not been informed when I would be arriving. She suggested I relax and rest up from my travels, as I am expected to start work Monday morning at 7:30 a.m. sharp.

Before closing the door, Nurse Bauer warned me that I will see it all here—not just birthing and your garden variety fevers and infections, but tuberculosis, hepatitis, encephalitis, all manner of bronchial diseases, gunshot and stab wounds, mental illness, murder, and suicides.

The latch snapped to with her warnings still ringing in the air.

NIKMAK 1
Rankin Inlet Nursing Station
October 11, 1970

Ayaiyaiyaaa.

Kublukuluk, paniga, daughter of my flesh, my sweetest child, joy of my days, this is your ataata speaking. I feel a pain so deep and sharp, it must be yours, the very pain you suffer. It is as fierce and piercing as the Keewatin wind.

How I envy you that sleep beyond sleep, while I endure these sharp stabs that slash at my heart, my belly, my brain. If I could drum and drum and drum like old Tautunngi, I know it would bring some relief. Perhaps the drumming would seep down into you where you could hear it, where you could listen to the rhythm of your ancestors, hear their song of survival. The beating of the drum might also chase the dark spirits from this white, white room.

But that nurse with the big nose has forbidden drumming in this place. "Old man—this is a place of healing, you must not disturb our quiet," she said to me. She does not know any better. She does not know how you need to hear the sounds of your own people, the voices of loved ones calling you back to us, reaching for you with *Inuktitut* words. So I sit here and rock, forth and back, on this hard chair next to your bed, softly singing the old songs to you and speaking Inuktitut to you. Softly, softly, so as not to disturb her and the other *Qablunaat*. Aiyayayeah.

Tukisinngittunga—I don't understand, yet I do understand, how this could have happened to you. You have walked around in a thick fog of sadness these past few months, ever since that plane crash.

When the baby was born, you were so ecstatic. I have never seen you happier, Kublu. Like a good daughter, you gave your first-born to your *anaana* and me to raise. Even though, for now, you live under our roof, so you lost nothing. We all gained that child.

I beg you: do not leave us, Kublu. The baby still needs you. Your anaana's breasts are dry. There is the bottle, with that milk powder from the Bay, but it is not the same—surely that white dust cannot grow a person. If you should die, they will hear your anaana's keening from the north pole to Winnipeg. I cannot even imagine the hole that would be left in my home without your spirit in it.

Your brothers, Sakku and Ivaluk, they need you, too, Kublu. Who will sew their *kamiit*, now that your anaana's teeth are worn flat to the gums and her eyesight is fading?

Your anaana does not dare to come down to this place. The last time she did, the nurses told her she had some foul disease. They flew her to the hospital in Churchill, then to some town even further south, and they kept her there for many months. She has that constant cough again, but she is afraid to come near here. She does not want to risk being wrenched away from her home like that again. My *nuliaq* can be hard headed—more so as the years go by, it seems. She would rather spit into that coffee can night and day than see a doctor. She clings to your baby, Kublu, trying to distract him, and herself, from missing you.

They say you drank liquor at that *Qablunaaq* party, then left without a word to anyone. The others thought you had gone home. But Ivaluk found you in the morning, on a snow bank not far from the bay, lying on your right side, as if you were just resting and admiring the view of the sun coming up over the boats frozen into the harbour. The fox fur around your hood clacked with icicles as he lifted you and carried you to this place, your nose black with frostbite.

They say it is a wonder you survived at all, a miracle you did not freeze to death, given how cold it was last night. They say you are in a coma now, sleeping very deeply. I ask when you will awaken. They say they do not know. They say I must be patient. They say just wait, just wait and see.

I am going to sing to you now, while you sleep this deep sleep. I will sing to the rhythm of your shallow breaths, calling you back home to us. I don't know what else to do. I close the door and sing softly, gently.

Aya-aya-ayayaaa.

IAN 1
Rankin Inlet, Northwest Territories
March 31, 1970

RE: Monthly Report to Keewatin Regional Headquarters, Churchill, Manitoba

After a relatively quiet start to the year (mostly due to the blizzards and magnetic storms precluding flights in January and February), there were a lot of arrivals and departures in March. We had two deaths (one natural, one suicide by shotgun) and three births, duly recorded by the RCMP. We gained and lost our new social worker in the same week, as he did not find the accommodations that were offered up to snuff, so he took the next plane out. Our Nursing Station staff expanded, with the addition of an attractive young lady from England, God help her. Two students from the north of Sweden hitched a ride up here on the mail plane. I don't know where they thought they would lay out their sleeping bags or take their meals, as there is no youth hostel or hotel here. I sent them over to the government-run Transient Centre, where someone took pity on them and let them have temporary accommodations in exchange for doing some work around the place.

A community organizer of some sort skidooed up here last week from Whale Cove and is billeting with a local family. He looks like trouble, so I shall keep an eye on him and do my best to make him feel unwelcome.

An American C-141 landed here last Friday, with fifty or sixty men in military gear on board. The airport manager was out hunting at the time, as we were not expecting any scheduled flights, so I went out to the landing strip myself when I heard the huge plane circling. The commander shook my hand and announced that he had arrived to conduct some kind of cold climate training exercises. I asked under what authority, and he alluded to some vague agreement between the U.S. military forces and DIAND but could not seem to produce any relevant paperwork. It was too late to reach anyone in Churchill and I had no idea who I might call in the capital at Yellowknife. The last thing I want is to have a pack of Americans accountable to no one prowling around this settlement in search of after-hours entertainment, so I told the commander I could not accept his mission here, and suggested he fly on up to Coral Harbour, where there is an excellent airstrip and more appropriate facilities at the old DEWline base. At first he was most unhappy with me and looked as if he might try to throw his weight around, but when I mentioned the heated bunkhouse with showers and a bar and movie theatre up there, he agreed that might be a more appropriate setting for his mission. For future reference, please inform me of any protocol I am supposed to follow in such instances.

Ian MacKenzie, Settlement Manager

ALISON 3
Rankin Inlet, Northwest Territories
April 1, 1970

April Fool's Day, and I am beginning to wonder if I have made the right decision, or if I am simply a bloody fool, adrift in this new sea of faces in an unfamiliar landscape. I am the last person on this planet I would expect to suffer "homesickness," unless that can be defined as growing sick of home. But here I sit, feeling utterly alone in this tiny hamlet north of nowhere. I've met a handful of people—Wayne Dupont, Ian MacKenzie, Elizabeth Bauer, Sherry Dunlop, and some of the native patients. But I can't claim to know any of them, and they know very little about me. And with my plan to forget my own past, what is there to know about me, anyway?

I sent a postcard to Liverpool, letting them know I had arrived and how they can reach me, should they need to.

On Saturday, I donned my denim pants and government-issue parka and took a walk around the community. I felt completely conspicuous. Children would peek at me from around the houses or from behind the snowmobiles, smiling and giggling, and occasionally calling out words I could not understand. Adults stared at me from the windows of the homes as I walked past.

I quickly learned that my footwear is totally inadequate for this place, so I went down to the Hudson Bay Company when it opened, to buy a pair of sturdy boots. An Eskimo woman was emerging from the store as I arrived. She was wearing a traditional parka made from shaved caribou skins, embroidered in bright colours around the edges, with a bulge on the back for carrying a baby. There was a baby in the pouch and another small child holding her right hand. In her left hand she held a bright yellow shopping bag that proclaimed: "Wise shoppers shop at the Bay!" Yet there seems to be no alternative here.

There were swarms of people inside the store. Some were shopping, but most were simply socializing. All heads turned to look me over, and soon I had a pack of children following me, watching me as I tried on boots. I learned my first words in the native language, as they kept asking me over and over: *"Kinauvit—what's your name?"* They would giggle when I replied, and they scattered briefly when I asked them back: "Kinauvit?"

A schoolteacher introduced herself to me as Janet Weber and welcomed me to the community. She had overheard the kids and explained to me that "kinauvit" is translated as "what's your name?" but it literally means "Who are you?" "There are no strangers in this town, no accidental visitors," she said. "They are curious to know what you are doing here. Tell them you are a *najannguaq*, a nurse, then they will be satisfied."

The next time I heard "Kinauvit?" I turned and faced the kids and said "Alison. Najannguaq. Najannguaq Alison." This time they did not giggle or scatter like birds. Their eyebrows arched upward over their mischievous brown eyes as they studied me, taking full measure of me. "Iiiiiiii," they whispered as they nodded their heads, seeming mesmerized by my speaking a few words of their language. Then they scurried off to tell the adults what they had learned about me.

I toured through the grocery section, past stacks of boxed potato chips and biscuits, towers of corned beef and Spam, boxes of Red River cereal and tea, and endless tins of evaporated milk. I was curious to see what kind of fresh produce might have made it this far north. There were the iceberg lettuces and eggs that Wayne had delivered, but little else other than some brownish celery and carrots, and a few apples and oranges. Children with runny noses would pick up an apple or an orange and suck it for a few moments, then put it back on the shelf. The fruit is twice as dear as a candy bar here, so I expect it is a rare treat for them.

As I checked out, I heard people complaining to the cashier about the dwindling stock of their favourite items—a particular brand of cigarette, a favourite sweet, or raisins. She shrugged her shoulders and told them to get used to it, as the annual sealift is still months away. I asked what sealift is and she told me that it is when a whole year's worth of supplies arrives at the settlement by barge.

I ran into Ian MacKenzie outside the Bay as he was plugging in a cord that ran from under the hood of his car into an electrical outlet on the side of the building. When I asked him what he was doing, he explained that it is necessary to use an electric heater to avoid having your engine block freeze while you shop.

A thin layer of snow had fallen over the gravel road and squeaked under my new boots. The streets were lined with rusty fifty-gallon fuel drums meant to collect rubbish; nonetheless, the roads were littered with soda cans, candy and cigarette wrappers, and the black plastic trash bags. Many of the pastel homes had sheets of plywood leaning against them, with scraped sealskins nailed on to dry. It seemed odd to see teams of Huskies chained up next to the snowmobiles that have been bought to replace them.

Some boys were playing a game of football in the street with a walrus skull. They paused for a moment so I could pass. I could hear them snickering and feel them eying me as I walked by. I hurried back to the station, where all was quiet. I napped and read in the afternoon, then helped myself to some of the chicken stew someone had left simmering on the stove.

On Sunday morning, I took another long walk. I heard singing coming from the Catholic Church, so I peeked in to see the Easter service in progress. Two of the Easter lilies I had flown up with had made their way onto the altar. The small building seemed jammed to the rafters with people, including many children. There were babies being jiggled on knees or riding on their mothers' backs, toddlers toddling, and older kids running in circles around the adults, most of whom were seated in folding metal chairs. The young ones didn't seem to distract the adults at all, as they listened with rapt attention to the catechist, who had to use a microphone to be heard above the din generated by the children, as well as the chorus of coughing. With a small pang of regret, I recalled the days when my family had attended Easter service together, our patent leather shoes shined to a fare thee well, anticipating the feast we would have at home later, with a piece of ham and some hot cross buns. I closed the door and walked onward.

From up on the hill where the fuel storage tanks loom, I looked out over the whole community. I could see the head frame, like a tall wooden shaft, towering over the abandoned mine site. Smoke was rising in plumes from many chimneys. I could hear the whining and barking and howling of the chained dogs carried on the constant wind.

Behind me was an endless expanse of frozen tundra, bluish-greyish-white, stark and eerie. I am used to seeing lights twinkling everywhere along the horizon, reflected off windows, or rivers and lakes—signs of civilization, like the muffled roar of hectic traffic.

Here, there seems to be absolutely nothing and no one out there.

NIKMAK 2
Rankin Inlet Nursing Station
October 12, 1970

Ayayayaaa.

Useless old man I have become. Sitting and singing. Not knowing if you hear me or not.

Today the head nurse complained even about my singing. You are disturbing the other patients, she said. What other patients, I asked, for your brother Ivaluk has told me there are only two young Inuit mothers and a child in the other beds, and I do not think they mind hearing these old songs. But that nurse is ignorant. She does not know Inuktitut or respect our Inuit ways. She is not a proper *Inuk*. It is too bad for her.

She reminds me of those nuns at the mission school: No native words may be spoken here, no native clothing may be worn, and you will earn a slap if you mention Sila or Nuliajuk or any other spirits. We were bound so tight with rules we could not move, until we ran away or failed to return from the summer fishing camps. Sometimes the RCMP flushed us out from under the furs in the iglus where our mothers had hidden us and herded us back like doomed caribou, captive again for a little while.

If I cannot sing, paniga, then I will tell you a story—a story about the winter without which I would not exist.

My mother's fifteenth winter arrived with unusual fury—an early storm that extinguished the sun and drilled the tundra with hail and ice for two days and two nights. It took Sukusi's camp by surprise. They had not had the usual warnings—sudden bird migrations, sky deepening in colour, a skin of ice on the lakes at dawn. They sought shelter in the biggest skin tent when the first needles of ice lashed down, never dreaming they would be confined there so long.

Through the storm they huddled together and slept and told stories and worried and sang. They lit the seal oil lamp and ate from their sparse stock of dried fish and the last summer berries. The women worked steadily to repair the winter clothing as best they could, grateful that their husbands had been able to trade some fox furs for metal needles.

On the third morning the camp roused and looked out to see the world transformed as if by a sorcerer. Rocks, moss, lichens, tents, boats, and sleds—all were frosted with a smooth coating of snow. The dogs looked like jesters, their thick coats bobbing with bubbles of ice that had frozen on the tips of their hair. As usual after a storm, they were yapping and squirming in anticipation of a hunt.

The fish fillets and strips of seal meat that had been left drying on the lines were ruined. The children got busy scraping up the shredded remnants to quell the grumbling in their stomachs, throwing the worst of the mess to the dogs.

The adults waited to hear what Sukusi, my mother's father, would decide. He was the leader of this camp, the *isumataq*. I have heard Qablunaat make some fun of this word, which means "the one who thinks."

"Oh it is easy to be Inuit—only one person in the group has to think!" they say. Of course everyone could think. But time had taught us well that the dog team that pulls in different directions goes nowhere. That is why one person in each camp was looked to for final decisions. In that camp, this person was my mother's father, my *ataatatsiak*, Sukusi. I remember him as a big man with a long silver moustache who could sometimes be very serious, but he was also quick to laugh, especially at me.

The camp consisted of nine people: my grandfather and grandmother and their three children, along with my great uncle Kavik, Sukusi's younger brother, with his wife Issa and their two sons. My grandfather was an experienced and skillful hunter. My great uncle Kavik was a good hunter, too, but he was also an *angakkuq*, a shaman who knew the taboos and rituals required to satisfy the spirit world and to influence the movement and behaviour of animals. Together they were able to provide for their families better than many. Also, the two oldest boys in the camp, Pangniq (Sukusi's eldest son) and Umilik (Kavik's eldest son) had both had their first kill and were beginning to be a real help to their fathers. With two grown women (my grandmother and great aunt) in camp to prepare skins and sew clothing, and my mother Missuk just coming of age to help them, they were a strong and stable group around the time they met the man who would be my father. These were good times, but still there was always something to challenge them, like the sudden appearance of strangers, or the threat of a mysterious illness, or changing game migration patterns, or bouts of extremely harsh weather, or unexpected troubles due to sorcery.

Sukusi decided that they should make haste, pack up the summer things, and travel overland to the winter sealing grounds, stopping to check on their caches of dried fish and meat along the way. He was concerned because winter seemed to have come so quickly. There was a long way to travel, and much to do, and the days were becoming shorter.

They stopped briefly to do some fishing through the river ice and to spit and rub a fresh coat of ice on the runners of the *qamutiik*. It was getting very cold, but there was not yet enough snow to build an iglu, so the men cut and hauled sheets of ice from the river to form a windbreak around the thin tents. After a few days of fishing they packed up again and moved on, pushing and pulling their laden sleds over the rocky terrain with the help of the dogs.

As they approached the winter sealing grounds, they saw a remarkable site: a huge wooden ship frozen into the ice near the edge of the sea. They set up camp at a distance, and grandfather sent my great uncle Kavik and his son Umilik to investigate. They returned the next day with some news—and a metal frying pan, which the elders had heard about, but no one in Sukusi's camp had ever seen or held one before that day.

Umilik reported that the huge ship was stuffed with more wonders like this pan, things made from wood and metal and leather and cloth he had never dreamed existed. The broken ship was a Russian icebreaker that had run aground. The early winter storm had destroyed visibility, and the men guiding the ship had made a wrong turn. The ice froze, and their boat was stuck in the unfamiliar inlet. They had some supplies, and even rifles to hunt with, but a mysterious illness swept through the ship, killing most of the crew. Perhaps like the ill-fated whalers of Hudson Bay, they would have died slowly of scurvy anyway, as a result of their foolish insistence on cooking all of their meat, burning the life force out of it. But the men on this ship had died quickly.

Sukusi decided they would wait several days, until the camp was more settled and they had caught a few seals, before allowing any further visiting with the inhabitants of the ship. There were iglus to build and dogs to feed, and tools to be repaired for the hunting season ahead.

When the men returned to the ship several days later, there was only one Qablunaaq left alive.

I have no memory of my father, only the stories I was told about him. They say he was born of a Russian father and a Japanese mother, who named him Nikita Makita. He grew to manhood in a fishing village somewhere far west of here, but he had a thirst for travel and eventually found work as a hand on the ships that patrol what the Qablunaat call the Northwest Passage.

Makita had witnessed the fate of his shipmates and had no idea why he had been spared. He also knew that his only hope of surviving the winter was to join Sukusi's camp, if they would have him. At first they were afraid of the disease that had killed this man's shipmates, so they made him sleep apart. Great uncle Kavik performed his rituals and ceremonies to dispel any *tupiliq* from their presence, and the stranger courted them with provisions he had brought from the ship—flour, lard, tea, sugar, canned milk, biscuits, and jam, as well as pots and knives and guns and ammunition.

Eventually, Nikita Makita was invited to join Sukusi's iglu and to share his family's sleeping platform, as well as their food and chores. His lack of traditional hunting knowledge was made up for by his skill with a rifle. As a result, there was an abundance of meat and birds and hare to eat that winter, and even a good stash of fox furs for trading. By spring, my anaana, Missuk, was swelling, which was a cause of joy in the camp. It meant there would be a new baby that summer, and Missuk would not have to go away to join the camp of her husband's people. They were ecstatic to learn some months later that her newborn baby was a boy. This meant there would be another future hunter to help assure the survival of the group. Grandfather gave me a strong name, Tigumiaq, the name of one of his favourite ancestors. My father gave me another name, a shortened version of his own—Nikmak. He thought it sounded like a good Inuit name, and everyone in the camp called me that to please him.

No one was surprised when Nikita Makita left on the first Russian ship to cut through the ice later that year. That is how it is. They had heard his stories, they had shared their food and home with him, but he was not their kin, he had not become one of them. He went off in search of more adventures, or to find his own people and speak his own language, and no one wished him ill. They were grateful for the pots and pans, the guns and ammunition, the winter's worth of shared stories and fresh memories, but above all they were grateful to him for bringing me, little Nikmak, your ataata, into their camp.

Taima—that is enough stories for now. Rest, paniga. I will come back later.

Aiyayaaa.

IVALUK 1
Rankin Inlet, N.W.T.
April 3, 1970

Dear Thomasie:

You asked me to write with the news from home so you won't get so homesick away at that hostel school in Churchill. So I am writing to you. Funny thing is here I find my self writing to you in English. You been away to school so long. I know you speak *Inuktitut* just fine but I think they never teach you how to write it in syllabics which is how I like to write out Inuktitut and prefer to sign my name. I don't like to do it the other way with so many English letters to sound out when one little squiggle is better. So I will try writing to you using *Qablunaatittut* words. Tell you what—if you help correct my worse mistakes I will teach you the syllabic way to write Inuktitut when you come home for the summer. That way we both learn something and maybe then I can read faster too not take all the day to read one magazine article about boats or the news paper.

The whole month of March was cold. I guess you don't need a weather report though since there is nothing to stop the wind between here and Churchill but a couple of musk ox. I bet you been dealing with the same wind down there just as sure as we see the same moon over our heads when we look up to the night sky. Too damn stormy off and on to go out seal hunting three straight weeks so we are making a big hole in our stash of frozen tuktu. Only one left stored up on the roof now so I will have to haul my rear end out onto the ice one of these days no matter. Even if the temperature still stuck past forty below zero and stalled there like a skidoo with no gas.

I don't mind the cold so much as the wind when even a tall guy like me has to fight just to stand upright. Every thing takes more effort then. I don't know how our ancestors did it in times like this. I guess if your belly is growling and the kids grow skinny you just have to get out there and stand over a breathing hole in the sea ice for hours. Hoping to catch a seal before your ass is frozen solid into a snowdrift.

I feel spoiled living in this government heated home with electric lights oil stove and even some cans of food from the Bay we can eat if we have to when all the tuktu and dried fish is gone. We have it pretty good. Even got a radio now to give us a break from Ataata's singing.

You should see the flag flying over the hamlet office. It has lost one of its red bars again from being whipped lashed and pelted with flying ice crystals. Little kids here probably think the Canada flag has only two parts—a solid red bar on the left and a red maple leaf on a white square at the right. I don't know why they bother to pull up that flag in winter. There is so little day time to see it flying anyway and it always takes this kind of abuse.

I don't suppose you heard yet that our *angajuk*, our big brother Sakku, has changed his mind again about what to call himself. Remember how the government asked all the Inuit first to use disc numbers instead of names because they could not keep track of us or pronounce our Inuit names. Then a while ago they ask us to quit using those disc numbers and instead make up a name they can pronounce maybe. Our brother did not want to pick the family name Tunu like our parents and you and me did. He needs a more modern name so he want to be called Jimi Hendrix after his favourite singer he discovered by listening to his girlfriend Carol's cassette tapes. You still haven't met Carol. She is a nice looking girl maybe a bit too skinny and a painter who found out she can't make a living from painting pictures down south so she took the CYA job to do community development work up here. I remember last summer Carol always walking around the settlement with her head in the clouds looking at our world through a little box she would make with her two thumbs and two fingers. When I ask her what is she doing she would say she is trying to put the tundra or sometimes the sky into a little frame because otherwise these are too big for her to take in all at one time. I guess she misses those Toronto skyscraper buildings slicing up her view into small bits though I find that hard to imagine.

After Carol and Jimi get together she went to work on community-developing him, try to build up his native pride like a bonfire. Maybe she does not want her own half-Inuit kids to get a family name like Hendrix. Anyway Jimi decide now he is going to have a traditional name after all so he plan to register himself as Sakkujuak Tunu when the Project Surname people come back to visit Rankin Inlet again. Also he and Carol say they plan to get hitch next time the Anglican minister comes through town so their brand new twin babies can share our family last name too. Those twins they are cute as little siksiks but it can sure get noisy when both of them are howling like they seem to do a lot.

Carol made up some names for the babies and Anaana had a fit. She picks artistic first names for them—Picasso and Mona Lisa. Then middle names she thinks are Inuit names but they are Inuktitut words for colours—*aupaluktuq* and *quqsuqtuq*, red and yellow. Yes she wants to register your niece and nephew as Picasso Aupaluktuq Tunu and Mona Lisa Quqsuqtuq Tunu. Anaana back at home asking "whose soul will reside in these babies? Who will they have to live up to"? She carry on until Ataata give the kids proper Inuit names—Uksukuluk and Palliq— even if that is not what their parents will call them every day. I try to keep out of the middle of these troubles and tease Sakku that if he and Carol have a few more kids they can get the whole rainbow done. When the twins are old enough to get a joke I plan to call them Orange when I see them together. See I learn something from art class in school.

Anaana and Ataata are proud of the little ones but also a little let down because it does not look like Jimi and Carol plan to follow our custom and let them adopt their first-born baby. Anaana and Ataata were hoping so especially since they have two babies so you think maybe they could spare one. But Carol is Qablunaaq so she does not think like that. She going to hang onto both kids and let Sakku deal with it. Pitsiark never sent her first-born home neither. But that's because she married that Padlirmiut Simeonie and they move to Eskimo Point and end up giving their number one baby to his parents down there. I have a feeling our *nayak* Kublu is working to fix this thing. She has always been sensitive and caring too much. Lately I see her hanging out a lot with a guy who flies bush planes up here and so I think maybe something is up.

Well those are all the news from here. I miss you *Nukaqtaaq* and I look forward to see you when you come home again.

△< ⅃'

(I-va-luk in syllabics)

ALISON 4
Rankin Inlet, Northwest Territories
April 20, 1970

I am doing better. Wayne invited me over for a glass of sherry on Sunday. I asked him lots of questions about his childhood spent on a farm in Saskatchewan. He showed me photos of his family and their property, acres of wheat fields tucked along a river. I thought it looked idyllic and said so. He said I should not be deceived—it was a hard life, with farm chores to do every day, before and after school and on weekends. He and his brother slept in an uninsulated attic room that could get so cold in winter that sometimes he would wake up to find his blanket frozen to the wall from the moisture of his own breath. Perhaps that is why he doesn't mind winter here too much. He is used to it. I find April bad enough and cannot even imagine what it must be like in January. And the darkness is even harder to imagine than the cold.

Wayne turns out to play the guitar. He sang a few folk songs for me, and his voice was quite good. It almost felt as if I were being serenaded. I wondered if he might try to kiss me, and I realized I hoped he would, but there was none of that. I wonder if I look drab or worn out these days. Perhaps I should have been bold and kissed him. I'm not sure what is expected here.

Work helps the time go by. I find myself exhausted by the end of the day, perhaps because I always have to be on my toes. Nothing is familiar, so nothing is routine. I have to learn everything, from the patients' names (and how to pronounce them properly) to where to find bandages and Mercurochrome and aspirin and splints. I've been helping Sherry run the prenatal clinic, which is swamped with patrons. I work in the daily drop-in clinic as needed, too, where mostly I peer into infected ears and throats.

Yesterday Nurse Bauer asked me to make a home visit, to check on an old man named Atayak. She told me to take his vital signs, but mainly she wanted to be sure he is taking the medication for his bronchial infection. She said there were several children in the home who speak English, so I would not need to take an interpreter along.

What I saw in that home shocked me. The home looked reasonably tidy, but it had an odd smell, and I could see that at least one of the children had scabies. While I was examining Atayak, one of the older boys went into the bathroom, which was plainly visible from the living room. He didn't bother to close the door, so we all could hear him taking a whiz noisily. I heard no flush of a commode. Atayak yelled something to the boy, and next I saw him wrestling a big black plastic bag out of the room, dragging it along the floor because it was so heavy. The stench of sloshing urine and feces was unmistakable. He tied a knot to secure the top, and then heaved the bag out the door onto a snow bank. I had witnessed my first "honey bucket," and I had to suppress an urge to retch.

I mentioned something about it when I returned to the Nursing Station, then regretted doing so, because I had to listen to Nurse Bauer go off again about how dirty the locals are. I don't see how she expects anyone to keep clean, when everyone in a household pees and poos into a plastic-lined receptacle—and some of the homes have fifteen or more people living in them. There is not even cold water to wash your hands. Hauling the full bags outside involves unavoidable stink and mess. Then these bags collect along the streets until someone comes to pick them up. I can just imagine all the lost or forgotten honey bags peeking out of the snowdrifts on the days when it is warm enough for snow to melt. Little boys and dogs surely must make a sport of seeing if they can get the bags to burst. Sanitation conditions here do not seem much better than nineteenth century London, with raw sewage practically running down the streets.

NIKMAK 3
Rankin Inlet Nursing Station
October 12, 1970

I am back again, Kublu, though it is late and the nurses say I cannot stay too long.

I wanted to tell you that I was a happy child, just as you were a happy child, though our young lives were so very different. I was born in an iglu. You were born under electric lights in a heated Nursing Station, and you have never known real hunger.

I was the last baby to be born into my grandfather Sukusi's camp—at least the last one to live and thrive—and so everyone spoiled and pampered me. My grandmother made my clothing from only the softest hides of the young caribou calves, and she chewed the sealskins for my kamiit longer than anyone else's, to make them very supple and soft. My mother would give me the choicest bits of seal meat or tuktu, and she would make sure I had my fill of char. I had the sled dog puppies to play with, and my grandfather made me a lasso and a snare, so I could practice catching hares or sea birds around the camp while the hunters were away. I do not remember anyone ever yelling at me or hitting me. They corrected me, if necessary, by teasing me for my childish behaviour. But mostly they patted me and held me and pinched my cheeks and wrestled with me and made me feel treasured.

When I was a bit older, I began to accompany my grandfather and uncles on their fishing and hunting trips. At first I just watched them go about their work. I would stay by the qamutiik and imitate them, throwing my little harpoon at an old whale vertebra, or fetching things for them, if they asked me to. When I was about ten, my grandfather showed me how to load and fire his rifle, and how to handle it with great respect. He did not have to tell me that ammunition was a precious thing not to be wasted, that our very lives depended upon it. So I would practice aiming the empty rifle for hours and hours, first at *inuksut* and later at things that moved, like siksiks and snow geese.

That fall, when the tuktu gathered near the lakes to begin their southward migration, my grandfather took me along hunting with the men. Of course I had seen tuktu before, wandering alone or in small groups near our campsites. But this time what I saw was a herd of tuktu blackening the tundra, as thick as a cloud of mosquitoes in July. My grandfather handed me the loaded rifle. All that practice at aiming, and I had never pulled the trigger before. I cannot describe the joy I felt when I pulled that trigger for the first time and a large buck fell to his knees, then his great rack of antlers crashed onto the tundra. Grandfather hoisted me onto his shoulders and pranced in a circle as great uncle Kavik cheered. My uncles teased that it would be impossible even for a girl to miss a shot in such a thick herd, and that anyone could use a rifle, but would I be able to fell a buck with a spear or a bow and arrow, as they had done for their first kill?

We packed up that tuktu to carry back to our camp, where the elders skinned it and divided it up. I did not touch or eat that animal, but sat glowing with pride as it was all given away, because I had shown that now I could hunt and contribute vital support to our group.

After that, I was accorded more respect, and more responsibility. I left my boyhood behind and took on the serious business of working with the other hunters to ensure the survival of our camp, using little more than stone and bone and our wits. Many days I felt thankful that I was born after the invention of the rifle, for I imagine that the life of the Inuit must have been much harder before that—but the old ones say the game was more plentiful in those times, and there was less illness, too.

There were some harsh times I had to endure as a young man. Times when the caribou would fail to appear, times when the winter storms made sealing impossible, times of hunger and sickness and death. But how can a person appreciate day without experiencing night?

ALISON 5
Rankin Inlet, Northwest Territories
April 30, 1970

Dear Nancy:

I am settling in here and learning to speak some of the local language, which is not called Eskimo at all, but "Inuktitut," meaning the language or the way of the Inuit, which is what the Eskimo people call themselves. I have learned a few words of the language from the children who follow me around, as well as from my patients. Yes is *ii*. No is *aakka*. A *Qablunaaq* is a non-Eskimo person, like you and me.

Inuktitut is unlike any other language I have ever studied. Not that I am fluent in anything but English, but I know a few words of German and French and Italian. Inuktitut is completely unlike those European languages. Each word or sentence is composed of a string of prefixes, suffixes and infixes—word fragments that are arranged in a prescribed order that is almost the complete reverse of how we would arrange them in the English language. For example, if you want to say "I didn't want to eat caribou meat" in Inuktitut, you would say *"tuktuturumalaunngittunga,"* which is composed of these bits:

   tuktu – caribou
   tuq – eat
   ruma – want
   lau – (denotes past tense)
   nngit – (signifies the negative)
   tunga – I

Thus, you are saying: "Caribou eat want did not I."

Don't you imagine that people who organize and express their thoughts so very differently from English speakers must see the world in an entirely different way than you and I do?

I have also learned some phrases that are important to my work. To ask a person "How are you?" you would say *"qanuippit?"* which really means "Are you sick?" If the person is fine they will respond *"qanuinngittunga,"* or "I am not sick." To ask a person how old they are, you say *"qapsinik ukiuqapit?"* which literally means "How many winters do you have?" And to ask where they are from, you would say *"nani nunaqapit?"*—or, "where do you have land?"

Counting in Inuktitut is a stitch. The numbers basically go: one, two, three, four, five, ten, many. I suppose if you were trying to communicate with a hunter about some caribou you saw over the hill, it would be enough to know if there were just a handful (one to five), or about ten, or too many to count.

Some of our English expressions have no Inuktitut equivalent. For example, there is no way to say "Hello" or "You are welcome" (in response to thank you, which is *qujannamiik*). This is not to say that the Inuit are rude—in fact, I find them terribly polite and sometimes very shy. Perhaps these types of courtesies are simply taken for granted among the Inuit and need not be spoken.

I hope you find this information about the native language here at least a bit interesting. Please say hullo to Mum and Dad and everyone else for me. I hope you are doing well in school.

Love,

Ali

IVALUK 2
Rankin Inlet, N.W.T.
May 11, 1970

Dear Thomasie:

I about drop dead to see Ian Mackenzie come up to my door this week. I thought maybe he come to arrest me for something but no. He has your telex message for me. Your note telling how your roommate was attacked and killed by a polar bear right there in the street of Churchill. I thought those bears in Churchill mainly hung out at the garbage dump waiting for the ice to get right for hunting seal pups or waiting for some tourist who is paying too much attention to his camera. I wonder why one would be wandering the road in search of a teenager student to snack on.

I wish I had been there to defend him and you. I wonder if I could do what our ancestors did. Stand calm and hold your spear steady with the butt end wedged in the ground as you are charged by a huge nanuq. I think my underwear would need a change after that.

I remember when I was little telling Ataata that I had a dream about hunting nanuq. He tell me never think or even dream that ever again. Inuit not supposed to do anything at all to attract attention from the spirit of nanuq because this is asking for big trouble and put everybody in danger. So do not think about getting even at all. Just take extra care and watch behind you and do not go out alone by yourself if you can help it. We want you to come home whole not missing any important parts when school is done.

I am not going to tell Anaana or Ataata about this. They would worry themselves sick over you. Right now they are really excited about Kublu's baby coming this summer. Pretty much everyone in town seem more happy now that days are getting longer.

I will miss you this summer but I am standing behind your decision to stay and do summer school so you can finish your studies and get home sooner next year. A lot of kids hate school but if you handle it I say stick with it and good for you for making a wise and grown up decision like that one. I am sure it will pay off for you in the end run.

I was sorry but not too surprised to hear stories you tell me about the fighting that goes on between the Inuit and Indian kids there at the hostel school. It seems like it has always been this way and I wonder if it will ever change. I had to deal with this when I took that GNWT heavy equipment course over in Fort Smith years ago. The class was mainly Indian and Metis kids from places along the MacKenzie River. Us Inuit kids from the high arctic and eastern arctic were not so many. They like to tease and call us names and play dirty tricks when the instructor is not looking. We give back some of the same thing you bet but on Friday and Saturday nights we have to lock ourselves up in our dorm room because Indian kids think it great fun to pound the shit out of some Inuit after they found illegal stuff to drink or sniff up. Fort Smith was supposed to be a dry town so even the vanilla extract was lock up behind the counter at the Bay. But if you want to bake some cookies and ask the cashier for the smallest bottle they got she go get the keys and bring out a quart.

Eventually us Inuit kids had enough of it. We used Wilbur Issaluk's stabbing as our excuse. We tell the teachers we fear for our lives but we were just plain homesick mainly. We want to be back somewhere we feel like we belong. We never got used to those tall trees waving in the wind up above us filled with noisy ravens. They seem creepy. We miss the open tundra and small hills dotted with inuksut. We miss our parents and siblings and friends and the hunting and fishing. We miss the taste of *uqsuq* and fresh seal meat and tuktu. We miss our home our land and our own people.

At least you are in a place not so different as Fort Smith was for us back then. I know Churchill can be strange but at least it is not so very far away and you have some friends and I know you are determine to stick it out.

It seems like education getting more and more important around here. The job ads always asking for more of it. Maybe when they move the government to Rankin Inlet you can end up with an important job running something right here. I am pretty sure your chance will be bigger if you finish school and not drop out like me and Sakku.

Maybe you should go to the Keewatin region office and talk to them about what kind of jobs will be coming with the GNWT when they move up here. Maybe they even give you some part time work right now just to try you out. I know you can leave a good impression on them.

Price of cigarettes going up again here so I am trying to quit hard. Keep your fingers cross for me.

△< ⊃ᶜ

ALISON 6
Rankin Inlet, Northwest Territories
May 12, 1970

One of my favourite patients, a woman named Uvitsi, told me her husband is a carver, so I expressed interest in seeing his work some time. On her next visit she brought some Polaroid photos of the man and his carvings. I was expecting to see carved seals or walruses, but his work was more abstract. He polishes the dull grey soapstone to a sheen somehow. This makes the light glance off the curved and angled surfaces of his pieces, which seem to be lumpy representations of human faces and animal spirits. I said I found his work interesting, so next evening Uvitsi came knocking on our door to introduce me to her husband. She had to translate, as he didn't speak one word of English. He produced two carvings from under his jacket and asked if I would like to buy them. One was of a woman with an eagle soaring from her back, and the other was a moonlike block of dark pitted stone with several faces seeming to pulse from it. I asked how much he wanted for them, and he said fifteen dollars. I bought the carving of the woman and eagle and paid him fifteen dollars, saying I would have to think about the other one. He pushed the second carving into my hand, as Uvitsi explained that he had asked fifteen dollars for both carvings, and then they were gone.

Later that evening, Nurse Bauer and Sherry walked into the common area and saw my new acquisitions on the dining table. Sherry came over to admire them, but Nurse Bauer simply said: "I bet you paid fifteen dollars for those." I said I had, and asked how she had guessed that. "Because it is the second Friday of the month," she said. "This is the day the Bay flies in the beer, which sells for fifteen dollars a case. There are all kinds of arts and crafts to be had in this town for fifteen dollars on beer day." So what, I thought sourly.

But I felt a proper fool the next morning when I saw Uvitsi at the Co-op. She turned away from me quickly, but I noticed that she had a bruised and swollen cheek with the unmistakable early colouring of a black eye. Later that day, we had to deal with a few split heads and a stab wound at the Nursing Station. Typical beer day, Sherry said.

ALISON 7
Rankin Inlet, Northwest Territories
May 17, 1970

Wayne had to fly a load of supplies up to one of the old DEWline stations last week, and he asked me if I'd like to come along for the ride. Of course I would. Sherry was good enough to trade shifts so I could go. What fun it was to get out flying and see more of the country round about, though much of it looks all the same to me. I'm afraid I'd be lost in a minute if I were to venture out on my own.

When we arrived at the DEWline station, the few inhabitants rushed out to greet us and to help unload the provisions. When the men saw me, someone yelled out, "There's a woman on board!" At first I wondered if they were sex-starved maniacs, but the men begged me to stay, because their cook had gone out on what was supposed to have been a week's leave but had never come back. They assumed that any woman can fix grub, so they were crestfallen when I explained that I am a nurse, not a chef. I asked if there weren't any Inuit around these parts who could cook for them. They said they had tried hiring an Eskimo cook before, and all they got was fish and caribou and seal served in various ways. They'd get braised walrus or curried seal or fish soup, when what they want to eat is steak and chips and pie.

Even though I did not want the job, it made me realize what a land of opportunity the north is. Almost as if, should you make the effort to show up here, there will be a niche for you to fit into somewhere. It is not like this in many parts of the world, especially for women. The pay can be excellent, because of the isolation and the difficulty of attracting and keeping talented people. It makes me wonder why the government and businesses don't expend more effort training the people who already live here.

Soon I could see that the men who worked at this station were starved for more than food. They followed me around like a cloud of gnats, sometimes leaning in for a good sniff or the odd pinch. It would be frightening to be left here alone among them, with weeks to wait until the next plane. I began to walk closer to Wayne, holding onto his arm, to give the impression that he might be my boyfriend or husband. That made them back off a bit.

On the return trip, I asked Wayne if he ever feels lonely, living so far away from his family. Not really, he replied, with an intriguing grin. He told me he intends to return to Saskatchewan some day, but at this stage of his life he wants to see some of the world. Mostly, he is so busy flying, especially in summer, that he doesn't have time to feel lonely. The winter can get long, he said. Then he blushed and confessed that he has an Inuit girlfriend, and that she is expecting a baby. I was stunned.

"But you said you plan to return to the south. Will you take her with you, then?"

"Oh, no. She would never want to go, and I made my plans clear to her from the beginning..." he argued.

I don't know why I felt indignant, but I did. I'm sure it was part sheer disappointment, because I have been feeling lonely, and I am somewhat attracted to Wayne myself, so it is a letdown to learn he is already taken.

I am no prude, but I do not like the idea of itinerant men taking advantage of local women, nor of them thoughtlessly contributing to the population explosion that threatens our planet. I actually yelled at Wayne for being inconsiderate and for not using birth control. He replied that he had wanted to, that he had tried to, but his girlfriend told him this was offensive to her values. Babies, she said, are valued and desired unconditionally. She insisted she would be completely delighted and honoured if she were to become pregnant. She *wanted* to have his baby, no strings attached. And if for some reason she became unable to look after their child, she assured him there were many other members of this community who would love to have the opportunity to do so. Their child would never want for love and attention or nurturing.

Wayne could see I had my doubts about what he was saying, so he suggested I ask his girlfriend about these things myself. He told me her name is Kublu Tunu, and that I know her already, because she is one of the patients in the Tuesday prenatal clinic at the nursing station.

Birth control as culturally offensive? That was a new one on me. I asked what about his cultural perspective? He said, "Well, I am not home now, am I? When in Rome..."

I crossed my arms and refused to speak to him the rest of the way home. When we arrived, I turned down his offer to give me a ride to the nursing station. Instead I walked all the way back to town. I didn't feel up to going straight to the nursing station, so instead I dropped by the Transient Centre, where I found the Swedes learning how to play Mah-jong with a few guests. I was invited to join them and was happy to have something to do that did not involve too much serious talk. The Swedes brought out some kind of clear distilled alcoholic beverage they kept stored in the freezer, and I drank more of it than I should have. I had a headache for two days afterwards.

NIKMAK 4
Rankin Inlet Nursing Station
October 13, 1970

Aieee, Paniga. They have chopped off three of your fingers. They had to do it, they say. They say those parts were frozen beyond recovery and will never come back to life again. They say they saved what they could of you. They say we are lucky that doctor came through Rankin Inlet when he did.

Lucky? Little by little I feel you being chipped away.

Your right hand now reminds me of the hunters in our old camps who had wrestled with *Ugjuq*, the big bearded seal with the square flipper, the favourite food of the polar bear. *Natsiq*, the common ringed seal, is challenge enough to hunt, but Ugjuq is the real fighter. She is so strong, she has pulled many hunters right down through her breathing holes in the ice. Only the lucky ones, the strongest ones, win such a contest, but they typically lose a finger in the process, as the taut harpoon line saws it off. Such a hunter returns to camp a hero, with a big seal to be carved up and shared around the camp. But people notice the new shape of this hunter's hand. As the meat is divided up, there are jokes about how he will have to do all sorts of things differently in the future, but everyone knows it is a very serious thing for a hunter to lose any part of his hand.

And your left hand...ach. It reminds me of a sad story my grandfather told me, about a particularly dark and dismal time that happened long before I was born, in a camp far north from here. There had been several bitter winters in a row, but this one was the worst. The hunting had been poor all summer, the caribou so sparse that there were not enough furs to go around. The hunters' winter clothing had to be made from old skins that had been used as bedding. There was some joking among the hunters about being clad like beggars, but they went out to hunt that winter more anxious than usual.

Several of the smaller camps joined together, in the hope that hunting cooperatively would improve their chances for at least a mouthful of seal meat. They had heard rumours from travellers, stories about bad times in other camps, stories about places where the caribou had failed to appear at all that summer, stories about poor fish runs, rumours of starvation and worse. At least, they thought, we have our winter sealing grounds. But there was an undercurrent of fear that seemed to rob the camp of laughter. Even the children were quiet.

As the sun was extinguished, storm after storm made it nearly impossible for the hunters to go out, and when they did, they found that the seal holes had been covered over by deep drifts of hard packed snow. Their stores of dried fish dwindled, and when they sent someone to get caribou meat from their summer cache, they found that their stores had been broken into, by men or wolves or bears they did not know, but what did it matter. Hunters returned empty handed.

A shaman named Ajjuktaq was part of this winter camp that Sukusi's family had joined. She was asked to provide more powerful amulets to the hunters. She was urged to perform more rituals so the group could regain favour with the Nuliajuk and the other spirits. But nothing seemed to work. The people began to doubt her power, to wonder if she had lost her abilities. Then they began to worry that she might be using her power against her very own people.

A woman in this camp delivered a baby girl and put it naked at the door of the iglu. This was not so unusual, especially in harsh times, when the thought of another mouth to feed was unbearable—especially a girl, a non-hunter. But this mother later took her sharp ulu and cut up that frozen baby and fed it to her family. It was the beginning of a slide into desperation that took the whole camp in its grip.

People began to hate and fear Ajjuktaq, as they became more certain that she had cast some kind of spell to bring these hard times upon them. People turned away from her. She became more strange, and then she went mad. One day she walked out onto the tundra to die, which was not uncommon for an old person in those days, especially in times of scarcity. But as Ajjuktaq went away, she cut off her fingers with her own ulu and sprinkled a bloody trail of them—perhaps as a final desperate plea to Nuliajuk, or perhaps to show the starving camp where they could find her meat. But the people were too afraid to have anything to do with eating her, no matter how desperate they had become.

The wind continued to howl, the children's stomachs grumbled, and tensions grew. Mothers started boiling old kamiit in their soapstone pots, slicing them into ribbons to give the fussing children something to chew on. An old rivalry erupted, and two men decided to settle a score with their snow knives. This was before the times when the RCMP started coming around asking questions about such acts, which they called murder, and began taking hunters away from the camps, sentencing their families to certain death. Those stabbings resulted in two more deaths in the camp, and still more hardship and fear, for now they had lost two good hunters.

Taimali—but that is enough about those dark times—I will speak of them no more this night.

Aiya-aiya-aiyayaiiee.

ALISON 8
Rankin Inlet, Northwest Territories
May 29, 1970

I haven't seen Wayne since the disastrous DEWline flight. Instead, I have thrown myself into language lessons. I found out there is a class being taught by some teachers at the elementary school, so I signed up. It seems a productive way to spend my evenings, as well as a good way to meet new people. My Swedish friends decided to sign up too, when I told them about it. In addition to the three of us, there is a social worker, a school administrator, and an Australian research biologist in the class. (The latter here for the summer to study the life cycle of the black fly).

I love the unearthly guttural sounds of Inuktitut. I have even mastered a couple of sounds that we do not have in the English language, like the 'q' sound that is pronounced so deep in the throat it almost sounds like coughing or gagging, and another sound that requires grinning and letting the air blow between your teeth and cheeks. The one word I have the most trouble pronouncing correctly is the Inuit name for Rankin Inlet, "*Kangiqliniq*" which means a deep bay or inlet. I feel I am in danger of swallowing my tongue when I try to pronounce that word.

I also learned that the Inuit are organized into many clans and sub-groups, and that each clan has a name for itself that ends in "*-miut*," which means "the people of." Thus, the "*Natsilingmiut*" are the people of the seal, the "*Aivilingmiut*" are the people of the walrus, and the "Nunamiut" are the people of the land.

"*Qapsinik*" is the Inuit word meaning "how many." The Inuit dubbed Qablunaat the "*Qapsinirmiut*" early on because of their obsession with counting things. The first Qablunaat they encountered must have been census takers, constantly asking questions such as how many people are in your camp, how many children do you have, how old is each one, and so on. I am embarrassed to think that this is exactly what we do with each patient in the nursing station. We want to write down numbers: how much do you weigh, how tall are you, how many times does your heart beat in a minute, how many teeth do you have, how many bowel movements have you had today, when did you last bleed? We are Qapsinirmiut, indeed.

Perhaps the French trappers and traders and missionaries didn't ask questions as compulsively as the English. They were simply called the *"Oui-oui-miut"* by the old-timers (after the French word for yes). And nowadays, civil servants are referred to simply as the *"Gavamamiut"* or people of the government.

I saw the MacKenzies in the Bay this week and they invited me over for supper, which was great because I am tired of eating in. Nurse Bauer can be a bear, and Sherry seems to prefer her own company. I usually just fix a sandwich and eat it in my room, listening to the BBC or practicing my language lessons.

I asked Ian about a strange thing I have noticed poking up through the snow lately—an above ground box that snakes through the town, connecting to various homes. He explained that it is the "utilidor" system that provides services to the government staff houses. Inside that linear box is a series of insulated pipes carrying steam heat and water and wastewater. He said the pipes have to be heated or they will freeze, and they are run above ground because the permafrost makes it impossible to trench and bury pipes underground. This system was built originally by the mining company that operated here decades ago, to provide modern comforts to the homes built for supervisors moving up from the south, whose wives would not want to live in a place lacking these basic amenities.

I asked if it wasn't considered discriminatory not to provide the same services to the Inuit. Ian said that this was not considered necessary at the time, because the Eskimos who came to work in the mine were used to living in tents and iglus on the land, so simply moving them into a wood frame house with an oil stove was thought to be a big improvement to their living conditions. He said the government eventually built a central bathhouse for the Inuit families to use for showering and doing laundry. That explains why the patients I see are never terribly dirty or smelly, in spite of the lack of running water in their homes.

Ian's wife drew a map for me, showing where the bathhouse is located. I dropped by to have a look at it on my way home, just to satisfy my curiosity. The hours posted by the door were most puzzling. According to the sign, the bathhouse is reserved for women only Monday through Friday, and for men only on Saturdays and Sundays. I wondered how it would be to have a date with an Eskimo man on a Friday evening, knowing there is no way he could have bathed since the previous Sunday.

IVALUK 3
Rankin Inlet, N.W.T.
May 31, 1970

Dear Thomasie:

You know I did not catch the Skidoo fever when it swept through this town these past years. I still think my dogs are the best way to go in this part of the world. They are loyal and hardworking and I can always eat one in an emergency if I have to. If your snowmobile breaks down far from home you are done that's it: taima. No use trying to eat spark plugs.

But you know that a snowmobile or even a qamutiik pulled by dog team is no good here in the summer time when there is no snow to slide over anyways.

A few weeks ago the HBC flew in a bunch of motor vehicles no one ever seen here before. Some two-wheel trail bikes and three-wheel tundra buggies that can really move. Crazy cost you bet to fly these things in but somebody at the Bay figured they would sell out fast and they were right about that.

The three-wheelers have a big sit area for two passengers and the two back wheels are set far apart to make good balance. The big tires have lots of tread to grab uneven ground if you go off the flat road and out on the tundra. It is a bit bumpy to drive over rocks and big clumps of moss but much faster than walking. You can even add a box behind the seat to carry supplies and fishing gear. This will make hunting and fishing in summer so much more easy. Not to mention most girls in town all want to be first to hitch a ride on these new toys.

You guessed it—I bought one of these things. Mitch Taylor snatched the red one right away for Co-op business he says. I went for the green one because this seems just right for a hunting and fishing help machine. The yellow and black and silver models all sold out by the end of the day too. I'm sure the Bay will order more to come on the sealift since these are so popular. This town was pretty quiet once if you ignore all the barking dog teams chained up but now you can hear motorcycle engines revving all night and day and everyone lines up along the muddy streets to watch or beg for a ride.

This new thing will be so big a help to me it is a necessity almost. It is one thing to hunt like our ancestors when the game was plentiful and the

Inuit lived in small nomad camps. Or even back when this community was smaller but now Rankin is grown so big—too many people to count. It means all the game is hunted out for too many miles around. You got to go further and further out to find any foxes or musk ox or caribou. It takes so long time but now this three-wheeler will make me faster.

Problem is now I have to get a job to pay for the damn thing. Most fish and meat I harvest I barter for stuff I need or sometimes to get a date but now all of a sudden I need money.

I put down all the cash I had and agree to pay the rest in instalments. The only job available in town this week was working with the driver of the honey wagon—riding through town to pick up bags of sewage that are lying next to the streets. It pays pretty well because no one wants to do this hard and stinky work. I guess I can do it myself for a while at least until this thing is paid off and I save up some more cash to buy fuel for her. Then I can quit and go fishing and hunting until the snow flies too hard again.

Take it easy,

ALISON 9
Rankin Inlet, Northwest Territories
May 31, 1970

Wayne invited me over to his house for dinner last night. He is making an effort to offer an olive branch and I suppose it is time to forgive him. What reason could there be to stay mad?

It was a sort of welcome party for his new roommate and fellow pilot, Jerry Duncan, a polite fellow from the east, from one of those "N" provinces—New Brunswick or Nova Scotia or Newfoundland. Jerry has come to help Wayne with the busy summer flying season, and just my luck, it turns out he has a wife and child at home. Wayne had invited another guest—Jean Philippe, a French Canadian man who has been hired to manage the Transient Centre. Jean said he plans to send the young Swedish couple packing and give the custodial work they have been doing to some locals, which makes sense of course but also seems a bit cruel. The Swedes have been good friends to me, and fun to have around. I don't see the harm in allowing them to stay a bit longer to support cultural diversity and international flavour around here.

Jean turns out to be a superb cook, and Wayne was clever enough to put him in charge of preparing our meal. We had fresh salad greens, home made noodles, boeuf bourgignon with buttered peas, and a delicious Tarte Tatin for dessert. Wayne opened a couple of bottles of Chateauneuf de Pape to wash it all down. And then Jean produced some real French chocolate truffles and Cognac and cigars from his backpack. The men were practically purring as they puffed and sipped. I felt as if I would burst if I ate one more thing.

I asked Wayne why he had not invited his girlfriend to dinner. He said that, for one thing, she shouldn't be drinking in her condition, and for another, he knew she would not really appreciate this type of meal, so he'd rather share it with someone he thought would enjoy it. I thanked him for picking me, as I really do appreciate a chance to meet some people who are not ill. The men joked about everyone in town being sick in some way, just some in more visible ways than others.

After dinner, Jean offered to walk me "home" to the nursing station, but Wayne insisted on coming along as well, saying he needed some fresh air. After we dropped Jean Philippe off at the Transient Centre, Wayne suggested we stop by his girlfriend's home to see if she was in, and she was. I shook hands with Kublu, and she introduced me to her parents, Nikmak and Ukpik Tunu. Nikmak shook my hand with a very strong grip, as Ukpik rushed off to fetch the kettle for tea. I was pleased to be able to exchange a few words with them in Inuktitut. Just small talk, but they were clearly delighted by my effort to speak their language. It felt as if it lifted some curtain that had been drawn between us.

Kublu was sitting on the floor, with her big belly resting over her outspread legs. She looked so young to me—mid to late teens perhaps— too young to be having a baby. My ambivalence about Wayne's part in this washed over me again.

There was a large piece of brown butcher paper on the floor that held hunks of a caribou, including a skinned head. Kublu picked up the caribou skull and began gnawing on the blood red parts of it. "Mmmmm—tuktu. You want some?" she offered. Wayne shot me a glance, as if to say: you see, this is the type of meal my beloved prefers.

I declined to gnaw on the skull, but then I accepted a small strip of meat that Kublu cut from a leg, after removing the hair and skin. I was surprised how much it tasted like beef, only a bit sweeter and not at all gamey like you might expect.

The way Kublu was sitting on the floor—among those hacked up parts of an animal—looked so primitive to me, like a scene that might have taken place a century earlier. But of course then it would have taken place on the floor of an iglu or a skin tent, not in a modern, oil-heated, wood-frame home with a linoleum floor, and with Johnny Cash singing the Folsom Prison Blues on a radio in the background.

I see these mind-bending scenes all the time. Like the Inuit women who wear traditional sealskin boots and parkas, but also carry bright-collared plastic purses they have bought at the Bay. Or a man in the street hauling a wooden qamutiik loaded with freshly butchered walrus meat to feed his dog team, but pulling it across the gravel with a shiny new Skidoo.

Wayne says that it would be a mistake to assume that, just because an Inuk is wearing blue jeans and eating chips with gravy or riding a bicycle, he has abandoned his traditional beliefs and become just like a Qablunaaq. I wonder how they do think, though.

I have not had any mail since I arrived here, two full months ago.

ALISON 10
Rankin Inlet, Northwest Territories
June 1, 1970

I was up in the night, suffering with a touch of indigestion, or perhaps too much wine. I fumbled my way to the supply closet to look for some Alka Seltzer or Pepto Bismal, and had no idea what a shock I was in for. When I flipped on the light, I saw Nurse Bauer and Sherry in a tangle up against the shelving at the back.

Sherry quickly unwrapped her leg from around Nurse Bauer's behind. They both stood up, hurriedly smoothing down their uniforms and blinking in the bright light. I gasped, flipped the light off, and ran back to my room. I locked the door and climbed into bed in the dark, my heart pounding in my ears.

I tried to go over what I had seen. Perhaps I was mistaken…but no, there could be no other explanation. Is Nurse Bauer some kind of predator, I wondered, and has she set her sights on me as her next victim? Or am I cooped up here a million miles from home in some kind of lesbian colony?

It occurred to me that the lock on my door is useless, as surely Nurse Bauer would have a duplicate or master key. I slid my bureau against the door for good measure, but lay awake all night long, anyway. I decided I would go to the Bay as soon as it opens in the morning and buy a couple more locks to install on the inside of my room.

How am I to work with my colleagues? Should I pretend I saw nothing? Am I expected to report this—but to whom? I have no idea who or where Nurse Bauer's supervisor might be, and I know that Ian MacKenzie has nothing to do with the running of the health department.

Is there some chance this news could get the whole lot of us fired? Would anyone believe me?

Yikes.

IAN 2
Rankin Inlet, Northwest Territories
June 5, 1970

RE: Monthly Report to Keewatin Regional Headquarters, Churchill, Manitoba

The HBC did an unusual thing last month. They paid air freight to have a dozen motor bikes flown in to this community. I can't imagine what that must have cost them. Apparently someone at their HQ decided this was a good market move, and they could not have been more correct on that score. Last month, there were exactly two motorized bikes or scooters in Rankin Inlet (one belonging to the RCMP constable and the other to the Fish and Game officer). Today there are 14. The cargo plane arrived around 9 a.m., and by noon the HBC had them all uncrated—mostly Honda 50 and Honda 90 trail bikes, a few black and silver higher-powered motorcycles for street use, and some yellow three-wheelers with balloon tires more suitable for tundra travel. They were all sold by the end of the day, and there has been one hellacious racket of motorcycle engines in the streets ever since. Young men speed around the gravel roads, giving rides to their friends, tearing out across the tundra, then back into the town. Impromptu races to Lake Nipissar and back. There are children in the streets day and night, jumping and cheering and clapping and begging for a ride, and even the dog teams tied up around town are howling with excitement. One big, loud, fuel-burning orgy under the midnight sun.

Which leads to a few questions. Do we or should we have any noise ordinances I am supposed to be enforcing? (I won't even ask about curfews, as there would be a revolt over that, I assure you.) And who is responsible for things like traffic signs and speed limits? Is there any budget for paving the roads, as these gravel ones will wear out faster now. And I hope it is not too late to order more gasoline for delivery on this summer's sealift.

We staged a big search party when an eight-year-old local girl was reported missing by her parents. Lots of GNWT staff time went into sweeping through the community and the surrounding hills looking for her over a three-day period, but she turned up safe and sound, sleeping under a porch with an empty box of hardtack biscuits. It turned out to be a simple runaway situation, happy ending I suppose, although we do not know what made her want to disappear from her family in the first place. The social worker is to investigate further.

We received a telex from the Housing Corporation in Yellowknife requesting a complete housing inventory (number and condition of units, number of occupants including age, sex, etc., and rent income histories) by mid July. Are they crazy? I don't have time to do this and the secretary of the local housing association has a sixth grade education, is not welcome in every home, due to clan affiliations and lord knows what other factors, and has gone fishing in any case and may not be back until August. It is another indication of how little the folks in the capital understand conditions out here in the settlements.

Ian Mackenzie, Settlement Manager

NIKMAK 5
Rankin Inlet Nursing Station
October 14, 1970

Aiyayai.

You see, paniga, what I am trying to tell you is that we Inuit survived those desperate times, just as you can survive the demons that are hammering away at your spirit now. Just as some of us survived the epidemics that swept through the hunting and fishing camps after the explorers left, or when the whalers came in their huge wooden boats to empty our great bay of the whales. Every time such strangers left, many people would fall ill and die from the boat sickness. But some would survive, Kublu. Some would survive, as I did.

When I was a young man, an illness struck my grandfather Sukusi's camp and almost wiped us out completely. In the early spring, Sukusi decided that we should go ice fishing at a big lake toward the eastern edge of our traditional hunting grounds, near the territory of the Aivilingmiut. Sometimes we would make contact and share tea and meals with members of that group, and my cousins and I would look them over to see if perhaps there might be a future bride among them. But they were never particularly friendly to us, and we would not stay with them too long, because they were not our kin. We were suspicious of each other, but we had to barter sometimes—soft soapstone for hard metal, or whatever was needed or new.

That spring, shortly after we had made brief contact with a small group of Aivilingmiut, my grandfather and great uncle and both their wives fell ill. They shook with fever and could not hold their food. They became too weak to get up and walk. Soon my two uncles and my own mother also became sick. After a few days, there were only two of us left alive in the camp: me and my uncle Qarmaq, Kavik's youngest son.

With broken hearts, we did what we had to do. The earth was still frozen, so we buried our family members in a rock cairn, with the women facing the land and the men facing the sea. We sang and wept as we worked.

Uncle Qarmaq and I could not afford to let our fear paralyze us, but without women to sew our clothing and prepare our food, we could not go on indefinitely. We talked about what we should do. Neither of us had the heart to raid another group and steal wives, as desperate men sometimes did. If we got lucky, we might be able to find and join another camp, particularly if we found one where we had some distant kin, but we would always feel like strangers and outsiders, compared to how we had been.

We packed our belongings and left that place with heavy hearts. We decided to travel to a new trading post we had heard about, to see if we could trade our spare dogs and equipment for some traps, so we could try our hand at trapping foxes for a while. We had heard that the traders paid well for fox furs—almost enough to keep a trapper in tea and bannock and bacon. It would be a change from hunting and fishing all the time. We thought just maybe two lone men could sustain themselves for a while in such a way.

We felt a bit discouraged with the ways of our ancestors just then, so our ears were open wide when we heard a rumour at the trading post about some kind of big building project going on at Repulse Bay. They said many Qablunaat had gathered there, and they were seeking still more able-bodied men to work. We tried to imagine if they were building a really large iglu or a huge inuksuk, or what it could be. It was rumoured that the Qablunaat would provide a warm place for sleeping and all the food you could imagine to eat, as well as shiny metal discs to use for buying goods, as long as you were willing to work hard. At first we thought this must be all hallucinations and lies, but given our dire situation, Qarmaq and I decided to go and see for ourselves. What did we have to lose?

We travelled all the way to Repulse Bay by dog team, making haste, as the sea ice was beginning to rot. We took turns mushing the dogs, and we stopped briefly only when the dogs needed to rest, or to hunt seals when we ran out of meat.

We arrived in Repulse Bay in late May, and learned that the rumours we had heard were true. It seems that America, that country way below the south part of Canada, had decided to build some kind of huge trap line across our land, with equipment that would catch flying weapons some Russians might want to send over the north pole. This sounded crazy to us, but the Qablunaat must have believed this to be true, because they hired me and my uncle the minute we arrived, and they put us to work right away.

This may be hard for you to understand, Kublu, but we had never seen a building except for a Hudson Bay trading post or a mission school until then. For men who had been born in iglus and lived all of their lives on the land, what we saw in Repulse Bay made our eyes spin in our heads. We saw huge machines made from enough steel to make thousands of frying pans fly in the air. We listened to voices from far away speak to us over the radio. We saw moving pictures shown on the wall of the hangar building that filled us with wonder and awe. We tried not to have our mouths hanging open in amazement all of the time.

We were not ready to go back to life on the land just then, so we applied ourselves to learning new skills. We learned to use hammers and saws, to read maps and other drawings. We learned to eat potatoes and bread and pie. We learned to sleep in a bed with sheets and blankets. We bought cotton shirts and wool pants and leather boots with our pay. We learned how to take hot showers without laughing about how it tickled.

We learned that the Americamiut were moving hundreds of tons of cargo by airlift, sealift and Caterpillar train to many traditional Inuit hunting grounds north of what they called the Arctic Circle, to build stations along a line called the 69th parallel on their maps. They were flying in thousands of heavy equipment operators and hiring hundreds of labourers—many of them Inuit, who were well adapted to working long hours in the cold. To support the new stations, they needed runways, hangars, warehousing, bunkhouses, office buildings, and more. Money was no object. Time was short. The Russians might attack at any moment.

My Uncle Qarmaq and I worked on that DEWline site all summer. We learned many things about the Qablunaat—how they talk, what they do in a day, the food they like to eat, the things they say as jokes. It was very strange for us, living in this camp of nothing but construction workers, waking at the same time every day to the sound of a horn, going to the job site at the same time, six or seven days a week. But we were being fed and housed in comfort, learning new skills, learning to speak a bit of Qablunaatitut. We missed our family, we missed the freedom of living on the land, but we also began to appreciate being freed from the hardships of that life—the constant struggle to find something to eat and to ensure there would be enough skins and hides to provide our clothing and tools through the year.

Then suddenly one morning we were told that the work was all finished and we would have to move on. Move where, we wondered. Move on to what?

Ayayaaa.

ALISON 11
Rankin Inlet, Northwest Territories
June 14, 1970

Nurse Bauer has been avoiding me big time, which is just fine with me. She didn't have the guts to confront me herself, but sent Sherry to have a talk with me. Some drivel about being caught in a moment of loneliness. I cut her speech off. By then I had already decided to live and let live, so long as it doesn't involve me. But Sherry cried and told me how badly she needs her job, and she begged me not to do anything to jeopardize it. Her husband took off with the sitter just after their second son was born, and now her mother is raising the boys in Halifax with the paycheck that Sherry sends her every month. This was the best job she could find, and she needs it badly.

We all need to do our jobs as professionals here, and I have decided that private lives are none of my business. Things could be worse. We three can and must co-exist at the station, but I do feel the need to get out of here more frequently.

I went to a going-away party for the Swedes that Jean threw at the Transient Centre. I have become fond of them and am sorry to see them go. My fellow foreigners. I wished them bon voyage and best of luck, then had myself a good cry when I returned to the nursing station alone.

Little by little, I am starting to build connections with the people who live in this community—not just the outsiders, but also the ones who have survived in this region for generations. I asked Annie Pilakapsi, a young woman who works as a nurses' aid here, if she might be willing to help me with my pronunciation now and then. She agreed readily, and has since invited me to her home twice. She lives with her parents and a younger brother in one of the tiny older wooden homes some people call the "matchboxes" or "coffins." It is basically one long room, with an oil stove in the middle. Sleeping mattresses are arranged at the far end of the room, behind some storage shelves. There is a formica table with four chairs around it near the only door. Annie introduced me to her family members, who participate in the lessons, encouraging me by clapping when I get it right, and laughing at me when I get things wrong. We drink litres of sweet, milky tea during the lessons. The hardest part is that the entire family smokes cigarettes, so the house smells like an ashtray and my lungs feel as though they are filled with clay by the end of our sessions.

I have been to events at the community centre several times now. Jean Phillipe invited to me to go for the Thursday movie night once, and I have gone by myself several times since, but each time I have gone they have shown the same movie—Easy Rider. Apparently there has been some kind of foul up with the service that is supposed to deliver new films to the community by airmail. No one seems to care that they have seen the film before. It is quite an experience to watch the audience, almost entirely Inuit, watching the antics of Peter Fonda and company projected onto a wall in this place, so very far from Hollywood. They talk and laugh about the strange scenery, the funny motorcycles, and the odd costumes worn by the characters riding them. A reverent silence falls during the psychedelic tripping portion of the movie, as if people are trying to make out what it was all about. The brothel scene and Mardi Gras events draw loud gasps of disbelief, and the crowd shouts at the projectionist to rewind and show the scene of the chopper blowing up over and over again.

Annie told me that there was to be a big dance this Saturday that I should not miss. As I approached the hall I could hear lots of rhythmic boot stomping and the bleating of a concertina. When I entered the hall, I saw that several square dancing rings had formed, and local men and women were reeling with enthusiasm. No one was calling the moves, but everyone seemed to know what to do and where to go. From time to time the women would stand in a circle facing outward, and their male partners would face them, making a most impressive racket as their heels pounded the wooden floor boards. It was thrilling to see—and feel—the spirited dancing. I was puzzled about the origin of this Inuit ritual, but a bystander explained that the whalers who hunted in the Hudson Bay during the late nineteenth century had taught this style of music and dance to the Inuit, and they still practice it today.

After I had watched for a while, a young Inuit man approached me and asked me if I'd like to dance. I said I couldn't—I had no idea what to do. He said that didn't matter, he would lead me and I should just hang on to his arm. So I tried it. Of course I stepped on a few toes and felt out of step much of the time, but I found I could do all right if I just kept switching my weight from foot to foot in time with the music and let Pauluusie and the others push me and pull me wherever I needed to go. It was great fun and a good workout, but after a while a thick cloud of cigarette smoke had built up in the room and I had to get out into the fresh air. I thanked Pauluusie for the dance lesson and headed for home. He winked and said he would see me around.

IVALUK 4
Rankin Inlet, N.W.T.
June 28, 1970

Dear Tomasie:

Our angajuk Sakku has taken up soapstone carving and now he looks down his nose at almost everyone including me. He keeps up teasing me about the honey wagon work I do these days. I tell him it is decent hard work and I need the money. I am paying for that three-wheeler with my labour and I am getting stronger in the process too which seems to make more girls want to hang onto me and take a ride so what is wrong with that picture?

But you smell like shit he says to me. You smell like stone I say back. Shit and stone both part of nature. Yah but one stinks worse he say. Yah but stink is in the nose of the smeller I tell him. We all human we all got to shit every one of us. Our Anaana handle your shit when we are babies then and I handle your shit now. It is work got to be done by someone and it is good steady work because no one ever stops shitting as long as he is alive. In good times or bad times everybody keep shitting. That shut him up some. Then he offer to lend me the money to pay off my balance at the Bay but I do not need or want to be in debt to him. I can take care of myself. He spit at me in frustration over my lack of concern about our family image.

Maybe it is Carol who does not like having a brother-in-law hauling shit around town. I do not care what any Qablunaaq think of me. Carol too. They are here today and gone tomorrow. It is the Inuit in this town who stay and who go through every thing together and who still going to be here in the future. We are mixed up ends of all kinds of groups here—some from the seashores and some from the inland places. But no matter where we come from this is our home now. When you survive so much sickness and starvation and then boarding schools and sanatoriums well you stick together after that. Sometimes fight but one big family.

I wonder if Carol has done something to our brother's brain. He seems different since they got together even though nothing has changed. Sakku puffs up and thinks he is a big important artist now but he is carving soapstone seals for the Coop to sell to tourists. He is no Tiktak but I will not say so. Let him think and do what he wants. I try to get him out on the land to hunt and fish every now and then so we can both get a peep at the Inuk still inside of him when his mind is not twisted up in little circles.

Maybe he gets crazy sometimes from his food. Too much Spam and chocolate bars and not enough fresh meat—the food his ancestors ate almost nothing but for centuries. Pure protein and not sugar and all that crap they put in food now to make it last for years on the shelf at the Bay.

Take it easy Nukaqtaaq and don't each too much crap so you too keep strong.

ALISON 12
Rankin Inlet, Northwest Territories
July 1, 1970

The Nursing Station is closed today (except for emergencies) for the Canada Day holiday, so I have an unexpected day off.

After my Inuktitut class last night, I decided to stay at the school and use the library for some extra studying. I was working away when I suddenly heard a sharp tapping at the window. I looked up and saw Pauluusie Nukilik, the young man I'd met at the community dance a few weeks ago, waving wildly and gesturing at me to come outside. When I did, I saw him grinning from ear to ear and pointing at his new Honda motorcycle. "Hey—I thought you might want to go for a ride and see some of the countryside around here," he said. How could I resist? Although it was late, it was still as light as mid-afternoon.

I hopped on the motorcycle behind Pauluusie. He tried to start it several times, without success. He turned and apologized, said he'd get it going next time for sure. That's when I noticed beer on his breath, but it was too late for reconsiderations. The motorcycle roared to life, and we were off, lurching in a cloud of dust along the road to Lake Nipissar. The tundra looked beautiful. The snow was all gone; so the land was a patchwork of green moss, grey rock, and blue ponds dotted with bird. It felt good to hold onto another person with the wind whipping my hair around my face. The air smelled so fresh and clean.

Pauluusie pulled off the road at a rock plateau beyond the lake. We got off the bike, and there was a sudden scuffle, and next thing I knew we were rolling on the moss, grabbing at each other's clothing. It ended quickly, and then I felt a bit nauseated. Was I this starved and desperate for intimacy? I don't even know this fellow, and I had taken no precautions. Stupid, stupid, stupid.

We sat up and leaned against a boulder. Pauluusie offered me a cigarette, and lit one for himself when I declined.

"I wanna talk, okay?" he asked. "Okay," I replied, still in a confused a daze.

Pauluusie told me that he lives in a house with nine other people. He is frustrated with living at home, and with living in Rankin Inlet, where there is no privacy. Half the population is under twelve years old, so children are everywhere, an efficient network of little eyes and ears. It is impossible to do anything outside their range. Gossip races through town as fast as a grass fire. Even now, he predicted, there would be rumours spreading through the community about the two of us, just because we rode away together on his motorcycle. No one ever knocks on doors. Everyone knows where you are at all times, what you are doing, and whom you are doing it with.

He asked me to tell him about city life. He wanted to know if what he had heard is true: that young adults there live in their own apartments, drive their own cars, watch television or go out dancing. Do whatever they want to do, whenever they want to do it.

I told him those things were true, but that city life is not all it is cracked up to be. It can be very exciting and liberating. But it can also be lonely and isolating. I told him that in some ways I was a fugitive from that very sort of life, that I had traded those freedoms willingly for life in a small place. I envied him his experience of a rich and intimate extended family life, a sense of belonging to both a family and a community.

"Ha!" he scoffed. "There is no fun here at all. My parents won't let me leave this place, not even for job training. Everyone watches every move I make. They try to keep me in line. I can't save money to travel on my own, either, because whatever I earn I have to give to my mother for food, or to my sisters to buy clothes, or to my uncle for Skidoo repairs. And all the girls here know me far too well."

We were quiet for a moment, watching pink and green wisps of the Aurora Borealis wave across the sky, glowing and fading and pulsing. Then Pauluusie grabbed my hand and asked me if I would marry him. I was stunned. I took my hand back and said I was sorry about what had happened, that it had been a mistake on my part, and I was sorry if it had given him the wrong idea. There was no way I could marry him, as I hardly know him at all, and furthermore, I am not looking for a husband at present. He looked sceptical. He pleaded with me some more. He begged me to whisk him away to a different sort of life, to his dream about living in a city in the south—disco dancing until dawn.

I told him I was flattered by his offer, and that he was an attractive fellow, and I hoped he wouldn't take it personally, but the answer was still no.

"But *nagligivagit*," he whined.

"What does that mean?" I asked, perplexed.

"It means I love you! I have been watching you ever since you arrived in this town, ever since I first saw you buying those walking boots at the Bay. I think you are beautiful and you seem really smart, too."

"But that's no reason to marry me," I protested. "You don't know me. I don't know anything about you. I am not ready to get married to anyone. And besides, I would lose my job—they don't allow married staff at the nursing station."

He grabbed my hand again and pulled me toward him, moving in for a kiss.

"Look, I have a boyfriend back home." I protested, and finally that seemed to do the trick.

"Well, why didn't you say so?" he asked, springing to his feet.

Pauluusie drove me back to town in a quiet gloom, his trail bike bumping over humps of tundra in the dusk. Even at that very late hour, there were numerous children playing and riding their bicycles in the streets. What a peculiar world I have found in this place, I thought. I wondered why I feel comfortable in it, and not as utterly foreign as surely I should.

Still not a word from home.

NIKMAK 6
Rankin Inlet Nursing Station
October 14, 1970

Ayayeah.

I am back, paniga. Your anaana sent Sakku to fetch me, to force me to come home and eat something. Now she is satisfied that I am not going to collapse, so I have returned to carry on with my story, our story.

When that work dried up so suddenly at Repulse Bay, Qarmaq and I were very sad for a while. We thought we had no choice but to go back to our desperate trapping plan, but we had heard that the foxes were now less plentiful and also that the price of the furs had dropped. This made us fear that our old plan might not succeed.

Then the Americamiut told us there might be more DEWline work available for strong and sober men like us, at the place the Qablunaat call Coral Harbour, on a big island further to the south, in the great Hudson Bay. So my uncle and I hitched a ride on a supply barge that was going to that place.

We found Coral Harbour to be even more remarkable than Repulse Bay had been. It was the big supply centre for many of the DEWline stations that were under construction in the region at that time. Once again, we were hired as soon as we showed up and they saw that we were fit. We spent most of our days moving here and there great sacks of metal nails and the longest pieces of lumber we had ever seen, and even big square posts made of steel. We did whatever the Qablunaat told us to do, and we were paid very well for doing so.

My uncle and I saved most of our money. We talked about one day buying a wooden home of our own, maybe even a Bombardier, and some guns to go hunting with just for fun, or maybe even a big boat to use for walrus and whale hunting in the great bay.

One clear summer day, my uncle and I woke up and noticed that the mosquitoes had died off in an overnight frost, which made us feel happy. Later that morning, as the Americamiut were unloading supplies from a big ship in the harbour, a cable snapped and a whole pallet of cement bags fell onto my uncle below. He was pinned to the ground from the waist down, his pelvis crushed. By the time they brought me to him, his spirit was already gone. Later that day, I carried him out onto the land and buried him under stones, and I lay awake there all night under the northern lights, wiping away tears and feeling as if my spirit was as crushed as Qarmaq's body had been.

There were other Inuit around at this place, but none of them were my kin. I felt as lonely as the north star shining in the sky above me, without anyone left from my very own family to cheer me, without any real connection to this world, with no one to care for, and no one left to care for me.

I resolved that the time had come for me to find a wife, and to make a new family of my own. This was an urgent matter.

There was a proper Inuit woman named Ukpik who worked at Coral Harbour in the bunkhouse, cleaning floors and making up the beds. She did not look all used up. So I returned to the work camp and proposed to her the very next day, even though her people were Sallirmiut. At first she must have thought I was joking. She giggled and shrugged and said "*Aamai.*" But I sat her down at an empty cafeteria table and told her my life story and about my savings and about my dream of creating a family of my own, since I had lost all of my people, including now my last relative, my uncle Qarmaq. I told her that I was a very hard worker, a strong and reliable man. I promised her she would not regret her decision, if she should decide to take me for her husband.

She told me then that she already had three children—two boys and a girl. Perhaps Ukpik thought this news would make me change my mind about marrying her, but I felt so lonely and alone in this world at that moment that the idea of gaining an instant family appealed to me all the more.

Her parents had promised her at birth to the son of a hunter in their camp group, and she had been married at a young age. Her husband was a good man and a fine hunter, and she had grown to love him. When their third child (your brother Sakku) had only one winter, the tragedy happened. The father was sealing out near the edge of the ice floe, with his family camped nearby. Ukpik was watching her husband from the shore, rocking Sakku in her arms, when she heard a loud crack. A chunk of ice suddenly broke free from the mass along the shore, and her husband had no chance to jump off. Suddenly he was speeding toward the open sea, the gap between them growing larger and larger. Like many traditional Inuit, he had never learned how to swim, so they both knew instantly what this meant: he was a dead man. Ukpik let out a loud wail as he gave her a final wave and then collapsed onto that white fleck and rode it toward the horizon until she could no longer see him at all.

Ukpik told me that her parents were at home looking after her three young children, and that is why she had taken a job at the DEWline station, to provide an income to help support them all. Her brother Amarok helped by providing fresh meat to their extended family.

I assured Ukpik that I still wanted to marry her, and that I would be honoured to help raise her children, as well as any of our own that we might have. She said she would talk to her parents about it that evening.

She gave me hope. I did not sleep all night.

The next day I was invited to the home of her family in the Inuit camp that had formed not far from the DEWline base. This camp was a collection of tents and shacks that had been banged together from scrap plywood and canvas tarps, to provide living places for some of the Inuit who worked at the station, or for their relatives who wanted to stay nearby.

Ukpik's family served me tea and dried tuktu, and then they asked me many hard questions about my origins, my family, my past, my skills, and my future plans. They watched me carefully, trying to learn what kind of man I was. Then her father began to speak. He said that Ukpik had already suffered much, and they worried about how she would be able to carry her burden after they were gone. They had hoped to engage her to a distant cousin who was hunting over near Pelly Bay and who was looking for a wife, but Ukpik had declared that she was not interested. She preferred making beds and washing pots to chewing hides and sewing kamiit. She insisted that she wanted to work at the DEWline station and use her wages to take care of her parents and her children.

At last, her father asked Ukpik, who had not said one word, if she would like to marry me. She blushed, then slowly smiled and said "Iiiii!" I felt happier than I had felt in a very long time, and suddenly I saw hope for my future. The children were called in from their game of hide and seek to meet me. Pitsiark stood bashfully looking at her feet while Adjuk poked at his baby brother Sakku, trying to make him laugh. I stepped forward and hugged the children one by one, and willingly accepted my duty to be their father.

Women were not allowed to live at any DEWline station at that time, so I moved out of the workers' dormitory and into the wooden shack that Ukpik shared with her family. It was crowded, but I did not mind. I felt as if I finally belonged to a camp group again. I was part of a new family. Ukpik and I made enough money to buy food and heating oil to sustain us all. A van came in summer and a Bombardier in winter to pick us up and take us to our work place.

We were happy together, and soon Ukpik became pregnant again, with your angajuk Ivaluk. But as the long nights of winter began to shorten again, we received strange and startling news from the Qablunaat. That was the end of our work at Coral Harbour. Taima. Just like that. And this time there was no other DEWline site to move on to, because the Americamiut had completed their whole trap line of stations across the north. They were finished with their project, and so they were finished with us, too.

Perhaps you think we were stupid not to see that coming, Kublu. But what did we know of these things? We knew only that once there had been hunting and fishing, and sometimes there had been starvation and hardships and illness in our camps, and then there had been wage work and heated buildings and food and money and comforts. Now there would be no more of this wage work, except for a handful of Qablunaat who would stay on to run the airport. We wondered how we would survive.

It was hard to go from construction work back to hunting, but that is what I did. I joined Ukpik's brother, and we did our best to provide fish and caribou and seal meat for the growing family. Amarok had married, and now he and his new wife had a baby on the way, too. It seemed there would always be more mouths to feed.

Everything about hunting felt challenging to me then. I had become spoiled by heated buildings and found myself complaining about the cold and the boredom during the long hours I had to spend bent over a breathing hole, hoping for a seal to come. And I was not familiar with the land around Coral Harbour. I did not know where the old fishing weirs were, or the best caribou crossing lakes, and so I had to learn everything about these things all over again from Amarok, as if I were a boy. I had become used to a different way of life, and I regretted its sudden ending.

I have talked so much today, Kublu, that my throat has become sore. And now the janitor has been sent to tell me that I must leave. I am worn out, anyway.

Until tomorrow, paniga.

Ayayaaa.

ALISON 13
Rankin Inlet, Northwest Territories
July 5, 1970

On one of my recent forays through town, a middle-aged man in a Department of Public Works uniform stopped me in the street. With a thick Newfoundland accent, he introduced himself as John Devers. He invited me to a party at his house on Friday night. It was to be a big send-off for the schoolteachers who get to bugger off south for the summer. He said most of the "ex-pats" would be there and there would be plenty of booze and grub. I accepted the invitation and got directions to his house.

When I arrived around 8 p.m., the bash was well underway. I could see that serious inroads already had been made into two oversized bottles of Seagram's whisky. John greeted me with a bear hug and then offered me a bowl of chocolate-covered ants with a flourish. "Something about living in this godforsaken place makes me crave exotic things I would never think of eating back home," he explained.

John yelled above the din to introduce me and he told everyone to introduce themselves to me in turn and make me feel welcome, in case my services should be needed to cure them of crabs or the clap or whatever else might inspire them to acquaint themselves with the nursing station. He gave me a generous pour of rye and steered me toward a buffet table arrayed with a variety of chopped fruits and vegetables, strips of grilled caribou meat, baked potatoes, canned mushrooms on skewers, chocolate cake, and a huge jug of California red table wine.

I fixed myself a plate while various people came and introduced themselves and asked me where I was from, etc. I met a German biologist who was doing her PhD research on caribou migration patterns, as well as a Polish-Canadian engineer who was doing research on the effects of permafrost on different types of building foundations. There were also several American men who had come to Rankin Inlet to salvage a sunken whaling ship in the vicinity.

When the music started, I was kept busy dancing. Married or single, many of the men wanted a dance, except for the cluster of hardcore cribbage players who sat at a card table in the corner, totally absorbed in their tournament.

Eventually, an Irish fellow named Ryan asked me to dance. He squeezed me tighter as the song progressed. Then he put his lips to my ear and suggested we retreat to one of the bedrooms in the staff house and take a little nap together to digest our dinner. As the song ended, he gave me a wink and a pat on the bottom. I said no thanks; I needed to be going, as I had to be on duty early the following day. I thanked the host and retrieved my jacket from the pile by the door. Ryan followed me outside and offered to walk me home. I declined, but he followed me down the street anyway. As we walked past the post office, he grabbed me and pushed me up against the door, pressing his hard cock against my belly. There was not enough room to pull my arm back and slap him, but I managed to jam him in the nose with the heel of my hand.

"Ooow," he wailed, as blood spurted from his left nostril.

"You nurses are all the same," he yelled after me as I hurried away toward the lights of the nursing station. "All a bunch of frigid bitches!"

ALISON 14
Rankin Inlet, Northwest Territories
July 12, 1970

Wayne and Kublu's baby was born at the Nursing Station early on Thursday morning this week, and I was thrilled to be the one to deliver him. A healthy baby boy, almost seven pounds, with a hearty scream to let us all know he had arrived awake and hungry.

It is the highlight of my career, delivering this baby. This is the first time I have caught a baby for parents I know personally. I experienced a rush of indescribable joy and a surge of inexplicable hope when I held that newborn boy. I'm sure there were tears in my own eyes as well as his parents', so it is just as well that Nurse Bauer was not around to witness such unprofessional demeanour.

As I was filling out the mandatory paperwork, I asked the new parents what they would name the baby. Wayne deferred to Kublu. Kublu said that her parents would pick a traditional name for the boy, but for the sake of the Qablunaaq paperwork, she said I should write down Radar Tunu. I asked if the name had something to do with the father's flying career. She said no. She had seen some previews at the community centre for a coming movie called Mash, and she thought a young Corporal named Radar O'Reilly was cute. So Radar would be his nickname, and a name the Qablunaat, including his own father, could pronounce easily.

I was still walking around in a cheery cloud over Radar's birth, when that vile man Ryan Dolan showed up at my clinic. He had been hanging around town for several days, up to who knows what mischief, and had finally came in to the nursing station to get someone to take a look at his drippy cock. Lucky me.

He turned out to have gonorrhoea, so then it became my job to grill him to find out where he's been poking his pecker recently, so we could call those poor women in for shots or testing. I also had to go down to the Hamlet office to use the radiophone, because we had to contact the nursing stations in several other settlements Ryan has visited recently, spreading his particular brand of joy. It tickled me to have to shout the news over the radiophone that Ryan Dolan had a confirmed case of gonorrhoea and it would be necessary to identify and treat anyone he has had sexual contact with. But my greatest pleasure was taking that big needle full of penicillin and jabbing it into his arse a bit more forcefully than was absolutely necessary.

(I can feel cocky about all this because the tests I did on myself after that incident with Pauluusie all came back negative. Whew).

NIKMAK 7
Rankin Inlet Nursing Station
October 15, 1970

Listen to me, Kublu, and I will tell you the rest of the story, how we came to be in this place and how our family managed to find our way in a new world once more.

Life in Coral Harbour became more tense and strange, without any wage work. I felt that Ukpik's family had looked at me a certain way when we both were earning good pay at the DEWline station, but another way when we had no income, in spite of my efforts to help feed the group. I'm not sure if this was true, but my heart felt heavy and I was not able to sleep well.

Then we heard about something else happening, down along the west coast of the Hudson Bay. A mine had just opened in a place the Inuit call Kangiqliniq but the Qablunaat had named Rankin Inlet. It was rumoured that they were seeking able-bodied men to come and work— this time to dig rocks out of the earth, so they could find metal in these rocks and use it to make coins and other things. I could not imagine how this would happen, but they were said to be offering good wages and even warm housing for the workers and their families.

Ukpik and I went down to the DEWline station to ask the Qablunaat about this mine talk, and they told us it was true. They said the mining company had an airplane that they were sending to Coral Harbour and other communities, offering free rides to Rankin Inlet for men who wanted to come and work at the new mine, as well as their wives and children.

We decided, my nuliaq and I, that the next time that plane came, we would get on it no matter how frightening it seemed. We would go to this place called Rankin Inlet, to earn money to support the family once again. All of us but Adjuk would go, because Ukpik's parents wanted to keep him, as was their right, since he was their daughter's first-born child.

So Ukpik and Pitsiark and Sakku and I were soon on an airplane, flying like birds along the coast of the great Hudson Bay, and Ivaluk was with us too, riding along in the belly of your anaana, who wept all the way to Rankin Inlet. She had never been away from her family and already she was missing them too much. But she stopped crying when we landed, because she was determined to accept this new life and make the best of it, even if it might mean never seeing her parents or her brother or her son Adjuk again.

Soon we were settled in a company house in Rankin Inlet. It was a huge house, with three bedrooms. One for your anaana and I, one for your sister Pitsiark, and one for your brother Sakku, although soon they would have to share those rooms with their new siblings, Ivaluk and you. Our home became filled with laughter and love.

Working in a mine was so strange, going down that deep hole in a noisy elevator, down into a darkness darker than winter, to blast and shovel rock so far below the earth. But all the Inuit men were doing it, right alongside the Qablunaat. We made good money, and there were many things to buy at the big new Hudson Bay store. We had our own mattresses to sleep on, with blankets and pillows, a spare set of clothing, pots to cook in, and food to cook in the pots. We had our children to raise. What more could we want? We were content then, for a while.

Aiyayayaaiieh.

ALISON 15
Rankin Inlet, Northwest Territories
July 27, 1970

I have seen lots of the countryside lately, so there is much to catch up on. I have done more hitchhiking around on bush planes, and I also had an unexpected trip to Marble Island by boat.

Wayne invited me to go flying with him on my day off, as he had supplies to deliver to a tourist fishing camp on Baker Lake. Because there is no landing strip there, he took the pontoon plane. How strange it felt to be rowed out to an airplane.

By now, the snow has melted, but the permafrost down below keeps the melted water puddled at the surface. As we flew over, it seemed as if a million small lakes were winking at us. We were flying among the clouds, yet they were also reflected in all the water below us, making it seem as if the whole world was made of almost nothing but sky and cloud.

Wayne pointed out several small fishing camps along the way, with just two or three tents each. He said a few Inuit families have gone back to living on the land year round, and many more spend a good part of the summer camping on the land, once the kids are out of school. Perhaps some time I will be lucky enough to go out with an Inuit family like that, to experience what living on the land is like.

When we arrived at the fishing camp, a motorboat buzzed out to meet the plane. There must always be a sense of excitement when a plane arrives in such a place, with the promise of fresh provisions or needed supplies, as well as a glimpse of new faces or the possibility of some good gossip.

I helped unload the boxes of milk and meat and vegetables and whisky and beer and cigarettes, and soon we were off again. On the way back to Rankin Inlet, Wayne made a detour and landed at the dock in Chesterfield Inlet, a small town with the look of a tidy English village about it. There were lots of well-maintained white buildings with red roofs that are owned by the Catholic Church. It seems the church established a stronghold in this place long ago and has made a considerable investment in it over the years. There was even a two-story hospital staffed by French-speaking Catholic nuns that put our small nursing station to shame. They were providing long term care for several special needs babies, as well as a few elderly people.

The nuns knew Wayne and seemed delighted to see him. They insisted we join them for lunch—homemade vegetable soup and corned beef sandwiches made from rye bread they had baked fresh that morning. They even opened a bottle of wine to celebrate their unexpected company, as well as the fact that the church had just been awarded the contract to keep the town's streets graded and ploughed for another year. Wayne declined since he was flying, but I enjoyed a glass of wine with the nuns, which made me fall into a contented doze on the homeward journey.

The next morning, I received an unusual nursing assignment. The American salvage crew out at Marble Island had radioed Ian MacKenzie to say there had been an accident. One of the divers had fallen from the mast and broken an arm and several ribs when he landed on the deck. It was not terribly serious, but the man was in considerable discomfort. They asked if we could to send someone to attend to the injured man, rather than have him make the 150-kilometer trip back to Rankin Inlet, bouncing around on the choppy waves.

Nurse Bauer appointed me to go. I was only too glad to get out of the nursing station and off on another adventure.

The RCMP boat was not available; it was out on some other assignment. Ian asked around and was able to hire a local Peterhead boat, so within a few hours we were motoring off toward Marble Island. The weather was mild, and the inlet is almost entirely free of pack ice now.

There were only three of us on board—Kanik, the owner of the boat, a young man named Ivaluk, and me. The men were polite enough to me, but there was not much conversation on the voyage out. I sat in the bow with my back to the wind and the salty spray, watching the community shrink in the distance until I could no longer see it at all. I was glad to be upwind, as the men smoked one cigarette after another.

After several hours, I saw Ivaluk pointing, and I turned to see Marble Island jutting abruptly out of the shimmering sea, huge and white and eerie. When we motored into the harbour, the archaeological expedition ship was plainly visible, anchored about a hundred meters from the shore. Two men leapt into a rowboat and came out to greet us.

I had begun to feel a bit queasy from the motion of the sea swells, so I was glad to set foot on terra firma again. I turned to see Kanik and Ivaluk roll out of the boat and crawl up the rocky shore on their elbows and knees. I wanted to ask what in the world they were doing, but Charley, the expedition director, hurried me toward the tent where the injured man was waiting for my ministrations. The poor fellow was groaning and sweating, though the tent was quite cool. I treated him, using the morphine and the brace and bandages I had brought along. The patient was very grateful to be made more comfortable.

Outside, it was windy. There was a harsh sun shining, but it did not feel warm. A definite sense of mystery seemed to hang over this rocky place surrounded by water as far as the eye could see. Charley invited us to spend the night on the island, if we wanted to. That sounded appealing, but I had not cleared any overnight stay with Nurse Bauer, and I did not know what kind of arrangement Ian had made for use of the Peterhead boat, so I said we should head back to Rankin Inlet after a brief tour of the island. I knew there would be plenty of daylight to get back before dark at this time of year.

Charley gave us the island tour himself. As we strolled, he pointed out all kinds of artefacts I might have missed—stone formations that marked the location of former buildings or tent rings, some old metal barrel hoops that had gone brittle with rust, and even the remnants of an ancient-looking amphitheatre. How sad to imagine those ill-fated whalers putting on skits and plays to entertain themselves while awaiting certain death, in clear view of the crosses and cairns that marked the burial places of their comrades.

As we finished our tour, the cook called out that supper was ready, and we (including the Inuit men) were invited to join them. He had fixed poached Arctic Char with hollandaise sauce, instant mashed potatoes, and tinned fruit salad. I suddenly realized I hadn't eaten anything since breakfast. I was ravenous, so the food tasted fabulous to me. Kanik and Ivaluk ate the fish, but picked at the rest.

We said our goodbyes, and walked back toward the rowboat. I asked Ivaluk why he and Kanik had crawled up the shore on their hands and knees. He told me the Inuit believe that the spirit of a quirky old woman inhabits Marble Island. It is necessary to crawl up to the high tide line the way they had, in order to show her proper respect, or she will get angry and bring you bad luck on the one-year anniversary of your visit to the island.

I am not superstitious, but both Ivaluk and Kanik had such a look of concern and dread on their faces that I went down to the water's edge and crawled back up to the high water mark, the way they had done before. Just in case. Better to be safe than sorry. The Inuit men looked relieved.

I let the waves of the Hudson Bay rock me into a light doze on the way home, but I was startled awake by the crack of a rifle. I sat up to see Ivaluk lower his gun as Kanik swung the heavy boat around to where a seal was bobbing in an expanding ring of bloody water. As we approached it, Ivaluk threw a harpoon smartly. It hit its target, and he hauled the seal into the boat, using a line that had been attached to the harpoon. As soon as the seal was on the deck, he poured a little water into its mouth from a canteen, then plunged a knife into its centre and ripped out its liver. He cut a piece off and ate it raw, then handed the remains to Kanik. Kanik gripped the bloody liver between his teeth and sawed a piece off with his pocket knife, working the blade so close to his face I thought he might cut the tip of his nose off, but he didn't. He smiled broadly as he chewed the bloody stuff.

"*Naammaktuq?*" Ivaluk asked.

"Iiii," Kanik replied.

"Tastes good," Ivaluk translated for my benefit. "You want some?"

I declined. He then cut another piece of liver and threw it into the water. I asked him if he liked it so much, why he was throwing it away. He said something about trying to please a goddess or sea spirit, who would become angry if he did not throw some bits back into the sea. This would help ensure a continued abundance of seals in the future.

There seemed to be a strong bond between the two men. I asked Ivaluk if Kanik were his father or uncle. "No," he replied, "but we are related somehow, through marriage and adoptions or something, like most everyone around here. It's complicated. We have so many ties, we might as well be blood relatives. Also, we just like to work together," he said with a grin.

I was surprised when the men turned the boat up into a small, unfamiliar inlet. We should be close to home by now, I thought, so what is going on? They anchored the boat near a rock shelf, and got out, built a fire and put on a pot of water. "Shouldn't we keep going?" I asked, "to be sure we get back to Rankin Inlet before dark?"

"There is always time for tea," Ivaluk replied. "If you think you do not have enough time for a cup of tea, you are in too much of a hurry and need to slow down." I was a bit annoyed, but had to admit that the cup of tea with a splash of evaporated milk and some sugar in it seemed to pick all of us up. Finally, we were underway again, warm and in good spirits.

Rankin Inlet came into view just as the sun was beginning to set. The stars and the lights on the harbour twinkled on the bay, as green and pink wisps of the Aurora Borealis swirled in the sky above us, reflecting on the water below. I could not imagine a more beautiful welcome home.

As we approached the dock, I saw Kublu and her new baby, Radar, walking along the shore. I began to wave madly to her.

Ivaluk's tanned brow wrinkled in surprise. "You know my sister?" he asked.

ALISON 16
Rankin Inlet, Northwest Territories
August 15, 1970

The annual supply ship sailed into the Rankin Inlet harbour in the late afternoon yesterday, and the community buzzed with palpable excitement. Apparently there is only a narrow window of time when the annual sealift can occur, having something to do with ships' liability insurance covering only the brief period when the Hudson Bay is reliably ice free—generally the last two weeks of August.

Nurse Bauer has witnessed the sealift many times, so she let me and Sherry have a day off to enjoy the festivities. I suppose she knew full well it would be a very slow day in clinic, as only the desperately ill would miss the fun of sealift.

The Bay put on free coffee and donuts, and it seemed as if the entire community turned out to watch the huge pallets of freight being unloaded. There were hundreds of people perched all over the rocks around the harbour, with children running and skipping everywhere. Kublu's brother, Ivaluk, came over to say hi. He said he would love to stay and watch the activities with us, but he and several other young men had been hired by the Bay to break down the pallets and move goods into the warehouse as quickly as possible. One of the elders came down to the waterfront with a traditional Inuit drum, which looked like some kind of skin stretched over a big round hoop with a short handle on the side. The afternoon was filled with pointing and cheering and laughter, with reverberating drumbeats echoing along the rocky shore, as various townspeople had a go at the native drum.

After hours spent marvelling over the towering crates of moon pies, diapers, cake mixes and baked beans, I felt the need to stretch my legs. Sherry and I took a walk along the road that leads to the airport. When we got to the terminal, we startled some young boys who were out behind the building, up to no good. Their shirts had holes torn in them, and it looked as if their hair was in need of a good combing. At first I thought they were just playing some game with the empty fuel drums, but soon I saw that they were opening them and purposefully sniffing the vapours.

"Hey, you little buggers, you're going to ruin your brains!" Sherry yelled at them. They sneered at her and ambled off, but I had a feeling they would be back at their mischief soon after we left. I couldn't imagine how hopeless these boys must feel, to miss out on the party going on down at the harbour only to come up here and get high instead. I wondered if Sherry was thinking of her own boys back home and what they might be up to...

As we strolled back toward the community, I looked over my shoulder. Sure enough, the boys were back sniffing at the fuel drums. One of them stuck his tongue out at me—a childish gesture, but it stung me nonetheless. It made me feel foreign, out of place and unwelcome, like an intruder or invader, or at the very least a voyeur.

IVALUK 5
Rankin Inlet, N.W.T.
August 17, 1970

Dear Thomasie:

I hope you are doing okay and it not killing you too bad to be stuck down there in school while the sun is warm and fish swimming thick in the rivers here. Not to mention the wild flowers more and bigger than I ever remember.

I met a new person. You will be surprise to learn she is a Qablunaaq—a nurse who works at our Nursing Station here. Her name is Alison. She seems different from the other nurses and also different from any Qablunaaq I ever met before. She is pretty and curious to learn about Inuit ways and language. She can keep quiet for long times too which is odd for a woman.

I spent some time with her yesterday. We took a walk on the tundra and I helped her practice her Inuktitut pronunciation and also show her some of my favourite inuksuks. I enjoy this day a lot. I have a feeling I will have some headache or scratchy throat this fall so I can go over to the Nursing Station and see if I can get this nurse to examine me. Ha. Funny thing is she seem to find me a bit interesting too unlike most Inuit girls these days who measure a man by the size of his pay check.

That motor bike is all paid off now so I cut back working for the honey wagon to do some fishing before the snow fly. I enclose a little spending money for you to go see a movie or something. Maybe take out a girl if there is some one you like. Just don't spend it on smokes okay? I trying harder to quit because I think nurses do not like it and I see their way of thinking when I hear Kanik coughing his lungs up.

Take it easy.

ALISON 17
Rankin Inlet, Northwest Territories
August 29, 1970

What a wicked week this has been. The school reopened last Monday after the summer recess. Classes haven't started yet, but the teachers are back, organizing their supplies and lesson plans, and they sponsored an orientation program for the youngsters who will be entering kindergarten soon. On Tuesday morning, we got a call from the principal, saying that a couple of the children had become ill, with vomiting and diarrhoea. Sherry went over and escorted the sick children to the nursing station, but she no sooner arrived than the phone rang again. It was the principal again—three more children had fallen ill.

Before long we had ten of them at the station. We only have four beds in here, so we had to double them up, toe to toe, and we moved the chesterfield in from our living quarters to accommodate the last two. It was a challenge for Sherry and me to manage all their trips to the toilet, which were so frequent that soon Nurse Bauer ordered us to use intravenous saline drips, to ward off dehydration. There were cries and tears when we inserted the lines, and then we had to manage all the bags and hoses too, as the little ones used the facilities. This went on without letup for almost thirty-six hours. A couple of social workers came by and offered to relieve us for a few hours, but I found I could not sleep.

The principal had alerted Ian Mackenzie, who had the DPW fellows investigate, suspecting something was amiss with the school's water supply, even though none of the teachers had become ill. He came by to see what was going on for himself, and said he suspected that the men who drove the "honey wagon" in town may have been washing it in the drinking water lake. Apparently an outbreak similar to this one had occurred in Eskimo Point recently, and that had been determined to be the cause. "Idiots," he muttered, shaking his head in dismay. He issued a community-wide alert, advising everyone to boil their water before using it for anything that might be ingested.

One of the children died on Thursday morning. Nurse Bauer got on the radiophone to Churchill and Winnipeg, but none of the medical advisers could shed any further light on what we were seeing. They told us to keep up the saline and issue large doses of antibiotics, which we did.

Word of the child's death spread quickly. The nursing station was mobbed Thursday afternoon with frantic parents and other relatives, and the sound of keening echoed through the halls until the RCMP moved the body down the street to the Catholic Church to await burial.

By Friday morning, the crisis had subsided. The other nine children recovered enough to go home, tired and hungry, to their relieved parents.

Today they buried Markusie, the little boy we lost, at the small cemetery that lies near the road to the airport. Everyone was there, and the mood was terribly low. Tears streaked many faces as the priest uttered some words that were meant to console us but did not.

At the end of the service, Ivaluk appeared at my side. "I want to talk to you," he said, rather firmly. I let him lead me away from the crowd that was now shuffling back toward the settlement. He told me he had heard that the outbreak was being blamed on the drivers of the honey wagon—something about letting sewage get into the drinking water lake. I nodded.

"I told Ian Mackenzie this is not true, but I don't think he believes me. All he said was that he noticed the honey wagon has been looking cleaner than usual lately. That is so, because I have been washing it, but not in the drinking water lake. How stupid does he think I am? I take pride in my work. I think the people don't have to look at a dirty truck, just because it is picking up bags of waste. Please, come, I want to show you where I have been cleaning the truck, so at least you will believe me."

He walked me out to an area near the landfill, where there were some rusty barrels arranged in a semi-circle just off the road. Ivaluk lifted the lid off one of the drums and pulled out a plastic bag that seemed to be full of clean cotton cloths, like old washed diapers. The next container held a plastic bag full of soiled cloths. Two other drums contained water he had scooped up with a plastic bucket from puddles of melted snow in the nearby marsh. He showed me the fuel pump he had borrowed from Wayne, so that he could spray the truck down before hand drying it with his cloths.

I told Ivaluk I was impressed with his efficient cleaning system and said I would tell Ian about it.

"I don't care what Ian thinks. I just don't want you to believe I would do anything to hurt a child or make somebody sick." He looked so stricken that I gave his arm a squeeze and told him he did not have to worry about me thinking ill of him.

IAN 3
Rankin Inlet, Northwest Territories
September 1, 1970

RE: Monthly Report to Keewatin Regional Headquarters, Churchill, Manitoba

The dysentery outbreak is over and the sealift has come and gone. The shelves at the Bay are stocked again. Thirty more motorized vehicles of various sorts arrived, given the popularity of the last set. I don't know how we will make it to next summer with the fuel we have, as no one expected the population of gas engines to explode like this. May have to set up some sort of rationing system or priority for government vehicles, and we will have to plan for much more heated gasoline storage capacity next year. And more gravel, as now it is being worn off the local streets at a rapid clip. Asphalt may soon become a necessity.

The sealift contractor ruined several containers of supplies meant for the Housing Corporation. Four pallets containing insulation and prefabricated panels for new modular homes were dropped, so there will be some materials to write off. No way to know yet whether it was walls or roofs or what, but there are bits of fibreglass blowing all across the tundra. DPW refused to help, saying it is now the Housing Corporation's responsibility to deal with all matters related to housing, but their regional manager is off in Sanikiluaq and cannot be reached, and the local board is sure this must be someone else's problem. I don't have the staff or warehouse space to move the damaged materials under roof to try to salvage them.

Received notice about the Commissioner's planned tour for early November and really appreciate the heads-up. Usually we find out about such things the hard way, without warning. Then we are expected to drop everything and deal with it, tour the muckety mucks around, feed them and put them up somewhere, etc. Please advise how long he will be staying and how big the entourage will be, and I will arrange for appropriate accommodations and feed. Let me know if there is anything else I am expected to say or do or arrange, such as native entertainment or what have you. I hope the press remember to bring pencils this time, so they won't be in a flummox when the ink freezes solid in their pens.

Ian Mackenzie, Settlement Manager

NIKMAK 8
Rankin Inlet Nursing Station
October 16, 1970

Paniga, you seem to be slipping down, down, down, further into the darkness, and I feel as if I am sliding down with you. Just as I slid all those years ago, down into the pitch dark shaft of the nickel mine, along with many other Inuit men, and even some Qablunaat, from as far away as Ontario and Quebec.

In Repulse Bay and at Coral Harbour, I had worked long day shifts for the DEWline, but in Rankin Inlet they ran the mine equipment all day and all night, seven days a week. Miners came and went at all hours, riding that groaning elevator down into the darkness as deep as winter. Sometimes we would emerge to see darkness outside, sometimes sun. It was confusing. I did not particularly like doing the loud, dusty work at the mine face, so far below the surface of the earth, where I used to hunt and fish. But I did not complain, because once again I was able to support my family well.

Our wooden house was painted pale yellow like the sun, and it had an oil stove in it for heating and cooking. It was not too far from the mine, so I could walk to work, and it was not too far from the inlet, so we could go fishing down there on my days off. Our neighbours were Inuit who had come from all over. We traded stories about the old days over endless cups of tea. We traded fish and meat when we had it. We talked about this new way of living, which most of us found acceptable, or even good. We settled into this new existence, feeling lucky. The years passed; our children grew.

And then came more strange and sudden news. The mine, which had been open not even five years, was going to close now. We always had known that the nickel ore was not an endless thing. The special rocks took up a certain space inside the earth, like a baby in a womb, with a definite shape and size. It would not go on forever. Still, we thought, given all the work and the Qablunaat money that had gone into building buildings and buying equipment and opening this mine, surely it would operate for many, many years, perhaps beyond our lifetime. Certainly longer than just four or five years. But we were told that the price of nickel had fallen so low that the company could no longer afford to pay the workers to dig the ore out of the earth and ship it away to be processed. So all of the miners were laid off. Taima. No more work, no more pay checks. Once again, we were told we were free to go.

But free to go where? Where were we to go this time? We did not want to move again. What would become of us now? We were afraid.

The Qablunaat miners flew back to their homes in the south, back to wherever they had land. A handful of Inuit miners went with them, to places with strange names like Flin Flon, desperate to keep earning pay as miners, even in foreign lands. Some went back to the places where they had lived before the mine opened, like Eskimo Point or Coral Harbour, if they still had family there, or the hunting was good, or if there was any possibility of work. But many stayed behind, not knowing what else to do, hoping it was all a joke or a big mistake, praying that the price of nickel would go back up, and the mine would reopen as suddenly as it had shut down.

But the mine did not reopen. There was growing depression and despair in the community. The Inuit who worked in that mine had all been born on the land, so hardship was no stranger to any of us. But now memories of the hard times returned to haunt us, while the future looked completely blank. Many of us did not want to go back to the land, back to uncertainty, back to the cold and punishing outdoor work, to the periods of starvation and worse. We were paralyzed.

The mine had provided a beer hall to quench the thirsts of the miners when they returned to the surface of the earth after their long shift in the stuffy darkness. Some of the men continued to drink beer, even though they could no longer afford to, and some were drinking even more than before, hoping to dull their fears. Meanwhile, more Inuit families were settled into the empty mine houses, as the RCMP rounded up the remnants of the inland groups who were suffering great deprivation. They were thin and gaunt and did little to cheer us.

A reporter from the CBC came and shone his light on the suicides taking place in Rankin Inlet, and then the federal government stepped in to do something. They sent counsellors; they sent social workers; they sent anthropologists to study us. They bought the abandoned houses from the mine company and told us we could continue living in them for free, at least for a time. Then they built more houses—just tiny shacks really—to accommodate other relocated families who kept arriving with nothing, not even hope. They built a school and a new store, and then some missionaries came and built a new church and encouraged the Inuit to come and sing hymns inside it and pray to Jesus for our salvation.

Aiiee, daughter, it is hard remembering all of these things. I am going to go outside to breath some fresh air. I will come back later to continue my story.

Ayayaaaa.

ALISON 18
Rankin Inlet, Northwest Territories
September 7, 1970

Things have been mercifully quiet at the nursing station, so Nurse Bauer agreed to let me have the entire Labour Day weekend off. Sherry had several days off earlier in the week, and she hitched a ride on a charter flight Jerry Duncan took down to Thompson, so she could do some shopping. I felt like getting away, too, so I asked Wayne if by any chance he would be flying down to Churchill or Thompson on the weekend. He said no, that he was planning to take the long weekend off. He and Kublu and the baby were going on a fishing trip with her two brothers, and her brother's wife and their young twins. He said he thought no one would mind if I tagged along. He checked with Kublu, and she said it would be fine. I was delighted to have this chance to go camping and fishing with a local family.

I bought a disposable camera at the Bay, as well as some juice and trail mix to share. I also nicked a couple of packages of dry soup mix and some biscuits from the nursing station kitchen and added those to my backpack.

It was a very slow day on Friday. The whole community seemed still, as if everyone had taken off to enjoy one last weekend on the land before autumn sets in and the children must go back to school. At five o'clock sharp, a Jeep pulled up. Sakku and Carol were in the front seats, and Wayne and Kublu in the back. Carol and Kublu each had one of the twins on their laps, and Wayne was holding little Radar, who was fast asleep. The back was heaped with coolers and tents and fishing gear. I was trying to figure out where in the world I would sit, when Ivaluk pulled up on his three-wheeled scooter. He patted the passenger seat behind him and invited me to climb aboard. There was nothing to hang on to except him, so I put my hands tentatively around his waist.

"No," he said, "You have to really hold on, or I might lose you on a bump." He took my hands and wrapped them around his waist, which required moving up closer on the seat. Then we were off with a roar.

What a strange caravan we must have seemed to any observer—an open Jeep and a three-wheeled scooter bumping across hummocks and through puddles side by side. By the time we reached the river, it was near seven o'clock, and my stomach was grumbling.

Ivaluk drove us right to the edge of the river and let out a gleeful yelp. There was an old stone weir—a series of big rocks that had been placed across the river—and he could see that there were some large fish trapped behind the rocks. He leapt from the scooter and hurriedly took off his jacket and shirt, then his shoes and socks and jeans. He jumped into the river wearing only his blue boxer shorts. He grabbed an old wooden gaffe that had been left beside the river, and soon he was spearing fish like a man possessed. He must have impaled twenty or thirty big fish, yelping with glee as he hurled them flopping onto the shore.

Wayne caught up with us and shouted "Oh boy—fresh Arctic Char for dinner!"

"I hope you're hungry," I said. "Ivaluk has caught an awful lot of fish." I turned and saw that Sakku was busy setting up a canvas tent, and Kublu was building a fire, as Carol watched the kids.

Ivaluk finally sat down on a rock to catch his breath. He scooped water from the river and threw it onto his face and over his head, then shook like a big dog. "Brrrrr... refreshing!" he shouted, though he was covered with goose bumps head to toe. I stuck my hand in the water and was startled to feel how cold it was.

Ivaluk walked back to where he had left the scooter. He opened a black bag that had been tied onto the luggage rack and pulled out a knife and some rope, as well as a towel. He quickly dried himself off, using the towel for privacy as he deftly removed his wet shorts and threw them over a rock to dry. He found a few scraps of driftwood to use as posts, and he strung the rope between them like a clothesline. He began to clean the fish on a rock with his pocket knife, throwing the heads and guts back into the river. He gave the filets, still attached at the tail end, a quick rinse in the river before flipping them over the clothesline inside out, so their deep orange flesh was glinting in the sun.

He asked me to gather bits of caribou moss and driftwood to feed the fire that Kublu had started and then to fill the aluminium kettle with river water. Soon I had the tea made, as Kublu was mixing up flour and water in a plastic bowl. She put a lump of lard in a cast iron frying pan over the fire, and then added the dough.

"What is that?" I asked.

"You have never had bannock? I feel sorry for you," she teased.

"If you've never tasted bannock, you are in for a treat," Carol added.

While the bannock sizzled in the frying pan, Ivaluk wrapped some fresh fish in foil and placed it directly on the fire to steam. Soon the aromas wafting in the air had me practically drooling.

Carol went to check on the napping twins and returned with a bowl of salad. All conversation ceased as we devoured our feast. Radar woke up and wanted his dinner too, so Kublu breast-fed him in front of us all. We talked and told jokes around the fire until the sun set.

There were three tents set up: one for Sakku and Carol and their twins, one for Wayne and Kublu and Radar, and a small orange nylon two-man pup tent that Ivaluk had produced from under the seat of his three-wheeler. He gestured toward it and said: "You take the tent; I'm used to sleeping outside." I was too tired to argue, and I am used to sleeping with a roof over my head, so I said *"qujannamiimmarialuk"* and climbed into the sleeping bag that had been rolled out inside the small tent.

In the morning, I awoke to the sound of chattering and scolding ground squirrels. I poked my head out the door and saw two of them sitting up on a rock, yelling at me about something. I saw Sakku and Kublu off a way, giving the twins walking lessons. Carol was busy cracking eggs into a bowl. Ivaluk strolled up and said good morning to me. He was carrying about a dozen freshly killed ptarmigan by the feet.

"How did you catch those?" I inquired. "I didn't hear any gun shots."

He explained his technique for hunting ptarmigan. If he noticed a flock of them, he would pick up some stones and crawl slowly toward them, then lie still. When a bird would get close enough to him, he would hurl a stone at its head. If his missile found its target, the bird would fall over, stunned momentarily. Then he would rush in, grab the bird and wring its neck. The rest of the flock would scatter for a minute, but would soon reassemble, so he was able to do this over and over.

After our breakfast of juice and trail mix and scrambled eggs and tea, we went for a long hike along the river. When we returned to camp, I volunteered to make lunch. Ivaluk cleaned the ptarmigans while I put a pot of river water on the fire, added the packages of dried soup mix I had brought along, and then the birds. The resulting concoction was fabulous.

I had brought along a novel I borrowed from Sherry, so after lunch I wandered off for a relaxing read, but once I laid my head down on a warm rock, I found I could not concentrate on reading. There was too much to take in sensually. Fat bumblebees buzzed slowly but steadily as they floated among the mosses and wild flowers, collecting the last of the summer nectar. The smooth slabs of grey rock poking out of the moss looked like a pod of grey whales breeching and cavorting around me. The sky above was a solid slate of bright blue colour, with four linear clouds that looked like bony fingers pointing northward. Lying there on the ground, I felt as if I were leaning up against another living creature, a very large one with a powerful presence. I closed my eyes and let my fingers probe the scratchy lichens around me until I found a round, flat stone. I slipped it into my pocket as a souvenir, so I could always keep a bit of this place close to me.

Late in the afternoon, the men did more fishing half naked in the river while the women chatted and played with the babies. I was glad that Carol spoke some Inuktitut, too, so both of us could practice our language skills with Kublu.

Saturday night was Wayne's turn to cook dinner. He boiled rice over the fire and then let it sit on a rock in the hot pan while he made us a curry from onion and celery and Arctic Char and chopped hard-boiled eggs and raisins. He produced a six-pack of beer, which he had chilled in the river. Kublu and Ivaluk declined, but the rest of us each had one, and then Wayne and Sakku each had another. During dinner, Kublu and her brothers asked Wayne how he had learned to cook, and he told them that, before he was strong enough to do serious farm work, he had helped his mother and aunt prepare meals to take to the men working out in the fields. He said he wished he could have stayed working with the women in the kitchen, rather than joining the men to do the backbreaking work stacking hay with a pitchfork.

After the children were tucked into bed, we watched the night sky begin to emerge. I marvelled at how many stars we could see and how bright they seemed, with no city lights to dim them. Carol started pointing out some constellations she knew: the Swan, Persius the king, etc. I enjoyed listening to her, as I have never studied astronomy, but Sakku became quite belligerent. He said that the sky overhead was the sky of his ancestors, the one they had watched and that had watched over them for centuries. Who had the right to declare that any particular configuration of stars overhead was a swan or a queen or some Greek warrior? How could Carol utter such crap without thinking first? Maybe what she had been taught to see as a swan was in fact a nanuq or a siksik to the Inuit. She should be more sensitive before uttering such nonsense, as if it were some kind of scientific fact.

It was an awkward moment. I could see his point, but it didn't seem worth making into such a big deal. Ivaluk suggested it was time to turn in. He walked me back to the orange pup tent. We could hear Sakku and Carol still arguing in the distance. He shrugged and said good night, and soon I could hear his soft snoring on the other side of the thin nylon wall that separated us. It took me ages to fall asleep.

I awoke Sunday morning to the smell of fresh-brewed coffee, which I was glad someone had thought to bring along. Wayne was up, sitting by the fire, poking a pan of Canadian bacon, while he soaked thick slices of bread in a bowl of eggs for French toast. He told me that Radar had had a bad night, so Kublu was trying to sleep in a bit. I could see that Carol had taken the twins for a walk on the tundra, holding one of their hands in each of hers as they stumbled along. Then I noticed that Sakku was dismantling his tent. Wayne shrugged and said they had decided to pack up and head home after breakfast, thinking it would be more relaxing to spend the last part of the long weekend in town, rather than camping.

I spotted Ivaluk near the river, checking on the drying fish. I walked over and said good morning and asked if I could help in any way. He said no, the fish were under control, even if the humans might not be. He was annoyed that Sakku had drunk beer the night before, when it is obvious that he can't handle it. I found it hard to get excited about a beer or two, since my own brothers have been known to kill a whole case of the stuff in one sitting, but I was sorry everyone seemed glum.

Ivaluk said he did not see the point of rushing back to town and, besides, the fish was not dry enough to pack yet. He asked if I would mind spending the rest of the long weekend out by the river. The others could go back in the Jeep; we could return later on the Honda. That sounded better to me than spending my remaining time off in the company of Nurse Bauer and Sherry, so I agreed, even though I wondered how it might look to the others. I decided I didn't care. I wanted to stay.

After a hearty breakfast, Wayne and Sakku finished dismantling their camp, and we all helped pack up the Jeep. They took the two big tents and most of the cooking equipment, but gave us some leftover bannock, though I felt as if I'd already eaten enough to last me for days. As we said our good-byes, Wayne winked at me and whispered, "Don't do anything I wouldn't do."

After they were out of sight, Ivaluk turned to me and, without a word, pulled me to his chest in a warm hug. There was room to escape if I wanted to, but I did not want to. "They are my siblings and I love them, but I am glad to see them go," he sighed. "All weekend long, I've been wishing I could just be alone with you." I couldn't find any words to say in response. I was lost in that hug that made me feel totally at ease, even with all my senses on high alert.

After a long cling, he slowly pushed me back just enough to get a good look into my eyes. I suppose he found whatever answer he was looking for there, because next thing I knew he was kissing me. I loved the feel of his moustache tickling my lips. His mouth tasted of mint. I realized I had not seen him smoking, so I asked him about it. "I gave it up for you," he said, "so you would love the taste of my kisses."

Soon we were writhing together, urgently yet comically, inside that tiny nylon pup tent—as if we thought there was still some need to protect our privacy. When the feeble tent poles broke, we cried out and laughed, then crawled outside and tumbled around naked on the caribou moss under the muted September sun.

I was surprised to feel how much I wanted this man, Ivaluk. I wanted to inhale him, to ingest him, as if I were a starving person. There was an intoxicating mix of scents emanating from him—a mix of sea and land smells—oyster shells, caviar, bird nests, lichens, and just a hint of that warm smell I associate with puppy ears, and perhaps a bit of toast with honey? I wanted to tell him I had never smelled a person with such a curious and interesting scent, but I thought he might take it the wrong way. And then there was the feel of him—all firm and muscular, yet wrapped in soft, mocha-colored skin with a sprinkling of fine, dark hair. He seemed like a paradox to me—hard, yet soft; firm, yet yielding; goofy, yet serious. I felt foolishly smitten with him, as I tried to control my trembling, and found that I could not.

Ivaluk confessed that he had noticed me in a special way the first time he met me, on that trip to Marble Island. I wanted to tell him that I had not noticed him then in that special way, but I began to wonder if perhaps I had. His crawling up the shore on his elbows had gotten my attention, that cute butt shuffling up in the air. His silence, his power, his serenity, his respect. His swift sureness in killing the seal, his certainty about following the traditions surrounding its proper treatment afterwards. His connection to Kublu, who is connected to my friend Wayne. Our pleasure at seeing each other at the sealift festivities, and then the sensitivity he displayed after Markusie's funeral. It was all beginning to make some kind of sense, though thinking about anything seemed an effort akin to slogging through thigh-deep snow without snowshoes. I just wanted to touch him more, hold him close to me and not let go.

"I..." I began, not sure exactly what words to choose.

"I know," he jumped in, "you don't have to explain. I did not say or do anything on that trip to Marble Island, because I knew it was your time of the month."

"What?" I stammered. "How could you know such a thing?"

"I'm a hunter—I know the smell of blood." He replied, and then he grinned in a way that made me think the sight of those white teeth against his tanned skin was the most beautiful sight I had ever seen. I hadn't noticed those dimples before.

"And I saw the bloody tissue in the honey bucket below deck," he added, and rolled away from me, laughing. I jumped on his back and pummelled him, then turned him over and kissed him some more.

I love the look of the land here, I thought, and the way I feel embraced by it. I have fallen in love with this place, and now I have fallen in love this man. Every day I spend here, and every encounter with him, seems to hold a new surprise.

We napped together for a while, and eventually got up and prepared a snack of dried fish and bannock. We took a long walk on the tundra, then returned to camp and rearranged our sleeping bags, zipping them together. We ditched the tent and lay under the open sky, watching the stars twinkle above us in swirling wisps of green and pink and yellow light.

The next morning, I awoke to the sound of sand cranes calling as they swept across the sky, one moment looking like a barrage of silver bullets as the sunbeams streaming through a puffy cloud reflected off their wings, then disappearing as they turned in unison, then reappearing. Ivaluk and I took our time waking up. We were quiet as we drank our tea and picked at trail mix and biscuits. We made love one more time before we began to pack up slowly. We carefully took the fish off the drying line and put it on a tarp, which Ivaluk rolled up and tied onto the luggage rack.

"I hate to leave this place, nurse Alison," he said, giving me a long series of quick kisses once we were packed and ready to go. "Are you sure you have to go to work tomorrow?"

"I don't want to, but I have to," I replied, leaning into him for one last hug.

I sat up extra close to his backside on the return trip and rested my head on his strong back in some kind of a daze. He stopped about halfway back, and when he began unpacking supplies I said: "I know—there is always time for tea."

"Ii," he replied with a laugh. We sipped our tea in silence, with one arm slung around each other, watching the sun begin to set over the tundra.

When Ivaluk dropped me off at the nursing station, I didn't dare kiss him, but I gave him a pat on the thigh as I dismounted, and I thanked him for introducing me to the wonderful world of fish camping by the river.

IVALUK 6
Rankin Inlet, N.W.T.
September 11, 1970

Dear Thomasie:

Everything is turned upside down here. Wayne has gone missing. He packed up a big load of supplies for one of the DEWline stations Tuesday but did not take off because of a magnetic storm. The kind you can't see but make all those dials useless. He took off early Wednesday morning and flew north but he did not come home like everyone expected him to that night. First they thought he might have gone visiting over to Baker Lake or Chesterfield Inlet like he sometimes do. But by Thursday evening everybody was really worrying what might have happened to him.

Wayne's friend Jerry got up a big search while the government still trying to figure out what to do next. I think Jerry called every bush pilot north of Thompson to come help. They study Wayne's flight plan and talk over his habits and now they take turns searching the land for any signs of him or his plane. Me and some other guys and even some sharp eye ladies are helping too.

I will call or send a telex when or if there is any big news. Kublu says please pray or send good thoughts or whatever you can do that you think might help. She seems really wound up or maybe just scared to the bone.

Take it easy,

△ ⊂ ⊃ '

p.s. - Before all this thing come to happen I had the best long weekend at our favourite fishing spot on the Meliadine River. Most everybody was there—Sakku and Carol and the twins and Kublu and Wayne and Radar. Ataata and Anaana were too tired to come or maybe want to stay home to have some peace and quiet for a change. And we had a special guest that nurse lady Alison Clark I told you about. Wayne invited her. I got to know them both better and can say to you for sure that I like her even more than I thought I did before. Now it seems like it was maybe all a dream.

NIKMAK 9
Rankin Inlet Nursing Station
October 16, 1970

Kublu—I have returned to continue my story.

So how are we to support our families and ourselves now that the nickel mine is gone, we wondered. Finally, the Gavamamiut came with answers. They said they would try some new economic development programs for us. They told us to be patient. They said we should trust them and that they would make us self-reliant once again.

They sent two Qablunaat from the south, men who knew how to organize a new business in Rankin Inlet. These men moved some of the smaller homes together and converted these into buildings for animals to live inside. When the buildings were ready, the Government sent us young pigs and chickens on the sealift. We were to become farmers, and raise our own food, and save a lot of shipping expenses that way. But all we had to feed these pigs and these chickens was fish and seal meat, and whatever walrus was not needed for men or dogs. The caribou was considered too precious—that was reserved for Inuit food only.

The meat from the pigs and the eggs from the chickens that were produced in Rankin Inlet did turn out to be cheaper than the food shipped in from the south. But there was a problem. It all tasted like fish or seal or walrus. The Inuit wouldn't eat it. "If we want to eat fish or seal or walrus, we will eat fish or seal or walrus," we said, "not pork that tastes like seal and walrus, or eggs with a fishy smell and yolks the colour of char."

The next year the sealift came with enough metal parts to build a small DEWline station, but it was all in odd sections that looked something like ladders. These things turned out to be parts for a cannery, a factory for wrapping food inside metal cans, so it would keep for a long time. Since the only thing we had a lot of was fish and seal meat, the Gavamamiut decided we should can those things and ship them to the south in the empty sealift boats, so Qablunaat could buy these things and serve them to their family or friends at their dinner parties in Toronto and Montreal and Ottawa, and maybe even New York.

For a while, many people in the community worked at the cannery. Some of the men thought this work was beneath them, as it required putting on a hair net and a white apron, something a man might not feel right about. So mainly it was the women who worked at the cannery, while the men hunted and fished, or stayed home to watch the babies or drink beer.

It soon became clear, though, that the Qablunaat in the south did not want to eat as much canned fish and seal meat at their dinner parties as the Government thought they would. Soon there were mountains of canned fish and seal piled high in warehouses in Ottawa and Winnipeg and Montreal, and they asked us please do not send any more. So the workers were laid off and the cannery closed. The pig and chicken houses, and now the cannery building, all sitting empty in the shadow of the head frame from the old abandoned nickel mine. We felt lost again.

Then the Government sent art instructors to teach us to make pottery and weave rugs and do leather work and make soapstone carvings. Many of us turned out to be good at these things, and we began to earn some money again, from selling art and crafts.

I liked carving. I had carved some simple soapstone lamps and pots as a boy, the hard way, using hard stone tools to hack at a block of softer stone until it resembled the shape we needed. It had been tedious work. But now the Government built a workshop and filled it with metal tools—files and hammers and chisels, and even electric drills and grinders that made carving much easier.

I made soapstone animals, like bears, and even some walruses with real ivory tusks, to be sold through the Cooperative to museums and art collectors in the south. This work did not pay as well as construction or mining, or even farming or canning, but it kept us alive and kept our minds from wandering to dark and frightening places. It was something to do, something to pass the time, a way to earn some cash and have something to show for your efforts.

Your anaana did sewing, making duffel slippers and purses from sealskin. Once in a while she would make an embroidered amauti for one of the Qablunaaq women who would come to our community for a year or two to teach or do social work.

We managed to scrape by and keep on living. We had food to eat and oil in the stove, and there was still enough love under our roof to sustain us.

Some other families were not so lucky as us. When polio and tuberculosis came to the Keewatin region, these diseases struck down many Inuit. Families were torn apart by the long absence of a mother or a father. Some children were sent away to hospitals in the south. Some were even sent to Winnipeg, over a thousand miles away. It may as well have been the moon.

Some families were forced to split up and send their young children to live with relatives. Parents had to adopt their children out to others who could support another child better than they could. This is how little Thomasie came to us. His mother was sent away with tuberculosis. When his father understood that his wife would be away for a very long time, he sent his daughter to live with her aunt in Baker Lake, and he asked us if we would care for little Thomasie, just until his mother returned. We agreed. But by the time she came back to Rankin Inlet, almost two years later, Thomasie did not know her at all, and we had grown to love him like a son. There were some hot tears shed, but in the end everyone agreed it would be best for Thomasie to stay in the place he had come to think of as his home, with the ones who knew him best now and loved him very much. Ukpik was so pleased about this that she gave Thomasie's mother her most prized possession, her electric frying pan, in a fit of thankfulness. His mother accepted it with surprise and glee, smiling sincerely as she clutched her new treasure to her bosom. She had lost a piece of her family—it could not be helped—but at least she had gained something of value in exchange. In a small way, it felt as if some balance had been restored, one treasure traded for another.

Kublu, it is time for me to go home now, before they send the janitor to sweep me out the door again. I am leaving another amulet that your anaana has made for you, though we are running out of places to tie such things onto your bed. I don't see these amulets helping you much, but all this sewing seems to help my nuliaq. It is her way of trying to touch you from home. We are lucky Radar gives her something to do, a way to feel needed and helpful and close to you.

Rest well, paniga. I will come back to you tomorrow. I beg you to come back to me too.

Ayayaiyeaaaii.

ALISON 19
Rankin Inlet, Northwest Territories
September 13, 1970

My head is pounding and feels as if it will burst from all the crying I have been doing.

Wayne is gone. He went missing September 9, and Jerry spotted the crash site yesterday, near the Ferguson River, west of Whale Cove. They brought his body back to town today, and once again a sad silence has fallen over this town. Even the children are quiet and still. I feel as though I have lost a brother.

Nurse Bauer has been horrid to me. She would not give me any time off this week. "It would be one thing if he were family," she said, "as we do have a family leave policy in place, though it is very rarely used, since most of the staff we recruit are loners or misfits whose families are far, far away, often in more ways than one." The hateful bitch.

None of my Inuit patients need to ask if I am sick. They know the reason for my red eyes and running nose. They try their best to be undemanding. Several of them have tapped my hand or squeezed my shoulder, murmuring sounds of sympathy, sighing and nodding in silent understanding. Or they softly utter *"ajurnarmat"*—it can't be helped. Their kindness only makes me more tearful. I don't know why I am finding it so hard to get a grip.

And poor Kublu. I dropped by her house after work to offer my pathetic and useless condolences. She was kneeling on the floor, sitting back on her heels and rocking back and forth, with little Radar in the pouch on her back, though I thought I heard her calling him "Fiasco." She was dry eyed, but seemed very sombre. She told me that Ivaluk had gone over to visit Jerry, so I dropped by that house, too—the house that is no longer Wayne's home.

Ivaluk was not there, so I did not stay long. It was too sad. Jerry was not really there, anyway. He was talking with his distant boss over the radiophone, reworking their flight schedules, as if it might be possible to blunt this discomfort by burying oneself in work. Over and out.

IVALUK 7
Rankin Inlet, N.W.T.
September 27, 1970

Dear Thomasie:

I been very worried about Kublu ever since Wayne crash his plane. She seem broken like a qamutiik with just one runner. Stuck and impossible to pull forward. I think she had convince herself that she did not love Wayne too much. He was just some man to bring a new baby into our home. But now everything different and she is not like her old self. Half the time when I speak to her she does not listen. Sometimes she walks around the community for hours and forgets that baby Radar is over there at our house crying for her. We all hope she snap out of it soon.

I have not seen so much of that nurse Alison because I need to stay around home more right now and also she seems almost more upset about Wayne's crash as Kublu. I don't understand that too well but I guess she was good friends with Wayne and maybe because they are both here alone without any of their own family around. Anyway she seems too sad these days. Almost like Wayne's death was a knife that open up some boil of stuff she needed to feel sad about and let it all weep out. Sakku says Qablunaat women need space to be by themself some time. So I wait even though I think maybe a big hug from Ivaluk would be best medicine to return a smile to her freckle face.

That's all from here. I hope things are more average for you down there in Churchill.

Take it easy

ALISON 20
Rankin Inlet, Northwest Territories
October 12, 1970

It is Thanksgiving Day in Canada, but everyone around here is as gloomy as can be, not finding much to give thanks for. The cumulative weight of recent events is too much—the death of little Markusie, then Wayne's crash, and now Kublu. Oh, Kublu!

I know she has been distraught and distracted—and with good reason. But now she is in even greater pain and trouble. It seems she wandered into one of those crazy parties at a staff house on Saturday night. Apparently she had a few drinks, which she is not accustomed to doing. No one seems to know how much she had. And no one seemed to notice when she wandered outside into the storm. They thought she had gone home. But Ivaluk found her the following morning, half frozen.

We've had some rotten weather recently, along with rotten luck. It was cold and cloudy on Saturday, with a harsh wind blowing ice crystals sideways all through the night.

Ivaluk brought Kublu to the nursing station at first light. She was unconscious, and her nose and bare hands were badly blistered with frostbite. We did what we could to stabilize her. We immersed her in a warm water bath and gave her narcotics for her pain, and then put her into a bed with warm blankets and intravenous fluids and some antibiotics for good measure. I asked if we shouldn't get Jerry to evacuate her straight to Churchill, but Nurse Bauer felt they wouldn't be able to do anything more for her there than we could do here. She insists the girl just needs warmth and rest and liquids and watching, and beyond that the outcome is out of our hands.

Nikmak, Kublu's father, has been practically glued to her bedside. He held her hand and sang and sang his old songs, until Nurse Bauer was driven nuts with it and told him to knock off the singing. I still hear him singing softly from time to time, but mostly now he just sits in a chair pulled up next to her bed, talking to her in that beautiful, flowing Inuktitut that rises sometimes but often falls into a barely audible whisper. It sounds like poems and potions and prayers all mixed together.

Kublu remains unconscious most of the time. I have seen her eyelids flutter and her lips move a few times, but unfortunately it never seems to happen when Nikmak is at her side. The poor man. I think even a second of recognition from her, or just one word, would cheer him immensely.

Ivaluk has asked me to send one of the local children over to the house to fetch him if anything changes, or if he is needed. He thinks he can be more useful over there for now.

Perhaps I have been a bit curt with him, but I just feel numb.

IVALUK 8
Rankin Inlet, N.W.T.
October 14, 1970

Dear Thomasie:

When I hear about our sister Kublu's fingers cut off I can't help but think of our legends about Nuliajuk, the sea goddess. There are many versions—you remember? Ataata's story says that when Nuliajuk was a small young girl she swam out to a raft where some other Inuit kids were playing. But these Inuit do not like or trust Nuliajuk, because she is not related to them and no one knows her very well so they are afraid of her. For this reason, when she swims to the raft and grabs hold of it to try and climb up from the water they chop off her fingers. She cries out and sinks to the bottom of the sea where her chopped off fingers turn into seals and walruses that swim around and multiply to feed us in the future. This Nuliajuk becomes a powerful goddess who controls not only the seals and walrus but also the caribou and this of course makes her real important for the Inuit to try to keep happy or at least not get angry. But because of what happened back at that raft she not necessarily have such warm and fizzy feeling toward us Inuit. We have to remind and encourage her to be generous and send the animals our way so we don't starve. This is why to this day us Inuit are so cautious not to offend her and why we are so careful to follow the ways of our ancestors who figured it out over time what rituals and taboos work to convince Nuliajuk we give respect for her and her animals.

Another version—maybe Padlirmiut story I heard through Pitsiark's husband Simeonie—says Nuliajuk was a young girl who fell in love with a bird. When her Ataata find out he is mad and takes her to an island to banish her. But the bird attacks the father. To save himself he tries to throw that daughter who brought harm on him and the group out of the boat. When she hang on to the side of the boat he cuts off her fingers and these fingers become the future sea mammals we eat. No matter which version is right it is these kind of thoughts going around in my mind when I do what I did.

I did not want my sister's fingers to be flush down some sink or toilet into a holding tank in the nursing station and then pumped off to who knows where. I did not want my sister's fingers to be haul away to the dump along with bloody towels and pill bottles or paper cups and empty tuna cans.

So I go up and have a talk with Davidee Pudlak who is cleaning floors up at the Nursing Station now and we work this out. Because he has a job he got to go to every day he cannot get out to hunt. He has no time. But I have time not to mention a three-wheeler now to get me out there where the caribou are grazing and the hunting is good. Even with the days growing shorter I can still get out and cover a lot of territory fast and do a lot of hunting while the sun shines even faintly in the sky. Davidee's father been sick and I know some fresh tuktu would help him. So I trade for a fat hind part and some good liver meat then I get what I want.

I rode my three-wheeler around the edge of town past the old mine headframe and up onto the cliff where the oil storage tanks sit with their bellies full since sea lift. With my back to the town all I can see is the sky and the water and the tundra now blown over with the tiny snow flakes. The gulls calling out above maybe cry for our sister and the wind blew my tears into my own face.

I hold those pieces of Kublu's fingers in my hand and remember all the times these very same fingers smooth my hair or pinch my cheeks or scratch my back or pat comfort onto me. I mutter some words I hope mean something over these finger parts and then with some noisy yelling I throw them out as far out into the sea as I can do.

Maybe I was hoping Nuliajuk can use them to bring our sister back and make her whole for us again. (Thomasie being honest I am afraid she maybe slipping away from us now). If not that well then maybe at least she can turn them back into some more seals to meet my harpoon in the future.

Even after all this I do not feel good. I do not feel like working. I do not feel like hunting. I take a long ride along the shore and then out onto the tundra just burning gas and looking for some place my heart might feel any bit better.

Finally I stop and sit down on a big flat cold rock near that inuksuk out past the airport. I sit watching clouds and looking for tuktu on the horizon just out of habit and try not to think about nothing. I stay out on the tundra like that really late with a emergency blanket wrapped around me like a piece of foil but the northern lights do not put on any kind of show. Just me alone with that moon white and cold and hard above me.

After a while I began to sing some of those songs Ataata has been singing all my life. I guess I have heard them so many times I learn them without knowing it. This singing makes me feel a bit better. Finally I got tired and cold but still I did not want to go home. The house crowded now even without Kublu. Radar is fussing and Sakku have some kind of trouble with Carol so sometimes he spends the night with us and sometimes he brings one or both of the twins along so it is more and more hard to find a quiet corner to sleep.

I sorry to write on about this to you Thomasie. I hope I am not boring you to crap or make you feel too pathetic for me. Preachers say all this will be past. I just worry how it will all come out at the end.

Take it easy.

△< ⊃ʹ

NIKMAK 10
Rankin Inlet Nursing Station
October 17, 1970

Aiyaiyayeah.

Paniga, they tell me you are gone, but I sense your spirit still with me in this room. A great sadness has come down upon me, because now I see that truly you will not be coming back to us this time.

Useless old man I have become. My hands are growing weak. My eyesight is failing. I cannot even call my own daughter back to me.

I feel so weary. I want to lie down in the snow and lose myself in sleep, as you did. But I cannot. I have my nuliaq and our other children and our grandchildren to watch over and care for. I can still hold a baby, wipe mess from his bottom. I am not too proud for that. I can teach a child to fish and to carve. I can still sing the old songs. Aiyaiyeah.

They want me to give your full name, for their government papers. How many of your names should we put down for this purpose? So many names, I know not where to start.

There are your Inuit names: Pangnirq, Idlout, Sakakuluk, Kublu. These include the name your mother gave you before you were born, the name of one of her ancestors, the name of my grandfather's cousin, and the name we called you at birth. Then there are the animal names we gave to you like amulets, so you would be cute and talkative like a siksik, proud and strong like a tuktu. Then there are all the names we have called you at home just for fun and amusement—pees in a pot, picks her nose, long toes, laughs too much. But you became mainly our Kublukuluk, our little Kublu, because you were small like a thumb, but also strong and agile, and lovable, and indispensable.

Then there is your *ujamik* or disc number, E3-756—the number given to you by the government of Canada, on a stamped leather coin you were meant to tie around your neck. It had Eskimo Identification Canada and the image of a crown stamped on it, along with numbers to show that you were person number 756 from Area 3 of the Eastern Arctic. At first we thought these discs were some new kind of amulet, a symbol of RCMP protection over us, a sign of Qablunaat goodwill, so many of us sewed them onto our clothing, along with the other amulets we kept. By now, most of these old discs are lost, but your sister Pitsiark still uses hers to keep her keys together in one place and I have seen Ivaluk's stored among his fishing weights.

Then there is the name the Catholic priest gave to you when he baptized you: Annie. Those missionaries, they always liked to pick out biblical names for us that were easy for them to pronounce. But that priest was the only one who called you—and ten other little girls in this town—by that particular name. And there is also the name the teachers called you at school: Karen, because it was a bit like Kublu, and easier for the Qablunaat teachers to remember.

There is the family name we share, Tunu, which came to us because of Project Surname, when the government decided to replace our disc numbers with proper last names. I picked Tunu, partly because I had known a good man with that name back in Repulse Bay, partly because I liked the sound of it, and partly as a little joke—because everything in my life has seemed "too new" to me. Including now your leaving us too early.

I will make it easy for them. I will say you are simply Kublu Tunu and be done with it.

Kublu, I am known to be a quiet man, yet I have talked and talked to you these past days. Telling you these stories, Kublu…it has brought back so many memories. The times of pain and suffering and hunger, times of uncertainty and despair, times of joy and wonder and gratitude and bounty. Sometimes even I forget all the things I have lived through, the things we Inuit as a people have survived. So many things throughout time.

Like most people my age, I was born on the land, and I lived with my family many years without seeing a single building or even one Qablunaaq. I became a good hunter, helping to feed our camp with only my harpoon and my spear and my hands and my wits. Then I became a construction worker, then a miner, working deep inside the earth. Then for a while I became a farmer, and then a carver. Very many changes, Kublu, but I have adapted to them all, meanwhile changing myself, too, from being a son to a husband and then a father, and then a grandfather. And now I will have to adapt to your loss, too, and become both a father and a grandfather to your boy. It is all a part of the same life, my life, and you will always be part of it too, even after this day. I will see a big part of you every day in Radar.

Daughter, the snow geese have gone, flown south in search of warm skies. Me, I am still here in this place of the long winter. The darkness is coming again; it is settling in very fast now. Already the wind is wailing and hurling small pellets of ice around our heads. The ground is hardening by the day.

They want to prepare you to be buried now, but I know soon you will fly to the home of our ancestors. Your spirit will float there among the moon and stars with the rest, in peace, I hope, until we call your spirit back and attach your name to a new life on this earth.

I must go home now, to comfort your mother and brothers as best I can. I must go back to face whatever the future has in store for me.

Aiyaiyaaaaaaa.

ALISON 21
Rankin Inlet, Northwest Territories
October 18, 1970

Ivaluk wept openly when he saw that his sister Kublu was dead. I have never known a man who can love like that, care that much, hurt so deeply, and express his feelings without a care about preserving someone else's image of his manliness. He heaved with sobs for several minutes, his head resting on Kublu's still form. Then he stood straight up, wiped his eyes, whispered "Ajurnarmat," and walked out of the room. I followed him out the door and asked him where he was going. He said he needed to do something—he was going to go out on the land and dig a grave for Kublu. He said he did not want her in the church cemetery next to the airport road. He was going to find a traditional site with a beautiful view over the land for her to gaze upon forever.

As he walked away I felt a physical pull, as if I were connected to that man by some invisible tether. I wanted to go with him, but I couldn't leave the nursing station. I had to finish my shift, of course, and obviously there will be no "family leave" granted to deal with Kublu's parting, as there had been none to deal with Wayne's.

I love that man Ivaluk, I thought, as I watched him stride away from me. And I would much prefer to spend every day with him, rather than be stuck here with Elizabeth Bauer and Sherry Dunlop.

And my next thought was: Get real, Alison. You are a British subject, a trained professional, and a nurse-midwife doing a two-year stint in a remote community in the Canadian Arctic, for heaven's sake. You have always been quirky and open-minded and a bit experimental, but you are definitely NOT going to get besotted with a practically stone age hunter-gatherer. That just doesn't make any sense. Don't be daft.

Yet I struggle with my feelings.

I have put in a request for vacation time off. I need to re-establish some professional distance, and give Ivaluk and his family—and this community—their space and time to grieve, without me getting in the way. I'm going to take a trip out to Winnipeg for a few days, and I shall try to get my head screwed back on properly before I return.

ALISON 22
Winnipeg, Manitoba
October 27, 1970

Back in civilization. I've been up north only seven months, and somehow it seems an eternity. What a different world this city is, filled with gadgets and electronic wonders. I felt like a complete bumpkin in the airport, marvelling at the big glass doors that sweep open automatically as you approach them. Electronic cash registers and vending machines, television sets in public places, coin operated telephones, and flush toilets everywhere. I fear my mouth must have been hanging open in amazement all the time, even though these things used to be so familiar to me that I took them completely for granted. I have to remind myself to mind the signals and look both ways for traffic before attempting to cross busy streets.

I got a room at the Holiday Inn downtown, handy to the shops and museums. I find the department stores overwhelming. I seem to have become used to the limited range of products available at the Bay store and the Coop in Rankin Inlet, and that selection seems completely adequate. Why does anyone need twelve brands of toothpaste to choose from, or thirty kinds of shampoo, or ten styles and colours of jumpers? A new pair of jeans and some underwear is all I've bought here so far.

I went to the Winnipeg Art Gallery, where they have an impressive collection of Inuit art, including lots of soapstone carvings. I felt proud to personally know some of the artists represented in the current exhibit. Seeing their work actually made me feel a bit homesick—for Rankin Inlet, of all places. I fear I am going native or something. Surely one winter there will cure me of that.

I telephoned home to Liverpool from my hotel room. Mum answered on the third ring. She sounded surprised to hear it was me on the line. She asked why I hadn't written. I told her I had written, I sent that postcard and the letter to Nancy, but I hadn't written more because I hadn't heard a word from anyone at home. You've had my address from the beginning, I pointed out. Well, you've had ours too, she replied. Then she quickly changed the subject, and told me that Dad was not doing very well at all. He's been diagnosed with a throat and mouth problem. She didn't want to say the "c" word, but I suspect cancer is what "the problem" is, given how much Dad smokes and drinks. She said he's had some surgery. They removed part of his jaw, so he is having trouble eating or talking, and he has lost quite a bit of weight. At least he is back home now.

I asked if she thought I should try to make the trip to see him. She said she didn't think that would be necessary, or even helpful, really. Travelling such a long way for a short visit would be a waste of hard-earned money.

I asked to speak with Nancy. She sounded terrific, and as if she had grown up a lot in my brief absence. She told me she is doing all right in school and has made some new friends and has been taking voice lessons and discovered she is good at it, and so she plans to try out for a singing spot with a local band. It would be just for fun, but who knows, with the British Invasion taking the music world by storm, the sky might be the limit. I felt happy for her.

Then she asked me what I'd been up to, which made me realize Mum hadn't asked any such thing at all. I didn't know where to start—how to describe the community I work in, or the majesty and power of the land there, or the people I have met, or the events that have unfolded over the past six months. How could I tell her about my colleagues, and about Wayne and Kublu, and about Radar and the rest of the Tunus, but especially about Ivaluk. In the end, I blurted out: "Please don't say anything to the rest of them, but I have fallen in love with an Eskimo hunter!" I heard a sharp intake of breath on the other end of the line, and then Nancy whispered "My word, that sounds quite thrilling and adventuresome of you. And don't worry, I will keep it to myself." We wished each other luck and rang off.

Of course I have been thinking a lot about Ivaluk, missing him tons. I catch myself wondering what he would think of this, or what he might say about that. I have dreams about him, too, some of which surely would be X-rated. I don't seem to be getting over it, or over him, at all. What am I to do?

Aamai.

ALISON 23
Rankin Inlet, Northwest Territories
November 1, 1970

I was due to be back in Rankin Inlet last Friday, but I got caught in Churchill by an early winter storm. It felt like déjà vu. I stayed at the Polar Bear Inn again, but this time there was no sign of my sullen native cabbie. A Sikh wearing a turban had replaced him. How did this man ever get so far from India, I wondered.

I walked over to the Aurora Borealis club, hoping for a drink and some company and a chat, but it was closed. It looked as if it had been badly damaged in a fire. I headed back to the hotel, just as it started to snow again—big fluffy flakes making halos around the streetlights and swirling across the pavement so fast that I could not see my feet.

I thought I would watch a bit of television—not that I crave it, but from tomorrow on I will be deprived of it again, back to listening to the BBC world service on the shortwave radio at the nursing station. There was nothing interesting on, so I turned out the light and opened up the curtains and crawled into bed, but I had a hard time getting to sleep. After the snow stopped falling, the sky began pulsing with streaks of waving light, yellow-green and pinkish purple. It was so beautiful. I wondered if Ivaluk was watching it too, and I felt a sudden sharp pang of missing him.

On Saturday, I sat in the airport terminal for several hours and finally was able to catch a commercial flight to Rankin Inlet. Of course I couldn't help but remember my first trip north, along this very same route, sitting in the co-pilot seat, next to Wayne.

When the plane began to circle the community, it looked much the way it had when I first arrived—rooftops dusted with snow, sculpted snowdrifts pushed up against the sides of the buildings. I realized how fond I have become of this place, how I have learned to read the subtle signs of life in this white landscape that can seem monotonous or unknowable to a stranger.

As we touched down, I noticed a man dressed in traditional caribou skin clothing waiting near the terminal, with his dog team staked close by. He ran straight to me as soon as I disembarked. It was Ivaluk. He grabbed me into his powerful arms like a drowning man clinging to a buoy.

"I have come out to meet every plane since you left," he said. "I was worried that you might not come back. I was worried I might never get to tell you this: Nagligivagit— I love you, Alison Clark."

I couldn't find any words to speak. I just clung to him, feeling dizzy with relief and joy, as well as nauseated with fear. At least I was not the only one who had gone completely mad.

"I know this might sound as crazy to you as it did to me at first," he went on, "but I want to marry you. I don't know what our future may hold, but I know that I want to face it together with you."

"Let's just take one step at a time," I said, feeling elated, yet overwhelmed. All kinds of questions began to swim around my brain. How would the rest of his family feel about this? Where would we live? Did we really know what we were doing? Was this true love, or just some passing fancy, or a wave of lust? And how would I earn a living, if I could no longer work as a nurse? Because it is the policy of the northern health service, for whatever reason, not to employ married nurses.

"Marrying you is so very different from any future I ever imagined for myself," I told him. "I love you, too, but I need to think about all of this some more before giving you a definitive answer. I'm sorry, Ivaluk, but I must."

"Too much thinking can get you into trouble," he grinned. "I think you should listen to your heart. But you take all the time you need to give me your answer. I can be a patient man, sometimes."

He took my suitcase and lashed it onto his qamutiik. The dogs were straining at their harnesses, anxious to be working again. Ivaluk sat me down in front of my bag and covered me with the extra caribou robe he had brought along. Then he stood on the back runners, released the brake, and mushed the dogs forward.

But he did not turn in the direction of town. Instead, we rode across the tundra to a private spot, tucked into a saddle between two lines of hills, where Ivaluk had built an iglu.

I had no idea how warm a snow house could be. We could hear a pack of foxes howling not too far away, and for a moment I thought their ecstatic yips were my own.

It was quite late when Ivaluk dropped me off at the nursing station. My dog team taxi was barking noisily as I opened the front door. Nurse Bauer didn't say a word, but I could see the questions lodged in her beady eyes. "You'll start work at 7 a.m. sharp tomorrow" was all she said.

IVALUK 9
Rankin Inlet, N.W.T.
November 8, 1970

Dear Thomasie:

It is a while since I write to you because too much is going on here. Anyways I talk to you on radiophone several times lately.

Do not feel bad about missing out on Kublu's funeral. I know it is hard for you now to get home. You can not stick out your thumb and hike a ride since there is no road to this place. And the sea is frozen over for boats now and air fare is completely crazy for a student or anyone.

You will be home for Christmas soon enough. I promise I will take you then and show you where Kublu is buried. I picked a spot on the rise above Nipissar Lake, close to an old inuksuk. Sakku and me bury her the traditional way with a white rock at her head and face looking toward the land.

Pitsiark came home from Eskimo Point with her two little girls as soon as she heard the news. She left her two boys with their grandparents so they can keep going to school. Simeonie and his brother brought them all up by snowmobile. It was a long trip but they have some relatives to visit over in Whale Cove so kill a couple of birds with one shot and help break up their journey. Simeonie agreed to let Pitsiark and the girls stay in Rankin Inlet for a while to help out while we all try to figure out how to go on next without Kublu.

It is good for Radar to learn his little cousins. Annie and Tessa treat him like he is their baby doll to play with. They are real sweet and shy and good about taking turns with him. They help give him a bath or feed him or just hold him or ride him around town in the duffle amauti that Anaana made so they can show off their baby boy to everyone.

Ataata has thrown himself into carving again. He goes to the Craft Shop for hours every day and sits there singing his old songs and chipping and filing away at the stones. He has been turning out more pieces even than Sakku and some of them are real good. I think the Coop would buy them from him but so far he does not want to sell any of these carvings. He just come home with them and put them up on the windowsill out of Radar reach.

So here is some big news. I ask Alison Clark to marry me. She is no fool so I am still waiting for her answer. I finally admit to myself that I love that woman hopeless.

I never wanted a child of my own before because there are always so many little kids around here need loving. But now I do want one—if it can be with her. Life seems more important to me now and time keeps going faster. Whether our baby is born a boy or girl I want to name him after Kublu to bring our sister's spirit back among us. That is if Alison agrees. She is a Qablunaaq after all and I got to be okay with that. I always tease Sakku about picking Carol and see now it happened to me so watch out who you tease about what Thomasie.

I don't think Sakku will be having more children to name after Kublu any time soon. Carol says no way until he come up with some kind of big pay job to support them all better.

You may think I am going too fast Nukaqtaaq . You have not even met this woman I talk about and must question if maybe I lost my mind. But I feel very sure about this thing. Like when the fish you want is in the water at your feet but not too near you throw the spear without hesitation. When the seal you been waiting for comes to the breathing hole in the ice at last you can not be standing there picking your nose and wondering if you should thrust the harpoon or not. Because then it is gone and you still hungry.

I feel that same instinctive kind of sure yes about this thing. So I took the chance before it pass by me and be gone. Nothing for me to do now but wait to hear and sure hope she will say yes. I let you know.

Take it easy,

ALISON 24
Rankin Inlet, Northwest Territories
November 15, 1970

Ivaluk has proposed to me. I'm deeply ambivalent about it. As much as I wanted to leap into his arms when he asked me and just kiss him until the sea ice melts again, I said I would have to think about it. Sleeping on it for a few nights rather than answering right away does not seem unreasonable. Yet I feel a bit badly about doing this, as if I am a bucket of cold water. Though I do not detect fear or sadness or insult in his eyes, which just seem to burn steady with joy and certainty when he looks at me.

But good lord this would be such a big step for me, I want more time to think it over. I know full well what I am feeling. It's just—well, can I trust my feelings? That is the question.

I have tried to bury myself in work for a few days, which is not hard to do, as our prenatal clinic is deluged these days. I see Ivaluk only briefly, meeting him in front of the Bay for a short talk or a quick kiss, taking small walks in the dusky light that comes for a short while only around noon these days.

I'd like to have a clearer notion of what our future together might be like, but his attitude is that the future will take care of itself and it will all be good, or not, but however it is, we are meant to deal with it together. Perhaps he is right—but what if he isn't? I have many questions…how will we live, where will we find shelter, what will we do for income? These are not trivial questions.

Can I really move straight from the nursing station into an overcrowded home with no running water or proper toilet facilities and say la-de-dah, I love my man, so whatever will be, will be? Our children could be poverty statistics—imagine that! It sends a shiver down my spine. It seems impossible, unreal.

I try to think about my options for earning a living here in the future. The government recently announced plans to build a big new school, as the old facility is quite outgrown. Perhaps they will need a school nurse. Or perhaps I could get some sort of civil service job when all those Churchill people quit and the regional government moves up here. I have even been wondering about the possibility of starting a business of my own, perhaps using my savings to open a little coffee shop, a place where lovers can meet or people can gather to talk outside of their homes. There could be some arcade games for the kids, a jukebox, maybe even some live entertainment once in a while, if someone is willing to come play the guitar and sing. Maybe Nancy and her friends could come and perform...

Or maybe I should just be sensible and go home right now. Except that home has never felt like home to me. How odd that I have come to feel more at home in this foreign place, among people from an entirely different culture, than I ever did with my own family, in my own hometown.

It's not that I feel I am one of the Inuit—I am not that daft. But I do feel I have become a part of this community, with its strange mix of outsiders who, for one reason or another, have chosen to make this place their home, for the short- or long-term. This feeling is both comforting and frightening. No one could be more surprised than me to see where my home might end up being—Rankin Inlet, Northwest Territories, Canada? A place where many of the adults were born on the land and lived in tents and iglus most of their lives. Can I, or any outsider, ever understand their perspective on the past, their accommodation of the present, and their hopes for the future? Can I ever truly be a part of this place? I just don't know.

Perhaps love is the only thing I can be sure about. I am going to sleep on this one more night, but if I wake up the same woman tomorrow, I am going to find Ivaluk and tell him my answer: ii. The rest will have to sort itself out.

NIKMAK 11
Rankin Inlet
November 15, 1970

Kublukuluk, paniga, the ground has frozen solid now. I wanted to check your grave to see that the rocks have not shifted, to make sure no wolf or bear has disturbed your brothers' work. I could have brought one of Ivaluk's dog teams, or borrowed Sakku's skidoo, but today I felt like walking. I wanted to go out onto the tundra like a real Inuk, with nothing but his caribou clothing and a bit of dried meat in his pocket.

This air is sharp as a slap. Inhaling makes little needles in my lungs. Exhaling coats my moustache and eyelashes with ice. It feels so good after being in that hot house. Your anaana is so afraid little Radar might catch a cold that she has me sweating day and night, stripped down to my undershirt. It feels good to move, to be out on the land, and to be with you for a moment. Sitting here in the almost-dark, stars making the snow glow beneath my feet, just a thin ribbon of pink light lying along the distant horizon like hope.

Ivaluk has asked me for permission to marry that Qablunaaq nurse, Alison Clark. By asking, he is honouring tradition, even though the days of arranged marriages are long gone. I know what he is worried about—already one of my sons has married a Qablunaaq woman, and that is not going so well. And one of my daughters had a baby with a Qablunaaq man, and now she is gone. Perhaps he thinks I am concerned that our heritage will be weakened, our bloodline thinned down to water. But this is not so. Look at me: Netsilingmiut mother, Russian-Japanese father, Sallimiut wife, Padlirmiut son-in-law, Qablunaaq daughter-in-law, and half-Qablunaaq grandkids. All this mixing may make us Tunus less Netsilingmiut, but does it make us any less Inuit? I do not think so. Not so long as we feel the same strong ties to this land and to one another, not so long as we love to hunt and fish, no matter what we must do to earn a living. Not so long as we love the look of the tundra in every season and crave the taste of seal meat and tuktu. I have no doubt that Radar will grow up to be such an Inuk, despite his drops of Qablunaaq blood.

Ivaluk thinks I know nothing about this woman, Alison. I could see he wanted to praise her, to defend his choice, but he kept silent, watching for signs from me.

I know enough about this woman. I know that when she and Wayne came to my home to visit you, her eyes were filled with curiosity and wonder, not disdain. I know that when I was in the nursing station singing at your bedside, she brought me a glass of water, a sign of her pitsirniq, her ability to anticipate and serve the needs of another. I know that when she told me about your fingers being cut off, she touched my hand to comfort me. I know that when she pulled up that white sheet to cover you after death, her own tears spilled onto the cotton like the tracks of an ukaliq across fresh snow. In my eyes, these things have shown her to be one of us, a real person, an Inuk.

I think she is worthy of our Ivaluk, and I told him so. I hope she is wise enough to see that he is a man worthy of her.

The wind is picking up, Kublu. I must head back before your anaana sends the RCMP looking for me.

I miss you, paniga.

Aya-aya-ayayeah.

PART II

TRANSITIONS

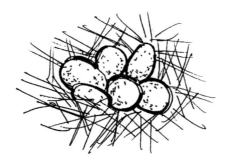

ALISON 1
Rankin Inlet, Northwest Territories
December 10, 1970

I bumped into Annie Pilakapsi in the Bay this morning. She approached me in a state of high excitement, pulling Pauluusie Nukilik by the sleeve. "Alison, I want you to meet my fiancée, Pauluusie," she said, her eyes glowing and her voice tight with pride.

"Hi, Pauluusie," I said, smiling as I shook his hand. He grinned and rolled his eyes.

I did not announce that I, too, am engaged to be married. Word about that will be out soon enough, and I am still trying to get used to the idea myself.

A bit later, Pauluusie shook himself loose from Annie's grip and found me browsing in the magazine section. "Alison, listen to me," he said earnestly. "I want you to know that my father arranged this thing, this marriage to Annie. I got tired of fighting about it. They wore me down. I have come to accept my fate, like a fox with his tail in a trap. I'm even beginning to think that marriage might be a good thing for me—to have my own home with a wife and some kids to look after. I am actually looking forward to having a son and teaching him how to hunt and fish. And Annie, she's a good enough girl. I'm lucky she agreed to have me."

I told him I thought so too, and that I was happy for him and Annie, and wished them both the best.

"Just because I'm getting married doesn't mean we can't still be lovers," he whispered. I managed to shake my head no as he ambled away, smiling over his shoulder at me, and leaving loose mounds of melting snow in his wake.

IVALUK 1
Rankin Inlet, N.W.T.
January 8, 1971

Dear Thomasie:

It was really good you could come home for Christmas and even come to my wedding with Alison. It is different to be a husband.

We have our own separate house now. It is good but it means now we got to come up with money to pay the rent for it every month. I don't think I can give the Housing Association my old collection of caribou antlers or a couple of sealskins in place of rent money. They want the paper kind.

Ataata and Sakku gave us two months' rent as a wedding present which was a big help. And Alison has more money saved up than any person I know. Several thousand dollars maybe. But I want her to keep saving that. In case she has to go home some day or have an emergency. I am a good hunter. I can keep us fed up but I also need to figure out how to earn some cash to pay for rent. As well as heating oil and chocolate and other things I learn Qablunaaq women can not live without.

I could hunt more but most of the people I supply with meat can't afford to pay cash. They have enough trouble to pay their own rent. We barter for stuff I need like new harnesses or even stuff I do not need but is nice to have like embroidery on my jacket or a homemade pie. I might try out carving like Ataata and Sakku but honest I think I do not have the right eye for it. I tried to carve a seal once but it come out looking mostly like a pregnant beluga whale.

Keep your fingers cross for me as I go ahead further into this marriage life.

Take it easy,

△< ﹍'

p.s. - been super cold this month with wind chill making outdoor work impossible. Good excuse for staying indoors and get to know Alison better eh?

ALISON 2
Rankin Inlet, Northwest Territories
January 10, 1971

Dear Nancy:

I appreciated your Christmas card more than you will ever know. I do think about you and wonder how everyone is getting on at home. So thank you very much for the holiday wishes and the family news. I can't believe it has been less than a year since I left home. It seems much longer.

I am married now, to the Inuit hunter I told you about on the telephone. Ivaluk and I had a simple ceremony on New Years' eve. Now the people in this community are making the transition from thinking of me as Nurse Alison Clark to knowing me as Mrs. Ivaluk Tunu, the improbable wife of one of the best young hunters here. Believe me, it's an adjustment for me too, a cause of amazement every day.

The Tunus have been wonderful to me. I feel fully and genuinely accepted into their family. The people in the community also treat me with respect, mixed with more than a little curiosity. If anything, it is the Qablunaat who look most strangely at me now, perhaps wondering about the mental status of a freckled redheaded former nurse who seems to have gone cuckoo and married one of the natives.

As feared, I lost my job because of a frustrating Nursing Station policy that prohibits the employment of married persons. I would have continued to work as a nurse-midwife quite happily. Instead, I've lost my income, my benefits, my pension, and even my room and board by marrying Ivaluk. So far, I have no regrets. I love him dearly, but we've only been living together a few weeks and my savings are not all spent yet.

I didn't think I could possibly adjust to living in a corner of Ivaluk's parents' home. I wanted to begin my married life with some degree of privacy. At first, Ivaluk wasn't keen on moving. He thought his parents would feel lonely, since his younger sister Kublu died just recently, leaving a baby behind to be raised. It all worked out, however, because Ivaluk's older sister, Pitsiark, and her two young daughters have come to Rankin Inlet to stay for a while. With Pitsiark at home, Ivaluk felt freer to leave.

Ivaluk got us onto the long waiting list for a home of our own, and then he practically drove the young housing secretary crazy, pestering him daily to see when something might become available. Perhaps the housing board took pity on the Qablunaaq woman who has been ousted from her accommodations at the Nursing Station to move into a public housing unit. Or perhaps Ivaluk did some bribing from his stock of frozen tuktu. Or perhaps they agreed to rent us the shack on the outskirts of town because no one else wanted it. The house is tiny and damp and badly in need of cosmetic work, and it is a long walk from the post office and the Bay store (the social centre of our community), but Ivaluk and I don't care about any of that. It is a space we can call our own—four walls and a roof over our heads, with complete, glorious privacy, except when someone enters without knocking.

We set about turning this shanty into our home with a vengeance. We cleaned and painted it, at least on the inside. The exterior will have to wait until spring, when the paint won't freeze solid on our brushes. Ivaluk has amused himself over the years by touring through the town dump and salvaging things that might turn out to be useful some day. Lately he has been pulling these treasures out from under his family's house, and we are using some of them to furnish and decorate our new home. He made us an unusual coffee table from an old ship's rudder. A couple of old railroad lanterns on chains (how these got to Rankin Inlet is a mystery, since there is no rail line within five hundred miles) have been made into electric lamps that now hang in the corners and cast beams of red and green light over our home, giving it the feel of a hippy crash pad—or perhaps a bordello.

We bought some rudimentary furnishings from the Bay—a mattress, a chest of drawers, and a formica dining table with four chairs. We also bought a used sofa bed from one of the social workers who is returning to the south—so now we even have guest accommodations, if we should need them in the future.

We have been enjoying our time together, hunkered near the oil stove as the storms howl around us in the darkness outside. We have a radio-cassette player for news and music, and we have stocked up on food, so I am not sure how long it might take to get this letter down to the post office, or how many weeks it might take to reach you after that, as the flights are erratic during this season of icy squalls and paltry daylight.

All the best for a happy new year.

Cheers,

Alison

ALISON 3
Rankin Inlet, Northwest Territories
February 12, 1971

Of course I was warned about the Arctic winter. It would be cold; it would be dark. But it was impossible for me to imagine just how cold and how dark. We have been right off the wind-chill charts for weeks on end now, with temperatures hovering around forty below zero, but sometimes we have forty mile per hour winds on top of that.

I was suffering from cabin fever one day and just had to go outside, storm or no storm. I decided on an outing to the Bay and the post office. Ivaluk insisted on accompanying me, saying it is easy to get lost and freeze to death at times like this. Much as even a break from him for half an hour sounded appealing, in the end I was glad he came with me. The sky was almost completely dark, even at high noon. There were snow pellets blowing sideways, drifting along the ground and obscuring vision to the point that I could not even see the buildings that I knew were right next door to us, or even my own feet. I had no depth perception, no sense of direction. Ivaluk told me that in these conditions sometimes people tie a rope to their door knob and walk off holding onto that, so that if they become disoriented, at least they can find their way home again. I thought he was kidding, but once I got outside I could see that it would be very easy indeed to lose your way and encounter disaster.

I learned that any exposed flesh can suffer frostbite in less than a minute. Well before we reached the Bay, Ivaluk yelled that I needed to stick my nose inside my parka hood, as it was beginning to freeze. I did as he told me, and found I could prevent my nose from freezing that way. I wondered if this is what rubbing noses is all about—sticking your face close to someone else's so the fox fur around your parka hoods can lock out the winter air to prevent your flesh from freezing.

It takes a great effort to dress to go outdoors. It must have taken me a good twenty minutes to put on my long johns, then jeans and a flannel shirt, and then wind pants, then duffle socks, then snow boots, then parka, scarf, hat, and caribou fur mittens. If we go to visiting, most homes have the oil stove cranked up, so it is necessary to shed most of these layers again, or you will be dripping sweat within minutes.

The twenty-three hours of darkness is disorienting, as well. It plays havoc with my internal clock. I feel sleepy as a bear much of the time, and go into a sort of hibernation—sleeping long hours to make up for all the frolicking we did under the midnight sun in the summertime. Now I understand the joy with which people greet the lengthening days and milder temperatures in spring. It will be a delight to step outside with merely a shirt or a jacket on, and no mittens and all the rest. If I survive that long.

THOMASIE 1
Churchill, Manitoba
March 12, 1971

Dear Ivaluk:

You are such a good hunter, it seems too bad you have to worry about earning money too. That's something our ancestors didn't have to think about—paying rent, buying groceries. Life has become more complicated.

I will be getting my high school diploma in just a few months. They have been bringing these guidance counsellors in to talk to us about continuing our education. Some government people also have come around to offer scholarship assistance. Peter Udjuk is the only one I know who seems interested right now. He has relatives who live in Quebec, and a cousin who is going to school in Montreal, so he is thinking about moving somewhere down there for a while to try out university. The rest of us feel worn out with school. We want to go home. Four years of being away is all we can stand.

I have missed being around my family and people who love me. I could go on and on about the things I have missed—hunting and fishing with you, drinking tea with Anaana, playing cards with Ataata, eating tuktu stew with Sakku, playing kid games with Radar. Maybe I'll go back to school later on, but right now I just want to finish these classes and get out of here, come home to Rankin Inlet.

With a little luck I should be there by early June. Can't wait.

Love,

Thomasie

ALISON 4
Rankin Inlet, Northwest Territories
March 14, 1971

We have had a blizzard going strong for four solid days now. Thank god for the oil stove, and for our stash of food and the four walls that shelter us. I cannot imagine spending these past four days inside an iglu, with little room to move around, and where the only source of light and heat would be a smouldering moss wick burning in seal oil. You could not heat the place properly or it would melt.

I've had no communication with any person but Ivaluk, and the wind has been howling so viciously that sometimes we have to shout to hear one another. At one point the storm tore off a part of our stovepipe, which crashed onto the roof before being blown somewhere in the direction of the North Pole. We lost power for several hours and had to use flashlights and emergency candles for light. I was able to cook a few things on the oil stove—tea, porridge, pea soup—but Ivaluk doesn't consider anything like that to be real food. He stored some char and caribou in our enclosed porch, where it remains solidly frozen. When he is hungry he goes out and whacks off a piece of caribou with the wood axe. Or he brings in a fish as stiff as a baseball bat and proceeds to suck on it like a popsicle, or shave bits off of it with his knife. I chuckle to myself at moments like this, and think how I might have married a beer belching, steak and kidney pie-eating Englishman, instead of this Inuit hunter.

Finally this evening, the wind let up for an hour or two. We peered outside, but it was pitch dark (street lights out) and still very cold. Ivaluk made me go out for a short walk with him, anyway. It seemed hardly worth the effort of putting on all those layers of clothing and fur just for a brief excursion. We started toward Nikmak's house, thinking we should check on the family and be sure all was well. Ivaluk tied a rope around his waist and then tied the other end around me, to prevent our losing one another outside. What kind of mad place have I come to, I wondered? I clutched the rope for dear life as we wandered blindly in the dark night, occasionally tripping over objects in the snow that might have been a frozen honey bag or a dog or a sled.

As we were groping and stumbling along, the wind picked up again, and sharp pellets of icy snow began to hammer at us. I thought Ivaluk must have a better sense of navigation under these conditions than I do, so I was surprised to find that, when we came upon a snow covered entryway, it turned out to belong to our own home.

"It's starting up again. No point in taking risks. We are better off staying in," he said.

Once we were indoors and had shed all the layers of clothing we had so painstakingly put on less than half an hour earlier, I asked Ivaluk how in god's name his ancestors survived in such a climate. It is challenging, he replied, because you have to respect the environment and pay tributes to Nuliajuk and watch out for evil spirits. But if you work hard and do things right, you can survive and enjoy the experience. He said he loves being outdoors for long periods of time, even in winter, dealing with whatever conditions nature throws his way.

He said the winter season can be tough, but if you are prepared for it and have cached fish and caribou meat and can go out and catch the occasional seal, you can provide for your family. Then spring, when it arrives, seems almost too bountiful. The sun returns, and as the snow and sea ice melt, the seal birthing lairs collapse, making it much easier to catch seals than standing for hours over a breathing hole, as you must do in winter. For a change from seal meat, you can go spring ice fishing on the lakes. And soon afterwards the caribou migrate in great numbers, the fish fill the rivers, and the snow geese and other migratory birds come north to nest and lay eggs and have their young. There are berries to eat. Summer is a time of abundance, but when the snow and ice return in the fall, everyone is happy, because once again you can travel long distances quickly by dog sled, and you can return to the winter sealing areas and hunt on the sea ice again.

I asked him why his ancestors didn't think about moving further south, to a more hospitable environment. He countered by asking me why my British relatives didn't move to Hawaii or some place where life might have been easier. I guess you learn to appreciate and master living in the environment wherever you are born. You get used to it, so that being anywhere else seems strange.

Much as I love the man, I was elated when the storm abated at last and he was able to get out of the house to go seal hunting.

"I will try not to be gone too long," he said.

"Take your time, darling," I called back. "Happy hunting."

I walked down to the Bay and bought a new magazine to celebrate the return of electricity, as well as a box of Cadbury Christmas chocolates I found in the discount bin. I dropped by Nikmak's house, and then Sakku's, but found no one home at either place. There were lots of people on the streets, strolling under the street lamps, but they were so bundled up it was impossible to tell who was who. I went home and turned on the BBC world report and read my magazine and listened to an entire Mahler symphony from beginning to end, imagining myself sitting in a big outdoor amphitheatre somewhere hot and sunny like Greece, wearing shorts and a tank top, with the sun heating my exposed skin. I slowly ate every single chocolate in that box, not leaving even one for Ivaluk.

By the time he came home a full day later, I was happy to see him again. I licked the ice off his moustache, and he made me happy I was not in Greece, after all.

IVALUK 2
Rankin Inlet, N.W.T.
March 31, 1971

Dear Thomasie:

I got your letter and wanted to reply soon. Maybe I am not one to talk about these things myself because I never finish school and did only a bit of vocational training. Still I see lots of ads posted at the Hamlet Office now for jobs with the GNWT and most of them except the secretary type jobs and repairing engines seem to ask for a college degree. Or they pay more money if you have one.

It makes me think this is become a more important thing. In the past I know some people got into a good job without a degree and just build up lots of experience on the job. I think that is harder now. But if you feel tired of school right now and want to take a break and come home please do that. Coming home is not closing the doors on your future. You could maybe still go to study more later if you decide you want to. Maybe still get a scholarship too. Your life is up to you. I feel pretty sure you will make good choices for yourself. And if not you probably learn something from mistakes. Like we all do.

Pitsiark went back to Eskimo Point with her girls. Ataata and Anaana are alone with Radar now. Sakku and I try to go visit just about every day but I can tell you they will love having you back home again.

It is so good to be out hunting more with sun coming back.

Take it easy,

ALISON 5
Rankin Inlet, Northwest Territories
April 5, 1971

I had a shock today when an official from the Housing Association came knocking at the door, demanding the rent. He said that we were a month in arrears already. I had no idea. I wrote him a check for March and April straight away.

When Ivaluk returned from visiting his parents, I confronted him. He stiffened and looked offended and said that everybody in this town is behind in rent. People pay what they can, when they can. This is how it is, so he was puzzled about why the housing officer was picking on us. Maybe because I am Qablunaaq, and therefore must be rich. He said he has not had any cash windfalls lately, but that he is working on some ideas. He as much as said you can't get blood out of a turnip.

I told him I was mortified and did not want to earn a reputation as a person who does not pay her debts. He was mad at me for paying the rent from my own funds, without talking to him about it first. I said the last thing we need is to be evicted. Then what would we do—go live in an iglu? He said he knows how to build one, should it become necessary, but he had never heard of anyone being evicted by the Housing Association, even if they owe years of back rent. I said I was not cut out for living in an iglu full-time and would not raise our child in one. His chocolate cheeks flushed with anger, and he stomped out of the house and vanished for two full days.

Why did we have to have our first fight over something as stupid as money? I can see we have different attitudes about it. I am hardwired to pay my bills promptly and to save for a rainy day, not live hand-to-mouth. In this land of few jobs and scarce income, the Inuit deal with things differently, by bartering or postponing payments due. Money comes in erratically, so it goes out erratically. I can appreciate that. It is not the end of the world, just a difference in perspective and habits. As long as we understand and accept that about each other, we should be fine. I hope...

When Ivaluk finally came home, he looked humble and as meek as a lamb, and so very handsome that my annoyance with him melted away at once. He pulled a single red rose out from under his caribou parka. It was plastic of course, or it would never have survived the trip from the Bay, but it is the thought that counts. "I heard Qablunaat women like flowers," he said, with a big grin. But of course it was not a rose at all but an olive branch, so I went over and kissed him and let him hold me in his arms for a long, quiet while.

Finally, he pulled back and looked me in the eyes and asked: "*Are* we going to have a child?"

"I think so," I replied. He said nothing, but he pulled me closer and held onto me until the wind died down and we were hungry.

ALISON 6
Rankin Inlet, Northwest Territories
April 16, 1971

At first I was so happy to learn that I am pregnant.

I decided to make a quick trip to Churchill to be examined, as I do not relish the idea of Nurse Bauer or Sherry Dunlop peering up my innards while they try not to think about my sex life and I try not to think about theirs. Jerry was kind enough to fly me down and back for free on one of his cargo runs.

Ivaluk met me at the airstrip when I returned, and we hurried home to make love to celebrate the happy news. Then, as I was making up our bed, I found a pair of women's underpants that were not mine.

"Ivaluk—whose are these?" I asked him in a panic.

"Uh, must belong to Agnes," he replied.

"Agnes Who?" I demanded.

And then it all came out. Agnes is a woman from Edmonton who has been coming to Rankin Inlet from time to time to work on some kind of anthropological study on culture change and the blending of different Inuit subgroups into one regional centre. Well. Isn't there some code of ethics to prevent such a person from fucking the subjects of her research? I have a mind to write to the government or whatever university she might work for about this, but it would just bring further embarrassment.

Ivaluk, it turns out, seems to think there is absolutely nothing wrong with having casual sex with another woman while your wife is away. It is just a convenience to him, like getting your back scratched. He says he meant nothing by it. He said it is a cultural tradition. In the old days, men would sometimes take long trading trips, or go off hunting for days or weeks at a time. Visitors from another camp might stop by. Borrowing someone else's wife under such circumstances was not uncommon. It is no big deal, just the traditional Inuit way, he claims.

Well, it is NOT my way, I retorted, and these are not the old days. My marriage vows mean something to me, including a commitment to be faithful to one another.

He swore he meant nothing by it. He said he thought Qablunaat behaved this way, too, because he sees it go on all the time in Rankin

Inlet. And he brought up that song we hear on the radio all the time, Love the One You're With. What about that, he asked.

I fell onto the sofa sobbing, and told him to get out. I am so mad I don't know what to do. Here I am pregnant with his child and he is messing around with other women the minute I am gone. What is to become of this baby and me?

NIKMAK 1
Rankin Inlet
April 28, 1971

Paniga—I have come to visit with you again.

It is a bright, crisp day and I had to get out of that stuffy house. Your anaana still likes to keep it as warm as summer in there. She says it helps her lungs feel better and she doesn't cough as much. And it is easier to change Radar's diaper if that is all he is wearing.

The back of the winter is broken and the days are growing longer. Soon the caribou will be thundering across the tundra again and the air will be thick with birds, and then with mosquitoes. The earth will soften and the siksiks will romp over our land. The ponds will melt and there will be pink flowers and purple berries once more. I wish you could be here to see it all happen again, Kublu. It is six months since you left us, and the pain in my heart is not quite so sharp.

I want you to know we are doing okay. Radar is crawling now, and he keeps us busy and amused. I think he is going to be a fine boy. He is cheerful and funny and does not cry much. We are happy to be raising him, and his uncles are also alert to his needs. Don't worry—I plan to make sure he pays more attention to Ivaluk than to Sakku, though they both have something to teach him and love to give.

Ivaluk has been visiting too much lately. It makes me think he is in some sort of trouble at home. I hope not. If he is, I hope he will figure out how to keep Alison happy and not try to drink away his troubles like Sakku. They are expecting a baby now, and I am pretty sure they will name their little one after you. Then perhaps I will no longer come here to talk with you. I will be able to talk to you as you learn to crawl among us once again.

I miss you. That is all I have to say.

Aiyayaaa.

ALISON 7
Rankin Inlet, Northwest Territories
April 30, 1971

Ivaluk and I have got past our recent crisis for now. He promised me he will never sleep with another woman again, although I can tell he thinks this is a foolish and unnecessary condition to place on any human life on this earth. We are reconciled, but there is still some residual tension. He occasionally goes out without telling me where he is going or how long he will be gone. He may come home an hour or a day later, without explanation about where he has been. I suppose it is his way of asserting independence. I do not want to make any more waves just now.

Sherry Dunlop paid a surprise visit to my home a few days ago, at one of those times when Ivaluk had vanished. Sherry and I were never close friends, but I felt pleased by her visit nevertheless. Perhaps I have been feeling a bit isolated and lonely, so the visit was all the more welcome. I made tea and biscuits and asked how she had found my home. She said it is easy to find anything in Rankin Inlet. There are no secrets that can be kept in this community; it is like living in a fish tank. In light of that, she decided she might as well tell me before I heard it from someone else: she and Jerry Duncan are having an affair.

I suppose she did more than go shopping when he flew her out to Thompson for a break last fall. What about his wife and kids, I asked? Well, these things happen don't they, she replied.

Jerry took over Wayne's permanent job and had planned to move his family to Rankin Inlet this summer. Now who knows what will happen. Sometimes we humans act like electrons circling on the outer ring of unstable atoms, flung about by invisible, powerful forces to slam together into all sorts of new arrangements. Or are we simply as randy as chimps?

Sherry also brought gossip from the Nursing Station. They are still busy mopping up the epidemic of venereal diseases spread by Ryan Dolan and his ilk. The Health Services Department has finally found someone to replace me—a woman from New Zealand who has been living in the States—but it will be another month or so before she arrives, so Sherry and Nurse Bauer have to work long hours for a while yet.

Their policy against married staff is idiotic. I'd love to be working, and it would benefit all concerned.

Sherry said she will stay on through the summer, but she is thinking about moving on to some place warmer in the fall, with or without Jerry, depending on how things go. Even Nurse Bauer is talking about retirement. She is under some investigation for dispensing antibiotics too liberally, which has led some patients to become resistant to them, so the drugs do not work when they are most needed.

Then Sherry informed me that another reason for her visit. She saw an advertisement in the Health Services bulletin that made her think of me. They are looking for a consultant to draft a guide on prenatal and perinatal issues in remote communities. The guide would be used in clinics all across the north country, to help standardize the care that is given to pregnant women and improve infant mortality rates. Sherry thought I would be just the right person to develop such a guide. I thanked her for thinking of me.

I told Sherry that I am pregnant, and she congratulated me and encouraged me to join a class for expectant mothers that she puts on at the Nursing Station on Monday afternoons. Not that I need to learn about the medical aspects of it, but it might be fun to meet some other expectant mothers, so we can build a network of future playmates for our babies.

I thanked Sherry for her visit and gave her a hug and wished her good luck, whatever that might mean.

IVALUK 3
Rankin Inlet, N.W.T.
May 31, 1971

Dear Thomasie:

Alison been getting some cabin fever attacks lately so I decided to take her with me to check my trap line. This was a really good idea. Being out on the land did us both a lot of good. We had a lucky cold snap. The weather was just cold enough to make the sleds run pretty good over the snow but not make your nose fall off.

Now that the days are long the sun is sure flashing off the ice and snow and can blind you some time. I don't know how our ancestors hunted in spring without Foster Grants. I've tried out the traditional bone eye mask with tiny slits cut into it. It helps a bit but also cuts down a lot how much you can see.

My traps were loaded with foxes. Mostly brown and grey ones but I impress Alison by getting six beautiful white pelts too. We took those pelts to the back room of the Hudson Bay store and Alistair look up on his charts what different size and type pelts are worth this week. Alison was all excited and whisper to me this must be how it was done in the old days. She doesn't realize the Hudson Bay trading post is still pretty new days to us. But I guess even twenty years ago Inuit would be stacking pelts up against the wall where those painted stripes show how much store debt you can pay off or how much tea and lard and ammunition you can get for your furs. Now you get store credit or cash. I took the cash because the rent is coming due again every time you turn around.

Did I tell you that we are expecting a baby soon? Well not that soon—sometime this fall I think. Still a long time off but we are pretty excited anyway.

Just a few weeks until you graduate. I knew you could do it and I know that it has not been so easy for you or the others either. All us Tunus looking forward to welcome you home and maybe we throw a big surprise congratulation party for you.

Take it easy,

△< ᗡ'

ALISON 8
Rankin Inlet, Northwest Territories
June 22, 1971

I won that consulting contract with the Health Services Department—what a lucky break, with the baby coming. I can fit the writing time in flexibly, picking my own work hours. I jot down my thoughts on a pad of paper at home, then go use a typewriter in the Settlement Office or the school library when the mood suits me. I could get used to being my own boss.

Ivaluk has found some paying work at last, too. The Arctic Char are running now, and he has been hired by the manager of a wilderness fishing business out of Yellowknife to guide avid fishermen to the Meliadine River. They provided him with a Jeep, so he has had to learn to drive it. He picks up the customers and their gear at the airstrip and takes them directly out to the river, where he pitches the tents and builds fires and makes sure there is bannock and tea, though the men seem to arrive with their own liquid provisions of another sort. He cleans and cooks fish for them, but God help them if they are gourmands, because Ivaluk can fry bacon and heat up baked beans, but his culinary skills are limited. He seems to exist on raw fish and seal and caribou and very little else. Once, when I was tucking into a fresh green salad, he asked me why Qablunaat eat so much grass. To him, any vegetable matter is grass—something for ungulates to graze on, perhaps, but not fit for consumption by humans, who are supposed to be higher up the food chain.

Living at the edge of town has turned out to be ideal for keeping Ivaluk's dog teams. He can stake them near the house, and their barking and mess don't bother other people too much. These days, more and more hunters in the community are switching to Skidoos; so many of them are shooting the dogs they no longer have use for. Not Ivaluk. He has continued to breed his, trying to develop the very best sled dogs possible. He has a bunch of beautiful pups now that he hopes to shape into two dog teams before winter. Having two teams seems excessive to me, but he claims it is good to have spare parts, as well as good breeding stock on hand. He says he plans to alternate taking them out on the land, or that he will get Sakku or Kanik to drive the second team and take them both out at the same time. With two good teams, he expects to be very successful in his hunting and trapping endeavours this winter. He barters or gives away most of the meat, but he is hoping that a few Qablunaat customers might appreciate (and pay dearly for) an occasional fresh tuktu roast or filet. He is taking advance orders from some customers, including the RCMP constable, the Transient Centre, and even the Nursing Station.

So, we are managing to keep our heads above water and the wolves from the door. I am growing as big as a bear, which makes it hard to get a good night's sleep. Ivaluk continues to assure me that he will not sleep with another woman, but I worry that he may think I am pathetically weak to need such a promise from him in order to feel happy and secure. Am I being too selfish and needy, I sometimes wonder?

ALISON 9
Rankin Inlet, Northwest Territories
October 1, 1971

Dear Mum and Nancy:

Just a quick note to tell you that I delivered a healthy baby girl last week. She is beautiful. She came out with a full head of hair and a dimpled chin, like Clint Eastwood. We have named her Kublu, after Ivaluk's sister who passed away a year ago. She has a strong pair of lungs, and she waves her fists like a boxer when she is hungry. She has completely disrupted our sleep with her demands, but we don't much care. Ivaluk is all smiles over her. My mother in law, Ukpik, has made me an amauti—the traditional women's parka used to carry a baby on your back. She took a lot of extra trouble with the embroidery and trim. Perhaps her way of thanking me for giving her son a child and herself another grandchild. The family seems to have transferred all the affection they felt for Ivaluk's sister directly to this new baby girl.

Ivaluk's brother Thomasie was here for the summer but now has gone off to Ottawa, the capital of Canada. He intended to stay put for a while, but after a summer of doing research for a new organization called the Inuit Tapirisat (or Eskimo Brotherhood), they offered him a position at their headquarters. He felt the opportunity was too good to refuse. He works for them during the day and takes university classes at night. His mother Ukpik is busy making him a new pair of sealskin boots for winter. I told her that he probably will not need them in Ottawa, but she has never seen a concrete sidewalk, so I don't think she quite believes me.

Wish you could see the baby. I know you'd love her. The enclosed photo will have to do for now.

Love,
Alison

THOMASIE 2
Ottawa, Ontario
October 16, 1971

Dear Ivaluk:

Adjusting to city life is a real challenge. There are so many people, they bump into you just walking down the street. Yet they are standoffish at the same time. You know how in Rankin Inlet, you pat or hug practically everyone you meet? It's different here. Strangers shove right into you on the sidewalk, but if you stop to talk to someone they stand back about two feet away, as if maybe you have bad breath. They don't lean in close like they do at home, as if they care about you and are real interested in what you are about to say.

I think I would be too homesick if it weren't for the other Inuit here in Ottawa. There are a surprising number of them—enough to form our own little settlement right here. They come from all over the north, not just Baffin Island and the High Arctic, but also Labrador and Quebec. ITC put on a party for all the Inuit they heard about who were coming to Ontario to study or to work this fall. They gave us useful tips about city living like make sure you look for cars before you cross the road, and they told us about some areas that might not be safe at night. They say we have to watch our money or it will flow through our hands like water, there are so many ways to spend it in the south. They encourage us to stick together and avoid isolation, because that can lead to depression. They also warned us about different kinds of drugs they have around here.

I'm working in the ITC office five days a week now and learning tons. There is lots of buzz about the Alaska Native Land Claims Agreement. It has everyone here in a spin. ITC is hoping to make a similar settlement agreement for us Inuit of Canada. Imagine that. So, there is lots of research work for guys like me, and it is mostly interesting.

I am taking an evening class in Political Science. This is a lot harder than anything at the residential school in Churchill, but I keep going because what I learn is fascinating and also useful to my job. I have to study and get lots of homework, so don't worry, I have no time to get into trouble.

Love to you and Alison and baby Kublu, and to Sakku and Carol and Picasso and Mona, and also Ataata and Anaana and Radar.

Thomasie

ALISON 10
Rankin Inlet, Northwest Territories
September 15, 1972

I have been too busy for diary keeping, with the baby and then the move and now a new baby on the way. Nikmak and Ukpik took the grandchildren out for a picnic, so I have a moment of peace to catch up.

Our big break came at last this year, and all because of a government mistake. Many new modular homes arrived on the sealift last summer. Some were simple homes for Inuit families, but many of them were the better made (and better insulated) staff houses to be assembled for the regional government workers who are moving up here. There was a frantic chorus of hammering in the town last fall, with crews working around the clock to get as many homes closed in before winter as possible.

The new homes stand out more than ever from the older Inuit homes. Some are even two-story models that tower above the rest of the community—for the coming bigwigs, I suppose. Most Inuit homes still lack even basic amenities like running water, but the new staff homes arrive fully equipped with modern appliances, and many are even fully furnished. You can almost guess the status or rank of the future resident by the quality of their furniture set.

I find all of this completely embarrassing, but none of the Inuit seem to notice or complain about it. They have coined a new word for the huge, two-story houses: iglurjuaq. "Iglu" is the general word for house and "juaq" means big, but it can convey the scale of difference you would observe between a kayak and an oil tanker.

Even Ivaluk just shrugs when I try to discuss these things. I guess since the days of first contact with whaling ships and polar expeditions, the Inuit have come to think of Qablunaat as possessing many more material comforts than their own people have or need. Or perhaps they simply have become inured to these inequities over the decades.

The error that was made was this: one of the three-bedroom homes being built for a teacher's family was accidentally put up on a pad that had been cut for an Inuit public housing unit. Only after the house was assembled did the contractor discover that it was in a spot that did not have utilidor service. They decided it would be prohibitively expensive to extend the utilidor system to that new home, or to take it down and move it to the right location. So there was a brand new home, complete with toilets and water heater, but no running water or wastewater service. The government felt that no Qablunaaq family would live in such a home, so it sat empty for several months, until a decision was made to write the unit off. Ian Mackenzie persuaded headquarters to try to recoup some of the losses by auctioning the building off. Fortunately for us, it was still winter when they held the auction, or one of the freight or communications firms that show up in the summertime surely would have snapped it up.

Ivaluk and I bid $2,001 dollars from my savings, and we got the house. We became homeowners before Kublu learned to crawl, which was a relief, because I was concerned that she might put her little hands on the glowing oil stove that heated our old rental unit.

This bit of good fortune has made Ivaluk and I feel very lucky. Just knowing that now we will have a roof over our heads forever, and that no landlord will ever again knock on our door demanding rent money or threatening to evict us has given us a new sense of security and optimism about the future.

No one in the Tunu family has ever owned a home, other than a tent or an iglu, until now. In fact, there are very few private homes in this community at all. There is one owned by the Hudson's Bay Company, one owned by the airline Jerry works for, and the catechist's hut owned by the Anglican Church. All the rest are owned by various government agencies.

We don't care a fig about the lack of flush toilets. We are used to the chemical toilet, and while I am not exactly thrilled with it, I do not let it bother me as long as Ivaluk takes charge of managing the honey bags, which so far he has done without complaint.

IVALUK 4
Rankin Inlet, N.W.T.
September 30, 1972

Dear Thomasie:

Don't expect more long distance phone calls from Anaana or Ataata. They been cut off by the telephone company like most families here.

When telephone service first come to Rankin Inlet a few months ago everybody signed up. The first few weeks was a blizzard of phone calls. You couldn't reach anybody by phone because all the lines were always busy. Like everyone else our parents enjoy catching up with their relatives back in Coral Harbour or down in Eskimo Point not realizing they are being charged each minute for all this catching up.

So just about every family built up a huge long distance phone bill in the first month or two. Once the phone company realize there is no way some customers can ever pay the bill they cut off their service cold. Everyone complains the phone company never explained right how the service works and what it cost. They just show everyone this great invention and hope they use it lots, which is what they did all right.

I guess the company decided not to fight the Inuit and make a lot of bad feelings. Easier to shut off the service and walk away instead. There are still some phones here but mostly for businesses and not for catching up news with the people who live far away. We still have a phone in our house because my nuliaq is smart and hardly let anyone use it.

We and the baby all are doing great. And now we got another one on the way. Not wasting any time.

Keep your news about life in the big city coming this way please. We love to hear from you.

Take it easy,

△< ⊃ᑉ

THOMASIE 3
Ottawa, Ontario
September 31, 1973

Dear Ivaluk:

It was great to be home for the summer, but it is fun to be here in Ottawa, too. The level of excitement at ITC is even higher than before. The Supreme Court of Canada just confirmed what they call "Aboriginal Title." It means that maybe the federal government does not own our land after all, like they thought they did. It might belong to the people who lived there for thousands of years, so maybe they will have to work with us to come to agreements about who has rights to do what, when, and where. It means they have agreed there should be some kind of land claims settlements with Canada's native people, including the Inuit.

ITC is now trying to put together all the bits of research people like me did these past summers, documenting the areas where our elders and our ancestors used to hunt and fish and camp. All that time we spent talking with people, especially the older ones, going over maps and making notes about where the big and small family camps gathered in various seasons in the past turns out to be useful.

Angajuk, sometimes I feel like I am playing a part in important history unfolding right in front of me. I don't spend all of my time hanging around the ITC office, though. I try to remember to get to my night class and study. I want to finish the program and earn my certificate, but what is going on in the headquarters of ITC can be distracting. I can't help myself from getting involved in it.

I get out once in a while too. One night last week I went out to a club to hear Charlie Panagoniak in person. He was amazing. Makes me think maybe when my course is finished and I have some more time, I will take up playing bass guitar, just so I can follow him around and hear him sing his country songs in Inuktitut and maybe be part of his backup band.

Love to all, and a special pinch to my new nephew, baby Missuk.

Love,

Thomasie

IVALUK 5
Rankin Inlet, N.W.T.
October 1, 1973

Dear Thomasie:

Glad I never listen to all those people who tell me what I should or should not do. Get rid of those nasty old sled dogs they kept telling me. They are noisy and stinky and out of fashion. Most everybody here has been shooting or giving away their last sled dogs and buying Skidoos instead.

Dog food was free—walrus meat. But now they have to buy oil and gas and plugs and belts and have repair bills to pay too.

I don't know why but I just knew I want to keep my dogs. I put down the weak ones and the old ones and picked up a few new ones no one wanted anymore. Now I have two real fine dog teams. Best teams ever. Even Ataata says so. They are a pleasure to work with and make me lucky in hunting. But there is more.

Since the regional government moved to Rankin Inlet I find myself and my dog teams in big demand. It turns out the Qablunaat moving up here think it is great fun to take a dog sled ride on the tundra and they will pay good money to do it. And the ones who like to hunt and fish pay me real well to act as a guide so they won't end up getting lost and freeze to death in a snowdrift out on the tundra alone. Some days I can't believe I am earning such good money for doing what I love. Maybe you feel that way too even though what you are doing is so different from me.

I get Sakku to help out with my dog business sometimes. He's a pretty good musher now and I know he can always use extra cash. Carol bugs him all the time about it even though he tries to explain to her that rent is on a sliding scale so when he earns more money they just pay more rent. Each time I hear about this it makes me happy all over again how we own our own home and don't have that problem any more.

Kublu is walking now so she gets into everything. She loves her new baby brother. We have to visit Ataata and Anaana even more now so they can hug and sing to their grandbabies. Sometimes we drop them and run so we can get some free babysitting and have a minute to ourselves.

Take it easy.

△< ⊃'

ALISON 11
Rankin Inlet, Northwest Territories
October 21, 1973

Television arrived with a bang last week. October 13, 1973 is a day I will always remember, because the streets of Rankin Inlet were absolutely deserted. It was spooky—as if someone had dropped a gas bomb on the town. We packed up the babies and went over to Carol and Sakku's place to watch the Ed Sullivan Show and a few Bugs Bunny cartoons. Nikmak pointed and laughed out loud at everything, as if he had never seen anything so amusing. Ukpik had tears streaming down her cheeks, she was laughing and coughing so hard. We had to keep pulling Radar and Kublu away from the set, as they wanted to be right in front of it, leaving hand and nose prints and blocking everyone else's view. When a crime show came on, everyone went silent, and the channel was changed quickly. Too much tension.

People have remained indoors all week, watching television relentlessly, day and night. I suspect this will continue for months to come, perhaps all winter, before the fascination wears off. Until now, we had only the radio and sporadic movies, so television has been a much-anticipated event. This summer the Bay brought in a mountain of television sets on the sealift, but so did the Coop. The TV wars ensued, with the Bay and the Coop trying to entice every household in the community to purchase a set, either at a big discount or on some type of a payment plan. For months, these television sets gathered dust, staring blankly into the living rooms of Rankin Inlet as people waited for the glitches with the Anik satellite to be worked out. But on October 13, they finally were. TVs switched on and brought a whole new universe of information and instant entertainment into the homes here.

I can't help but wonder if Nikmak has flashbacks to his days of living in an iglu, in an era when there was not a single electronic device around, as he watches a tribe of half-dressed, painted and feathered natives dancing around a fire in Papua New Guinea on the National Geographic show, or as he watches a space shuttle launch on the TV news. I tried to tell Nikmak that men have actually walked on the moon, but he doesn't believe me. He is sure it was all a Qablunaaq stunt, as unlikely as a rabbit standing up and asking "What's Up, Doc"?

IVALUK 6
Rankin Inlet, N.W.T.
November 29, 1974

Dear Thomasie:

I am sorry you will not be coming home for the Christmas holiday. Are you sure you are not keeping a secret from us like some big love thing or some thing else? The kids will sure miss you. We all will.

We are doing okay here. We are short on sleep some days with three little kids in the house but I wouldn't trade them for anything. I am sending a picture Alison took of the three of them naked and all lined up on a polar bear skin I got from Simon Arluk in exchange for some fresh tuktu.

I worry some about Sakku lately. He is keeping up with his carving so that is good. But sometimes he loves to drink his quota of beer just as soon as it arrives. He goes down the Bay store first thing to wait on beer day and can't save his two cases to stretch over the two weeks until the next shipment. Like some other people around here he doesn't handle alcohol too well. Carol usually ends up not talking to him for several days after. I have been trying to work on him about this but he doesn't like to talk about it. I'm an adult he tells me—mind your own business.

Most folks think it is great that Rankin Inlet finally hooked up to the rest of the world with television. I am not so sure. Before television came here people visited each other all the time. They would have tea and talk about things. Now they stay at home instead as if they are hypnotized by the TV and can't stop watching it just like Sakku can't stop sipping his beers til they are done. Nobody is outside looking at the stars in the sky anymore. They just want to see the Hollywood stars instead.

Alison hates TV and won't let one in our house. I don't feel so strong about it but don't want to fight over something like that. The kids are too little to complain and anyways they see plenty of it over at Sakku's place and every other house in town. Even Anaana and Ataata got one now.

I guess another thing that is different is that we see a lot more folks from Whale Cove than we used to. They pride themselves on staying small and isolated and traditional and refusing TV service, but now there is a skidoo parade coming here every Saturday to watch Hockey Night in

Canada, maybe drink a few beers and then head back home on Sunday. They are not too traditional to love hockey.

I keep busy giving dog sled rides which is good because the hunting is not too good lately. Game seems more scarce than ever around here. Maybe too many hunters in one small space. Or maybe the musk ox and caribou are scared off by the lights and sounds as our town grows bigger and brighter and louder all the time.

Lots of Qablunaat coming and going. That head nurse lady went away and the one they hired to replace Alison did not last long. Also Sherry ran off with Jerry but I guess he dump her because now she back again and in charge of our nursing station. Ian said this community getting too big and crowded for him so he took the open Settlement Manager job for Pond Inlet. Same kind of thing at the school and other offices here. Lots of people coming and going.

Next time you write please explain more about this land claim you are working on. People here don't understand it too well but there are lots of rumours. Everyone keep asking me about it because they know I have a brother down there in Ottawa, so they think I know everything going on in our Canada capital.

Some people here want me to run for the Council. I don't know. I have a lot of responsibility with dogs and kids right now and I am not as smart about how government supposed to work as you are. But then I been to some meetings lately with Alison because she is trying to get permission for a home business. I hear all kinds of things come from the mouths of the people who make decisions for the rest of us. Most of the time I think I could do at least as good a job as they are doing so I go forth and back about it. What do you think?

Take it easy,

ᐃᐦ ᓴ ᐅ ᑊ

ALISON 12
Rankin Inlet, Northwest Territories
December 8, 1974

Dear Nancy:

I want to get this card off to you early, because the Christmas season is going to be crazy here, with the three children plus my catering business, which seems to be booming.

When I became a mother, I began to take more interest in cooking and nutrition than I did in the past. I've read some of those trendy books like *Diet for a Small Planet* and *Confessions of a Sneaky Organic Cook*. I began experimenting in the kitchen, baking healthy breads, making yogurt from powdered milk (Kublu will eat anything if it has enough jam in it or on it). I even grow bean sprouts in jars on the windowsill; although Ivaluk refuses to eat them, claiming it is like nibbling moss. I grow fresh herbs under a grow light, and use them in my soups and stews.

I took up cooking with a vengeance last winter. I would empty the leftovers out of the refrigerator and add a few things from the Bay and turn out some unique stews and casseroles. Our friends and neighbours began to comment on the aromas wafting from our house. Several people suggested that I should open a bakery or a restaurant, but with three small kids at home, there is no way I could go out to a job all day or evening.

Then a couple of single teachers asked if they could pay me to cook for them several times a week, as they don't feel they have time to do it for themselves. (Apparently the open classroom system at the new school is wearing them out). I spoke with the Settlement Council about the idea of a small take-out and catering business that I could run from my home. They gave me tentative permission, provided we could find a way to get hot running water and a dishwashing machine installed at the house. So we built a heated enclosure and put in a water holding tank, which has to be filled by a water tanker truck weekly, and hooked it up to the unused water heater and piping that came with the house originally. Then we got another tank to collect wastewater, which has to be picked up by a different pump truck. (We are fortunate that these trucks already exist in the community to service remote locations like the airport terminal). It is an elaborate system that required some investment, but now we enjoy indoor baths and showers, without having to march over to the bathhouse or use the school gymnasium. It seems luxurious. I don't know how I managed the babies before this bathtub came along. Of course now we get more visits from Ivaluk's relatives, who do not have such facilities of their own and are fascinated by them.

Word of my business spread quickly around town, so it was a hit from opening day. I make original dishes with local ingredients, like caribou goulash or curried seal flipper soup, and dark loaves of bread filled with whole barley kernels and molasses or brewers yeast. People come by to purchase the soup of the day and bread to take away between 11:30 and 12:30 daily, or they can call to arrange a special pickup time. Sometimes they send the taxi van over to fetch enough food for a staff meeting or house party. I take special orders for dinner entrees, which customers can pick up between 5:00 and 6:00 p.m. The business has been so successful that we just added an insulated porch at the side of the house, with a service window cut through the wall into the kitchen, to keep customers' messy boots out of the house.

I got many requests to bake cinnamon buns, brownies, pies, and such sweets. At first, I resisted. I felt determined to make only things that I think are actually good for people, not empty calories, especially given the mountains of junk food available at the Bay already. But then I relented. I admitted that I am addicted to chocolate myself, and the kids love a cookie now and then. Why deprive people of what they want, if it makes them so happy? Anything in moderation. So now I am practically running a bakery, as well as a restaurant. At least my sweets don't have a lot of preservatives in them.

Give my love to mum and everyone else. Wishing you all a happy holiday season. I guess it will be a different Christmas with dad gone. I hope it is not too gloomy for you.

Love,
Alison

ALISON 13
Rankin Inlet, Northwest Territories
July 1, 1976

I have been married to Ivaluk for more than five years now, yet I still have things to learn about him and his beliefs. We made a family outing recently, to have a picnic in a pretty place Ivaluk knows about, down by the water, in an area where thousands of birds nest in the cliffs in the summer time. He borrowed the outfitters' Jeep to take us all there.

The children (5, 4 and 3 now) giggled as we bumped along over the tundra. Ivaluk built a fire when we arrived, and I made tea and bannock. Ivaluk went off to gather gull eggs, taking Kublu along with him. I kept an eye on Missuk and Kavik, who were pitching stones at some ptarmigan nearby. When I looked up at some point and noticed where Kublu was, my heart flew into my mouth. She was following her father as he scrambled along the edge of a cliff to fetch eggs. She was picking her way along the edge of a twenty or thirty foot sheer drop. I couldn't run to her and leave the boys to drown at the water's edge. And I didn't want to shout out, for fear I might startle her and make her lose her balance. So instead I leapt about, flapping my arms like a mad woman, trying to attract Ivaluk's attention. When he didn't notice, I tried banging some pots together in a slow, steady rhythm. He finally looked my way and I waved frantically, pointing at Kublu. He looked over at her, and then gave me a puzzled look. I motioned more frantically. He gathered some eggs, then finally walked over and took Kublu's hand. The two of them came ambling into camp as if nothing unusual had happened. I was furious at Ivaluk and wondered if I could trust him to keep our children out of harm's way.

I didn't want to cause a scene and frighten the children, but we had a big talk about it after they were in bed that night. Apparently, the Inuit believe that when you name a child after a deceased person, it is not just some kind of honour or remembrance. They actually believe that the deceased person's spirit inhabits the new child along with the name, and so is able to direct the child's behaviour. Children are not considered mature enough to make wise choices for themselves, but there is no need to worry if the child has an old spirit dwelling in it. Ivaluk seems to think it would be presumptuous to correct Kublu, or even to worry about her playing at the edge of a cliff, because to him it would be like correcting his sister Kublu, who certainly would know better than to fall off the edge of a cliff.

I told Ivaluk I want to respect his cultural traditions and beliefs, but mine are different, and he has to respect them too. I can't afford to assume that adult sensibilities are guiding my babies, simply because they are named after his ancestors. I cannot risk having them fall to their deaths or drown, because someone else is supposed to be in charge of guiding them. I asked Ivaluk, for my sake, to act as if perhaps there might not be a mature spirit guiding our babies, even if he believes there is. He said he would try to see things my way, but I think he would have done anything to calm me down at the time, as I was pitching a fit. He must think I am truly a nut case sometimes, a woman with very strange beliefs and extraordinary demands of him. He slipped away early the next morning and didn't return until midnight. At least I knew enough not to pepper him with questions about where he had been and what he had been up to, though I do wonder and worry about it.

I know we both mean the best and love our babies with all of our hearts. I just hope we can manage not to love them to death.

Occasions like this make me feel like the foreigner I am, even in my own home.

IVALUK 7
Rankin Inlet, N.W.T.
March 19, 1977

Dear Thomasie:

Times are changed. Some people (me included some days) thought I would never be able to make a living from hunting and fishing and dogsled adventures. I am not a millionaire but we are doing better than okay.

Now people all over are getting nostalgic for the old Inuit ways. The government and ITC and other groups are funding new culture education programs, to teach the kids about our traditional way of life before it is gone. This spring they hired me to take a bunch of school kids snow camping. We loaded them up on the dogsleds and showed them how to drill a hole in the ice for fishing and how to build a good iglu. Ataata sang some of his old songs for them. We got paid to have this fun.

All those guys who shot their dogs are sorry about it now and want to build up teams again. Some Qablunaat want to run a team, too, just for fun. And guess who is breeding and selling the best sled dogs? They seem to be in demand all over the Northwest Territories now and wait until you hear this—I am even shipping frozen sled dog semen off to other places as far away as Alaska and Greenland. That's how famous my dogs have become. Who could have guessed this would happen, eh?

It is interesting being on the Settlement Council. A lot of agendas are simple stuff like votes on how often garbage pickup should happen or what to do about dogs barking at night or whether we should have a stop sign on the road by the Bay ever since that head-on collision of two Skidoos happened there. I been trying to get the Council to pay more attention to bigger stuff, like the sale of liquor in this town and the problems that come from that. I know some communities have outlawed booze all together and most days I think it does more harm than good here. The Bay boys are mad at me over this talk not to mention my own angajuk Sakku who thinks I should keep my nose out of this business and stick to voting about dogshit and streetlights.

Take it easy,

THOMASIE 4
Barrow, Alaska
June 15, 1977

Dear Ivaluk:

I will try to tell you what happened here these past few days, but I'm not sure words can do it. ITC sent me to Alaska to attend a big meeting called the Inuit Circumpolar Conference. Inuit came here from all over the Arctic—Greenland, Siberia, Alaska and all across northern Canada. Even some Saami people from Finland. I felt a strong sense of brotherhood with all these people. We look similar, we play similar games, we sing similar songs, and many of us share the same language with just little dialect differences. But most important, we are all descended from ancestors whose survival depended on understanding the Arctic environment and treating her with respect so she would keep us alive.

The Alaskans from the North Slope were the main force behind organizing this meeting. They feel their homeland and traditional livelihood are threatened by offshore drilling proposals, so they want to band together with other native people to develop more political strength. They want to find ways to make sure that our traditional knowledge about how ice and snow and animals behave in this part of the world is respected and to ensure that the people who have been the guardians of these lands and waters for thousands of years continue to be involved in decisions that will affect us and our children in the future. Some of these people worry that one great big environmental disaster could ruin our game harvesting and our livelihood forever. Others worry that vegetarian environmentalists might work to ban our traditional hunting ways, with a similar result. These are threats to us. They say we need to be more than vigilant; we need to take action. There are probably 100,000 Inuit in all this world now. I am beginning to see there is strength in our numbers.

After a long day of speeches and study groups yesterday, everyone was too excited to sleep. Instead, we built a big bonfire outside and put on a sort of culture and arts festival. We sat up under the midnight sun listening to each others' traditional songs and poems and dancing some native dances. I felt so moved by all of this that I had to hug onto something. I found this cute girl from Greenland who had tears in her eyes too, listening to poetry by the fire. We stayed clamped onto each other for most of the night. I think I might be in love.

Up until now I thought of myself as working for a better future for our Inuit people in the Northwest Territories. Now I am thinking bigger than that. Sometimes, like you, I can hardly believe I get paid for doing the work I do. I'm excited to get back to Ottawa and work even harder, except first I might need to take a little side trip to Greenland.

Love to all,
Thomasie

ALISON 14
Rankin Inlet, Northwest Territories
December 13, 1977

Dear Nancy:

First and foremost—belated congratulations on your recent wedding. I wish I could meet Reggie. From everything you have said about him, I think I would like him very much. I wish you all happiness together.

We are much the same here, except that the kids keep growing by leaps and bounds. Kublu and Missuk are in elementary school now, and Kavik is in kindergarten for a half day. It allows me to devote more attention to my catering business, which remains very busy. Ivaluk is doing well too, and now he is on the local Council, which means lots of evening meetings and phone calls from his constituents at all hours to discuss various problems.

The community continues to expand. It has probably doubled in size since the regional government offices moved here a few years ago. We have several kilometres of paved roadways now, and even a stop sign, so civilization marches forward.

It is going to be another very busy holiday season, as I have over a dozen parties to cook for. I've had to hire two assistants.

Please stay in touch. I am happy for you!

Love,

Alison

THOMASIE 5
Ottawa, Ontario
May 1, 1978

Dear Ivaluk and Alison:

I was sorry to hear about the big school burning down. What a shame—it was not even that old. What happened? Please tell me it was not arson. I know some kids hate going to school, but burning the building down would be kind of extreme. Besides, going to school in Rankin Inlet is a lot better than being shipped away to a distant boarding school, like we were. Are Kublu and the boys upset, or are they happy to have some unexpected days off?

I don't know anyone here in Ottawa who can find funding quickly to rebuild the school in Rankin Inlet. As I understand it, each regional Department of Education is responsible for schools and the federal government tries to keep out of it. I will ask around some more but I have a feeling there is no way to get a new school built in time to deliver on this year's sealift. I think you parents and the teachers are going to have to find temporary spaces to use for teaching kids, at least for this year. Sorry not to have better news.

I don't have plans to come home anytime soon. I spent too much money travelling to Greenland last winter, only to find out my girlfriend had a few Danish boyfriends already. Plus she is not so traditional after all, wears miniskirts and likes to snort white powder off a little mirror.

So I am back to focusing on work. We are really pushing here to put together a package to present to a parliamentary committee this fall. That may sound a long way off to you, but you would not believe the amount of effort that goes into these things. We could use more help, but there is never enough money, so sometimes most of the weight falls on too few shoulders.

Love to all,
Thomasie

IVALUK 8
Rankin Inlet, N.W.T.
May 17, 1978

Dear Thomasie:

No one knows exactly what happened with the school. The RCMP think it was burned down on purpose or arson but they have not charged anybody yet. Kenny Ipatok made some sort of a confession but the police don't believe him because they think he is not smart enough and would have had to get help from others. Picasso is making himself scarce these days. I have a bad feeling about that.

Radar claims to know nothing about nothing. He is a good boy, but I wonder if he is covering up to protect some friends or maybe his own cousin. I plan to take the two of them hunting next week and see if I can learn any more.

The sad thing is that there are a couple of new teachers here who were pulling together material for a Cultural Inclusion course, so Inuit kids can learn about the old ways even if their parents are not living on the land anymore. It was a good idea but the stuff they were working on all went up in that smoke.

I admire those teachers—they haven't given up. Instead of going on summer vacation, they are staying here to try to redo the material before they forget it all. That is above and beyond and more than anyone expect. Also, they are trying to set up an Elders' Society here. Both Ataata and Anaana have been asked to join up. You should see them smile over that one like they are King and Queen of England. The teachers have helpers who are trying to write down Inuit oral history and stories and songs before all the old folks die off.

I am going to tell those teachers to get in touch with you because maybe some of the stuff they are doing and what they are recording could be useful to the land claims you are working on. And maybe you have some things they would like to see too.

Take it easy,

p.s. — sound like you are better off without that Greenland girlfriend.

NIKMAK 2
Rankin Inlet
August 2, 1978

Ayaiyeah.

Paniga, it is a long time since I have come here to visit your grave. There is no real need, since your spirit is among us once more. I wanted to come anyway, for the walk and the view, and for the feeling I get when I am alone here and the land and the sky and me are like one.

The mosquitoes and biting flies are thicker this summer than any time I can remember. But I have not come down here to complain about that. I have troubles to report about your nephew and your own son. At least Mona and Kublu and Ivaluk's boys are staying out of trouble. But with Picasso and Radar, it is different.

The RCMP have their way of pressing in on everyone, sniffing and digging like wolves at a cache until they find what they want. And here is what they found out. There were five boys involved in setting the school on fire, and Picasso and Radar were among them, not just Kenny Ipatok. The police decided that the two older teenaged boys must have been the leaders. They said they ran away from home and got cold and so built a fire at the school to get warm, but the RCMP do not believe this. Those two were expelled last year. They must have been wondering how to get back at the teacher for humiliating them that way. But they did not choose wisely and now it seems they will be sent away to some kind of jail for young people for a while.

The other three will not be sent away. I went to the RCMP hearing, where they kept talking about IQ. Radar has been teaching me the Qablunaaq alphabet, so I knew these letters. I thought they were talking about "Inuit Qaujimajatuqangit," or traditional Inuit knowledge, like we discuss at the Elders Society meetings all the time. Later, Alison explained to me that is not what they meant. They were talking about some kind of scale the Qablunaat use to weigh intelligence, and they were saying Kenny does not have too much of it and so he should not go to jail. Kenny's uncle agreed to give him a part-time job in his delivery business and keep close watch on him, so the RCMP agreed to that.

As for Picasso and Radar, maybe they let them go because they are younger than the others, or because Ivaluk offered to help them raise their IQ—by making them do some ice fishing to provide char to the old people in town this winter, and also have them run their own trap line and sell every fox fur they catch to raise money for the new school. The RCMP thought this was a good plan that would keep the boys busy and out of trouble, but they warned that if they do anything bad like this again they will be very rough on them.

Picasso and Radar both said they were very sorry they had any part in this disaster. They did not strike any matches, but Picasso held open a window and Radar held a flashlight, and so to the RCMP of course they were helpers, even though the boys said they thought the others were just going to steal some pencils and not burn the school down.

It is all too easy to get talked into doing something that does not seem quite right. Maybe it is good that the boys learn this lesson sooner, rather than later. I hope now they can grow to become men who think for themselves and not do whatever someone asks them to do.

Ivaluk and Sakku and I, we all try to make sure they will succeed, but there is no travel over the land without hitting bumps. We will watch them closely for the next couple of years. It would be good if you could help watch over them too.

Aiyayaaaa.

IVALUK 9
Rankin Inlet, N.W.T.
September 11, 1979

Dear Thomasie:

I was re-elected to the Settlement Council by a landslide. What do you think about that? Shows you how hard up we are for leaders here, eh?

I've been taking politic lessons from you. I worked hard to get support for a referendum to outlaw alcohol sales here and it finally passed on the third try. Sakku was so pissed off he wouldn't speak to me for a couple of weeks but then he figured out how to order beer from the liquor store in Churchill all by himself and get it flown up here. I can think of better ways to spend money.

At least this vote sends a message to people. We don't want to make it too easy or cheap to just walk into the Bay and buy your beer when you get in a mood to get drunk. Even the quota system was causing all sorts of problems. The alcoholic men were pressing their wives and aunts and daughters to go buy their two cases and hand it over to them, so there have been some ugly fights and beatings. We got Social Services to provide more counselling and even start up an AA group here. But now we have some drug problems and gambling problems starting up too. Always some thing.

No money yet to rebuild the school so our kids are spread all over town again this year. Kublu's class meets in the Anglican church office and Missuk's is an old store room at the Co-op. Soon we are supposed to get a bunch of architects come talk to us about how to have a state of the art school here with fancy gym and welding shop and all. Maybe for this reason no one is giving Picasso or Radar too hard of a time about everything.

Some of us trouble maker Council members had buttons and posters made up to protest mineral exploration plans and plans to mine uranium around Rankin Inlet and Baker Lake. We sure need jobs that is true but we don't want to do things to the land that will disrupt the caribou migrations so we starve. Or get a paycheck but glow in the dark. Alison says I'm turning radical like my little brother.

Take it easy,

ALISON 15
Rankin Inlet, Northwest Territories
December 3, 1981

Dear Nancy:

How is that baby boy of yours doing? Please give him a hug for me. I have no idea if we shall ever meet the young chap, or see you again. We are busy all the time, and the cost of air travel is frightening.

We have been through a tough year here. My mother-in-law Ukpik died. She had become more and more frail over the past few years. She never had much appetite, and she developed chronic bronchitis and a constant, wracking cough. She and Nikmak gave up smoking years ago, but she loved to go to the Community Centre on Friday nights to play bingo, and the room would fill up with a thick cloud of cigarette smoke that would hover overhead and descend further and further as the evening progressed. I couldn't stand to go to bingo with her for that reason.

Ivaluk took our boys on a spring hunting trip, and he invited Nikmak and Radar and Sakku and Picasso to go along, too. They wanted to do a guys' overnight camping trip while the snow was still good enough for building iglus. I dropped in later that day to check on Ukpik, and she seemed fine. She was sitting watching TV, drinking tea. She called me Kublu at one point, but I didn't think much about it at the time.

When the men returned, they found Ukpik dead on the chesterfield. It turned out she had developed a simple urinary tract infection that, without treatment, turned into a blood infection. She became septic and her organs failed. She could have been cured readily, if only she had complained and let me take her to the Nursing Station to be seen, but she feared and detested that place. I felt very badly afterwards, for not having picked up on that early sign of her disorientation. I am (or was) a nurse, after all. One can only hope she died painlessly, since it happened so quickly.

Then this summer, my sister-in-law Carol packed her bags and left Ivaluk's brother Sakku. I suppose she had finally had enough of his verbal abuse. He didn't seem to drink alcohol all that frequently, but he had a real knack for getting himself into trouble every time he did. He seems to be one of those persons who does not tolerate alcohol well. Carol had begged him to quit drinking, on more than one occasion, but Sakku does not want a woman telling him what to do.

Carol must have been planning this for a while, because she had arranged to stay with some friends in Montreal until she is on her feet again. She landed a teaching assistant job at an art school there.

Picasso and Mona Lisa are barely into their teens, and now they are motherless. Perhaps Carol thought they were finally old enough to look after themselves, or that they would not do well in the south, or perhaps she thought that she simply could not afford to support them on her meagre earnings. Whatever her thinking, she left the kids behind with Sakku, and that family has been like a three-legged stool ever since. It has been hard to watch the effect of this on them—on Ivaluk's entire family, really. Ivaluk and I have tried to be more involved in their lives, but it isn't easy. We go over to visit in the evenings, but generally Sakku and the kids will be fighting over which TV channel to watch. Sakku likes to watch the northern channel but the kids always want something racier than that.

Since Carol left, Sakku has been drinking more regularly and more heavily. In the fall, Picasso started cutting school and getting into trouble, and Mona seemed to be keeping bad company. Ivaluk is fiercely loyal to his brother, despite (or maybe because of) his weaknesses. He thinks we should do more to help. I want to be generous and helpful too, yet I worry about the negativity that is so palpable in Sakku's home spreading into our home and affecting our children, as I am sure you would understand. We have had some rows over it.

This summer I shut the catering business down entirely so I could go fishing with Ivaluk and the kids. That was a grand idea, so I hope it will become an annual tradition.

Love and happy holidays to all,

Alison

NIKMAK 3
Rankin Inlet
June 12, 1982

Ayayayai.

How much I miss you, nuliaq. A whole round of seasons has passed since you died, and still I feel like a lame man who has lost his cane, lurching forward without the support that had been there for so long that perhaps it was taken for granted, but now is gone. I had forgotten how hard it is to walk on my own two legs only. No wonder toddlers stumble. The sound of your quiet humming and murmuring is no longer there in my home, or even your coughing and spitting that helped to mark the passage of hours, your voice constantly whispering like a breeze at my back. Now silent. I don't know what I would do without Radar to keep me company, to give my life purpose.

Ivaluk and Alison seem busy all the time. Kublu is growing into a young lady now. She comes over to visit with me and Radar a lot, always bringing food that her father caught or her mother made. Sakku keeps asking Radar and I to come over to his house to spend time with him and his kids. But it keeps Radar from doing his homework, and you would not believe the noise that happens in that place—crashing pots and pans and loud laughing at cartoons, and many screeching and banging noises that those kids call modern music. I prefer my quiet home, but I am worried that the Housing Association is planning to take it away from us, since we are just two people living there now and there are many larger families in need.

Thomasie is coming home for a visit, but I don't think he plans to stay for long. I don't understand why all this being away from us is so important, as Ivaluk believes.

That is all I have to say for now, nuliaq, except that I am grateful for the time we shared. You made me a happy man. You gave me a family and restored my life, and it is still going on through our children and grandchildren. Still, of course I miss you.

Aiyaiyaaaa.

THOMASIE 6
Ottawa, Ontario
December 1, 1982

Dear Ivaluk:

I still plan to come home for the holidays, but not for as long as I had hoped. There is too much happening down here ever since Pierre Trudeau passed the new Constitution Act recognizing aboriginal title and the rights of native groups to negotiate land claims agreements with Canada.

The latest news is that Peter Ittinuar, our first-ever elected Inuit Member of Parliament, suddenly quit the New Democratic Party, because the Liberals now say they will support an independent new Inuit territory in the north. He felt he had to change parties. We want to make the most of the sudden media attention to this idea of an Inuit homeland and get the word out as far as we can.

I know you and Alison don't care about television, but you should take a look at the new kind of programs they are showing on the Inuit Broadcasting Corporation. I don't find much time to watch TV, either, but when I do now I learn all sorts of stuff they never taught us at school. We were too busy reading that Dick and Jane and Spot stuff developed for kids in Calgary and New York. I know that school in the north is not the way it used to be, but these changes did not happen soon enough for you or me. The IBC shows let me catch up on stuff I should know.

Anyway, if you say the word, I will bring a nice television set home for Christmas. Otherwise, I have no clue what you guys would like to have, so please let me know if you have ideas. All I want is some good tobacco for my new pipe, but I can get that here.

Love,

Thomasie

ALISON 16
Rankin Inlet, Northwest Territories
December 9, 1983

Dear Nancy:

It has been another rotten year. This time because my brother-in-law Sakku died in a most tragic way. He became depressed after his wife left him, and alcohol added to his problems. One cold day in early October, he got on his Skidoo at dusk and drove it at full throttle down to the edge of the Hudson Bay. He rode out onto the ice, as if he were planning to go seal hunting at the floe edge. But it was too early in the season; the ice had not frozen solid yet. He and his skidoo vanished from sight in seconds. Any sort of rescue was quite impossible under the circumstances. It is awful to think of Sakku lying somewhere out there under the sea ice, which is frozen solid now.

Ivaluk took the loss of his brother hard. Perhaps the cumulative loss of his sister, his mother, and his brother was too much for him. His father Nikmak murmured "Ajurnarmat"—it can't be helped—and seemed to carry on all right. He moved Sakku's two teenagers, his grandchildren, into the house with him and Radar, where he can keep an eye on them. He gets Kublu to come over and badger them to do their homework.

Life moves on, but it seems as if we have been under some kind of dark cloud lately.

Please send a photo of you and Reg and the kids. Hope you are all well and that you will have a good Christmas.

Love,

Alison

IVALUK 10
Rankin Inlet, N.W.T.
January 13, 1984

Dear Thomasie:

Ever since Sakku left us I have been feeling older than Ataata. I can't seem to pull myself up. It is like having a bear sitting on my chest. Sometimes I can hardly breathe. I keep thinking even if I could not stop him from falling through the ice with his skidoo that day, maybe there were some other days when I could have saved him from his own drinking so this thing would never happen. I feel like I failed him some big way. His death has left a dark hole in my centre.

There is no point in you coming home just now. We did not find his body so we cannot bury him. I feel his spirit continue to swirl around me full of troubles. Why why why I keep asking but I cannot seem to find any good enough answers. I would like to give my right arm to go back in time and make this thing turn out some other way but I know I am powerless to do this. The loss of a parent is one thing—it is expected and natural. But to have your own siblings die off when they are still young, this is not right.

Even though you are not right here and I cannot see you every day I feel your presence more than ever in my life, and you are more precious to me than even before. Please promise to take good care of yourself, Nukaqtaaq . Don't drive too fast and stay away from booze and drugs and bad women, okay?

Love,

ALISON 17
Rankin Inlet, Northwest Territories
August 28, 1984

Dear Nancy:

I am writing to you with the most remarkable news. I delivered a healthy baby girl a week ago. Ivaluk and I thought our family was complete with Kublu, Missuk and Kavik. We were very surprised to find out (with our three kids almost in their teens) that we had another baby on the way. After the recent string of family tragedies, the promise of a new life around here gave us all something to smile about again.

I can't keep track of the traditional names her father and grandfather have loaded onto our tiny baby girl, but I call her Ukaliq, which is the Inuit word for the white Arctic hare. Nikmak approved, because he wants her to be as fast as a hare and outrun any danger that might threaten her. I like the name because she is as cute as a bunny and as lucky as a rabbit's foot charm in our home.

Kublu is most thrilled with her new baby sister. Because the two boys came along so quickly behind her, she was too small to carry either of them in an amauti. Now she carries her sister around town and gets to experience the unique attention that the Inuit shower on little ones and on those who care for them.

I'm enclosing a photograph of the new baby. It will have to do since you can't be here to hold her yourself.

Cheers,
Alison

NIKMAK 4
Rankin Inlet
June 1, 1986

Ayayaaa.

Ah, nuliaq, here I am babbling on the tundra to a dead woman and a pile of stones. I cannot seem to help myself. It does me good to get out of town. The sky is so big out here, and the tundra restores me. So, I have come to tell you our news.

Mona has left Rankin Inlet—gone to Montreal. She wants to be an artist like her mother. Picasso has been dating a local girl, and I think he will marry her soon. They seem good for each other.

Ivaluk has pulled himself together. That new baby, Ukaliq, has helped everything and all of us. Kublu adores her little sister, but now she has won some award that means she will be leaving us soon to attend university in the south.

Radar is doing well in school too. Some days I wish he were not so smart, because I am afraid he is going to get money from the government to go to university like Kublu. That means he will have to go south, and I will miss him very much. I don't know why our young people have to move away like this. It is enough to miss the ones who die.

If Picasso and Radar go, I am sure Ivaluk will invite me to come live with him. I am feeling too old for a lot of moving around. But there are other things I want to talk with you about.

These young generations puzzle me, nuliaq. One minute they are ashamed of their heritage, they don't want to be called Pudluk or be seen wearing caribou skin mittens anymore, then the next day they are filled with fond ideas about it and want to hear tales of the glorious old days. At least they say they do, but I notice it is not often they take those music plugs out of their ears to listen to anything a person might have to say.

They say the Elders' Society is a way to respect those of us who were born on the land and really lived the old way of life in times past. Living off the land. The way they say it, with that faraway look in their eye, they make it sound like it was living off the fat of the land. There was no fat on that land. There were no bananas or coconuts falling from the trees, like you see on the TV—programs about islands in a warm sea somewhere, where you do not even need to clothe yourself to keep from getting cold.

The old way of life was not like that for us. Many times, it was hard work and struggle to find something to eat, to keep warm, to stay alive. "But you were free of all these problems we have today," they say, "like having to pay rent, having to make payments on your boat and skidoo, having to pay for fuel all the time, the phone bills and travel expense, and needing enough spare change to go to the coffee shop or a fast food restaurant once in a while."

Every now and then I want to say to them: you have no idea. You cannot have it both ways. You can own practically nothing, except for a few basic hand tools and your dog team. Then you can work very hard every day, eat nothing but seal meat for six months at a time (if you are lucky to have anything to eat at all), have no toys and no sweets, take no vacations, walk almost everywhere you go, use moss and fat for your light and heat, and die if you get an infected cut or catch the flu. Or you can have these things you have, your house, your entertainments, your suitcase full of clothing, your hot meals from a restaurant or from cans heated on an electric stove, a school and a hospital close by. If these are the things you want, then you have to figure out how to work at something modern to pay for all these modern things, instead of whining for a simple and easy life that never existed.

But there is no use in fighting or being unpleasant. If they seem eager and attentive, in the end I show them how we used to make harpoons from driftwood and bone and caribou sinew. I show them how to test the snow with a sabgut, to see if it is the right kind of snow for making an iglu, and if it is, I show them how to use the pana to cut and shape and place the blocks. I know they are thinking—see, quick and cheap and easy housing—you were so lucky. I know they will go home and make a bad iglu for themselves, one our ancestors would laugh at, to show off their new skills to their friends and family. And this iglu will be used for a playhouse or maybe for overnight shelter on a hunting trip, and they will still have no idea what it was like for their ancestors to live in this cold and tiny home for many months at a time. They will have no idea what an iglu could smell like, after months of burning seal fat in the stone lamp, the seal guts spilled on the floor, the unwashed bodies, the lice, the piss pot in the corner, and how all these smells would linger and ripen with the coming of spring.

Ach! I am becoming just a cranky old man with aching and leaking parts, and now they wish to look up to me. I suppose it is better than looking down on me, except I am not sure there is anything here but just me, Nikmak, your husband, a man who has survived through fate and fortune, work and luck, with no special secrets to relay. No magic formula for living. Put one foot in front of the other, that is all. That is life. If you fall, get up, keep going. Rejoice each time you see the sun return. Rejoice when the caribou find your camp. Treasure the love of a good partner. Teach your children to be proper human beings.

They seek wisdom from me, but all I can do is sing some old songs and show them how to make some old tools. How old songs and harpoon heads will help them survive in this new world of theirs today, I do not know.

Perhaps I am forgetting how to laugh, especially at myself.

Aiyaiyeah.

IVALUK 11
Rankin Inlet, N.W.T.
June 15, 1988

Dear Thomasie:

There is lots happening with the kids so I want to keep you up to date. First Radar. He has been accepted into that new program called *Sivuniksavut*. This program is to help good students from all over the Northwest Territories get used to living in a city in the south and help them to succeed in university. Radar will be going to Ottawa to start this program soon, so I know you will be seeing him some times. You will both be busy but at least you will be close by each other.

Kublu is too smart and wants to go to law school now. Maybe because of everything she has been hearing about you and what ITC is up to. Law school is okay with us if she can find some scholarship money to help pay for it. Otherwise I think she could come home and run for MLA right now or maybe be our first lady Prime Minister of all of Canada.

Our boys Missuk and Kavik they like school okay but not like Kublu does, so I don't think they will want any more of it after they finish high school. It is good they can do that here now and not have to go to the hostel school at Churchill like you and me did.

Mona took some art classes in Montreal and now got a government grant to find her roots. She is up at Cape Dorset on Baffin Island where they have a big studio and smart people so she can study print making up there using Inuit designs and ideas.

Picasso is different from his twin sister. He doesn't like to go too far from home. Alison can't make up her mind if he matured fast or never at all. Anyway he has been dating Angela Tautuk for a while now and looks like they have a baby on the way so we think they will get married pretty soon.

Our own baby Ukaliq is still too young for school. She stays home and tries to help Alison with her cooking and baking business. This makes her easy to find when she goes hiding, because she is always leaving little flour footprints through the house.

Those are the news from here. Me and Alison are doing good.
Love,

RADAR 1
Ottawa, Ontario
May 15, 1989

Dear Uncle Ivaluk and Aunt Alison:

I wanted to let you know about something, and you can decide if Nikmak should know, or if it would give him a heart attack.

This year I got a bright idea, that I would like to track down my biological father's family and maybe try to get in touch with them. I know I have cousins in Rankin Inlet, but it was a little bit lonely for me growing up with no brothers or sisters around and my real mother and father both dead. Of course I had Ukpik and Nikmak and you guys and my cousins, but I never got to know my parents, Kublu and Wayne, at all.

The program staff helped me do the research, and we found out that Wayne's mom and dad are still alive and living in a small town outside Regina. I sent them a letter, then after a while they sent me a reply. I guess it took some time to sink in. It must have been a shock to learn their dead son had fathered a child. I think he planned to go back to Saskatchewan and settle down and have a family (besides me) some day, but then he died instead.

They asked me if I would mind doing a blood test, so they could be sure in their minds that all this was true. I said sure. So we got the results, and then they knew that what I claimed was the truth, and that they had a grown up grandson they had no idea was alive. They have invited me to come spend a few weeks with them on their prairie farm so we can get to know each other a bit and I can meet some of my uncles and aunts and Qablunaat cousins.

I hope you understand that I do not mean any snub to my Tunu family. I love all you guys. I was just curious about the other part that I never knew anything about, and it didn't feel right just to forget all about it.

I plan to leave here and travel west in a few weeks, when my courses are over. I should be back in Rankin Inlet by the end of June. I look forward to seeing you all then. Maybe it would best if I explain everything to ataatasiak when I get there. Meanwhile, just tell him I love him and that I'll be home soon.

Love,
Radar

ALISON 18
Rankin Inlet, Northwest Territories
December 5, 1990

Dear Nancy:

It is ever so much quieter in the house, with Kublu and Kavik now both off in the south pursuing their studies and careers. Kublu is in law school in Ottawa and has a part-time internship with the federal Department of Indian and Northern Affairs there. Kavik is in the Engineering School at the University of Manitoba in Winnipeg. I guess I have harped about the inequity of the utilidor system here enough that he decided to become an engineer and try to figure out what to do about it.

Missuk is working with Ivaluk in his guide business. He seems to love it. Perhaps he hopes to take it over some day, if his father ever decides to retire. He has a girlfriend these days, so we don't see much of him weekends and evenings.

Our youngest, Ukaliq, is seven years old now. She loves to paint and draw and does well enough in school. This week she wants to be a ballerina, but last week she wanted to become a heavy equipment operator.

Mona Lisa is back in Montreal and living with a new boyfriend down there, pursuing her art career, with the help of some grants from the Canada Arts Council. Picasso is eking out a living here making ceramics, and he watches his baby son while his wife Angela works her shift as a clerk at the Bay.

Radar spent some time last summer with his biological father's family on their farm in Saskatchewan. One of his uncles taught him to fly the crop duster, and he was hooked. So now he is following in the footsteps of the father he never met. He won a career development grant from the Government of the Northwest Territories and is training to become a bush pilot.

Ivaluk and I are well. Ivaluk's brother Thomasie is working for a new Inuit organization that is dedicated to negotiating an Inuit land claims agreement. He travels a great deal, so we see a bit more of him these days.

Happy Christmas to all.

Love,

Alison

TRANSCANADA NEWS AGENCY
FOR IMMEDIATE RELEASE

NUNAVUT LAND CLAIMS SETTLED

July 9, 1993. Today the Canadian Parliament passed the Nunavut Land Claims Agreement Act and the Nunavut Act outlining the terms of the biggest indigenous peoples' land claims settlement in history. The federal government has agreed to pay $1.2 billion dollars to the Inuit people over a period of fourteen years. This money will be held in a trust fund and managed to ensure the future well being of the Inuit people.

The Northwest Territories will be divided into two territories. The western portion will retain the same name, and the new territory in the east will be known as Nunavut, meaning "our land" in the language of the Inuit. Nunavut will encompass 1.9 million square kilometres, or about one-fifth of Canada's land mass. The new territory will have a public government serving both Inuit and non-Inuit residents, but entitled Inuit will retain certain recognized aboriginal rights, including the right to hunt and fish in the new national parks that will be established in Nunavut.

The Inuit people have historically been a minority population within the Northwest Territories, representing only about one-third of the territorial population. In Nunavut, they will become the strong majority—approximately 85 percent of the new territory's population. Inuktitut is to be the official language of the territory, but residents needing communications in English or French will receive them in those languages.

The Agreement gives the Inuit outright title to about 350,000 square kilometres of land, including all mineral rights to about 35,000 square kilometres. No resource development activities will occur without the consent of the Inuit people, and no mining will be permitted in places the Inuit hold sacred.

An organization called Nunavut Tunngavik Inc. (NTI) will continue to work with federal representatives on the details for implementing this historic agreement.

#   #   #

THOMASIE 7
Ottawa, Ontario
July 10, 1993

Dear Ivaluk:

We have been so busy working up to the big referendum that I feel as if I have hardly slept for months. At last it is done—the Nunavut Land Claims Agreement has become real now, after it was ratified by an overwhelming majority of the Inuit last month and signed into law yesterday. It will take a few more years to put everything into motion, but we are over the hump.

As part of the agreement, the Inuit are guaranteed representation on resource and wildlife management boards. Want to guess who I plan to nominate? I can't think of anybody better cut out to oversee wildlife management issues.

The excitement among the Inuit here in Ottawa is sky high. How are people taking this news at home? Does it seem like just another day, or do people realize the importance of what has happened? From where I sit, the world will never be the same. Our future seems entirely new and very much more secure.

I am exhilarated, yet I feel completely exhausted, too. I have some things to wrap up here, but I want to come home in a week or two and take the rest of the summer off. I hope you have some fishing planned and could use an assistant.

After that, I plan to move to Iqaluit and go to work for NTI, the new group that will manage the Inuit trust fund and set up a new government for Nunavut.

Love,
Thomasie

ALISON 19
Rankin Inlet, Northwest Territories
June 20, 1996

Dear Nancy:

Our daughter Kublu shows no sign of settling down. She is enjoying her career too much. She is now working for the Department of Indian and Northern Affairs in Ottawa, while Thomasie has moved to Iqaluit, which will soon become the capital of a new territory to be called Nunavut. Have you heard anything about this? It is very big news here.

Both of our sons are getting married this summer. Kavik finished his Engineering degree and is marrying a French Canadian woman who is an elementary school teacher here. Marie is about five years older than Kavik and has an adopted Chinese daughter who is something of a novelty here. She goes to kindergarten with the local children and is often mistaken for an Inuk.

Missuk is going to marry a local girl whose family moved here from Baker Lake several years ago. We like Annie very much. I got the biggest shock at their engagement party, however, when that awful Irishman Ryan Dolan showed up. I knew him from my nursing days here, when he would come in all too frequently to be treated for some venereal disease or another. I thought for a moment he must have crashed the party in search of free booze or something, but no. He took me aside to explain that he is Annie's biological father and he expects to give her away at their wedding. You could have pushed me over with a feather. I'm sure he never paid a penny of child support for Annie (or any other offspring of his who may be scattered around the north), so I am not sure what his motivation is for showing up at this late date in her life. Guilt? Regret? Seeking more opportunities for usury? He had the nerve to say to me "Don't look so shocked about it; I see you've been fucking with the natives yourself." With a wink, he nodded toward Ivaluk and our son.

I am so annoyed that somehow my life has become entangled with this man's. Though I detest him, it looks as if he will be the grandfather of my son's future children. For Missuk's sake, I try to contain my feelings about this as best I can.

I'll send wedding photos later.

Love,

Alison

PART III

KIVALLIQ

NIKMAK 1
Rankin Inlet
October 12, 1998

Aiyayaya.

Nuliaq, I need to talk to you again. There is no one who listens and understands right to the bottom of what I am saying like you always did.

So many changes we saw in our days together, Nuliaq. I am slowing down now, but the changes—they keep coming, faster and faster. Remember when these wild ideas arose in our children and our grandchildren, forcing their way to daylight like air bubbles rising from fish in the river: land claims, homeland, self-rule? They called it a vision, but to us it seemed like some kind of mirage. So many far-fetched dreams that eventually you would have to wake up from. Don't get your hopes up, I wanted to tell them. Don't get your spirit whipped up into a blizzard of expectation, only to be disappointed.

I feel as if I am the one who was asleep for a long time, only now I am waking up to find those crazy ideas our children and grandchildren had are coming into being. While I was not paying too much attention—just making my carvings and raising Radar as best I could—the young generations of Inuit were forming into new groups like char running to the sea—these groups with names like COPE and ITC and NTI and so many other letters. Who could keep up? I could not keep up. I did not bother keeping up. These were just so many fancy words and letters to me, empty promises. I thought they were pissing in the wind.

But now I realize they were not just pissing in the wind. It is as if they have been beating a huge skin drum all this time, in the way of our ancestors, starting out soft but steady, then a little bit louder and more insistent all the time until the sound fills the air like a curtain of cranes beating their wings as they rise up.

I failed to hear it, but they heard it. Our Thomasie heard it, and young Kublu too. The young ones kept up this drumming, passing the katuut from one to another. There were no ugly fights or yelling. None of those marches or sit-ins that the Qablunaat are accustomed to doing. That is not the Inuit way. There was just that persistent drumming—that grabbing onto an idea and holding onto it until it becomes real, keeping the beat going and going, even when your arm is so tired you think it will fall off.

And now this thing they called land claims seems to be happening.

Nuliaq, I am not a stupid man, but it is hard for me to grasp this thing. They say we are to have our own land, Nunavut. They say Canada will pay money to protect our land and our traditional ways. They say there will be more jobs, so the young people will not have to go away to find work. They will not have to pull up their tents as often as we did.

Nuliaq, I don't know whether to believe these things, or not. I wish you were here to wonder with me, as I see the world transformed before my eyes, as if I am watching snow fall over the tundra for the very first time.

Snowflakes fat as ptarmigans are spinning down from the sky now. By the time this winter is over, they say our new homeland will be born. And our region will no longer be called Keewatin, after a Cree word meaning north wind. I guess we were north to them—but they were south to us. Now our region will be called by the name our ancestors gave it—Kivalliq, meaning that area to the south.

Life is full of surprises.

Aiya-aiya-aiyayaaa.

IVALUK 1
Rankin Inlet, N.W.T.
January 3, 1999

Dear Thomasie:

I always felt sure you would make a success of your life but still I have trouble getting used to you being such a big cheese over there in Iqaluit—soon to become the capital of our new territory of Nunavut. Just look at you now—the Deputy Minister of the Environment for Nunavut. I can't tell you how that makes me feel.

Our new settlement manager in Rankin Inlet moved here from Iqaluit. He tells me there are tunnels you can walk through to get from one building to another over there. Heated up so you never ever have to wear mitts. I don't think I can believe that. Why would you want to live in this part of the world and then never go outside to feel the wind on your face, say hi to the huge sky? It's all about what's outside. I think I'd go nuts if I had to walk from one building to another all week and never sniff the clean fresh cold air stab at my lungs to let me know I am alive and breathing fine.

Thanks for helping Kublu get that job in the Government of Nunavut. She always did want to follow in your shoes. Alison and I were hoping she might come home and maybe settle down and have some kids but she seems determined to get an important career with Nunavut like you. I feel a bit better knowing you two will keep an eye on each other there. Maybe she will cook you a decent meal once in a while. I hope.

The land claims settlement is moving ahead so fast now it makes my head spin. I try to explain about it to Ataata but he just shakes his head and mumbles Nunavut Nunavut over and over as if he is in some kind of trance. I'm not sure if he is moved beyond speech or just scared shitless of what will become of us now.

You would not know Rankin Inlet these days. There is a building boom going on makes me sometimes wonder if I should have gone into a construction business with my sons. The town grew like a pregnant lady when the regional government moved up here from Churchill and now we are getting Nunavut staff too. And people keep having kids. The old drinking water lake is surrounded by buildings now right down to the shoreline, and there are houses stretching halfway out to the airport. On weekends there is a traffic jam on the road to Nipissar Lake with every body trying to get some fishing in on their day off. I see people in the Bay sometimes and I don't even know who they are, and I don't mean just the Qablunaat who are always changing over. They come and go. But now there are even Inuit who are strangers to me. Sometimes I ask them who they are but sometimes I feel too nosy so I leave them alone but then it seems strange not to know them.

People here can't wait for April 1, but Alison says this is April Fools' Day in the rest of the world or at least her old part of it. So we are wondering why you guys picked April Fools' Day as the day to reveal our new territorial flag and make it fly from our flagpoles for the very first time. Some people are mad about the big hush up about what the new flag will look like but others think it is kind of exciting not to know. Sort of like not knowing whether your baby is going to come out a boy or a girl.

We have lots of celebrations planned for April 1 here. There will be traditional singing and drumming, then an old style square dance, then a modern dance for the kids so they can flail their arms around to big noise. Both my sons have been practicing for the cultural games and contests. Missuk hopes to win a prize in the high kick and Kavik is really good at the cheek pull. He never did complain about pain as a kid and was always able to endure it longer than anyone. Even Ukaliq is going to play a part. She is helping to put on some kind of a fashion show of traditional fur clothing up at the school.

I wish you could be here to celebrate with us, but I guess there will be even bigger events happening over there in our new capital. Please write and tell us about it and give a big hug to Kublu for me.

Love,

ALISON 1
Rankin Inlet, Northwest Territories
February 6, 1999

Dear Nancy:

I am sorry to be writing with some bad news. I have been diagnosed with breast cancer.

I felt a small lump in my left breast several weeks ago and had a bad feeling about it. I went to the Nursing Station, where the staff are all strangers to me now. Fortunately, there was a visiting doctor who was able to do a needle biopsy and have the sample flown to a lab in Winnipeg for analysis. I just learned the result—it is malignant.

I have not said a prayer in years, but I find myself muttering Hail Mary's again these days. It seems to calm my nerves and chase off the other thoughts and fears that hover, waiting for a chance to crowd in. It's not that I am a fair weather Catholic or that suddenly I have become a true believer. The praying just feels like some form of meditation to me, and I figure it can't hurt.

I am scheduled to fly to Winnipeg to see a specialist later this week, to determine what should happen next. The Nursing Station here is bigger and better now. There is even a new state-of-the-art Birthing Centre. But there are still no specialists of the sort I need anywhere in the Kivalliq region, or even in Churchill. I don't know what will happen in Winnipeg, or how long I might have to stay there. They will do at least a lumpectomy, but perhaps a full mastectomy, and afterwards I will need radiation treatments and/or chemotherapy.

So many Inuit men and women (and children) have travelled this road before me—having to leave their families for long periods of time to seek medical care. This was especially true during the polio and TB epidemics in the '50s and '60s. I just never thought it would happen to me.

I have been packing a few things to take with me to the hospital. I can't seem to resist the urge to lug one of my soapstone carvings along with me, as sort of a good luck charm. It is an old carving that I bought from Arvalak years ago, not long after I first came to Rankin Inlet. I saw Arvalak working arduously in a workshop near the post office and I poked my head in the door. He invited me to come in and look around. He was just starting out as a carver then, so he didn't have much of an inventory, and some of his pieces were awful. He told me that he had just sold a few pieces to the Co-op, and that basically the things I was looking at were the rejects. But there was one piece that caught my eye. It was the figure of a woman, solid and strong, done in a very dark, highly polished soapstone. The striking thing was that she was missing one breast. I kept pondering the artistic significance—perhaps she was half male; perhaps she was one of those Amazon warrior women who had lopped off one breast because it obstructed her archery; or perhaps we were meant to ponder the meaning of womanhood, both with and without breasts, which can be symbols of nurturing or just plain sex symbols. I told Arvalak I was intrigued with this piece and asked if I could buy it. He said I could have it for free, but when I insisted I would not take it without paying him something, he agreed to take twenty dollars. I paid him cash, then asked him to explain what he was thinking when he carved this woman with one breast.

"Oh, nothing," he explained. "She had two breasts originally. One got knocked off by accident when my chisel slipped." I laughed along with him over that. I have always liked that carving, even knowing that it came about by accident (some would argue that the best art always does). Knowing now that there is a possibility I might lose one or both of my own breasts, I treasure it even more, and wonder if Arvalak couldn't make a fortune reproducing his "mistake" for the numerous breast cancer patients in this world.

I will keep you informed as I learn more. Please don't say anything to the family yet. I can't bear the thought of them feeling sorry for me.

Alison

p.s. - I am no longer in the catering business. The managers of the new hotel here have made offers to buy me out in the past, but I was not particularly interested then. I decided the time has come, however, to give up cooking and catering, and fortunately they were still interested. I couldn't just take off for months with no one to cover for me. So that is over. It is good to have the extra cash on hand for emergencies and unexpected expenditures—not that the tiny empire I built was worth any great fortune. Thank heaven three of our four children are through with their schooling and well on their way in life. There is only Ukaliq left at home to worry over.

UKALIQ 1
Rankin Inlet, NWT
February 11, 1999

Mom's been bugging me to keep a diary. She thinks I spend too much time alone.

There has been a rash of suicides lately, even two kids from my own school, and I know that has her concerned. I keep telling her I don't have any thoughts like that, and besides I think my life is too boring to write about. But I'm going to give this a try, because right now the last thing she needs is to be worried about me. I see her smiling and nodding at the stove right this minute, just because I opened up this notebook she gave me and started writing. So, I guess this diary is doing somebody some good already.

Mom can't help herself. She was trained as a nurse. I know that what happened to my Aunt Kublu and my Uncle Sakku weighs on her mind, though she doesn't talk about it much, at least not in front of me. But I heard her talking to Ataata in a hushed voice about the recent suicides, and I heard her mention the phrase "family history." I know what that means: she's afraid that whatever made my aunt and uncle run off the rails might be genetic, so it might show up suddenly in me, too. But I look at her and Dad and my sister Kublu and my two brothers, and I don't see anything to be worried about.

Mom says that these days my Aunt Kublu would be treated for depression, and it probably would have saved her. (Maybe she also thinks Aunt Kublu would have been fine if only she had kept a diary). As for Uncle Sakku, I don't think pills or a diary would have saved him. I think maybe something like Alcoholics Anonymous could have helped. But maybe not. At school they say that no one can help an addict but him or herself.

I never met my aunt and uncle. Aunt Kublu died a really long time ago, and Uncle Sakku died a few months before I was born. My sister Kublu (who is named after my aunt) told me she didn't like going over to Uncle Sakku's house much, because you never knew if he had been drinking or not. And if he'd been drinking, you never knew if you'd find him passed out, or friendly, or mean. She told me about the day he died. She had gone by his house to visit our cousins, but Uncle Sakku was there alone. He told her Picasso was out playing street hockey and Mona was visiting a friend, and he invited her in to watch some TV with him. She took off her parka and kamiit and sat on the sofa. She could tell he had been drinking by the way his breath stank, and his eyes were watery. She told me not to tell this to anybody, but he threw his big arm around her and pulled her closer. She got a creepy feeling about it, so she stood up and said she'd better get home. He said okay but come give your Uncle Sakku a kiss first. She went over and gave him a peck on the forehead, but he grabbed her and smooched her on the lips, grasping hard at her shoulders. She pulled away and ran out the door, grabbing her parka and kamiit and running out into the snow in her sock feet. When she got home Mom scolded her for having wet socks and no mittens. Kublu just went to her room and said nothing. She said she'd rather let mom think she was a nitwit than talk about what went on at Uncle Sakku's house. Even after what happened to him next, she never said a word about it to anyone—until she told me when she was home for Christmas.

My dad and a DPW maintenance guy were the only ones who actually saw it happen.

The DPW guy was doing something up at the oil tank farm and happened to look out toward the Hudson Bay about the same time my dad was coming home from a hunting trip. Dad was heading for the inlet to tie up his dog team, when suddenly Uncle Sakku came ripping down from town on his Skidoo, going full speed, maybe a hundred clicks. He drove his Skidoo straight out onto the sea ice and kept moving out toward the open water in the distance. Finally he reached the part that was not frozen enough to support a snowmobile. The ice cracked like a thunderbolt, then split open, and he and the Skidoo both went straight down into the freezing waters of the Hudson Bay.

My dad raced down to the inlet, set the brake on his qamutiik and jumped off with his harpoon in one hand and a coil of rope in the other. He ran out onto the ice and threw himself down and slid on his stomach to the place where Uncle Sakku had vanished, almost sliding right into the dark hole himself. He poked around with the handle of the harpoon, this way and that, but didn't feel anything. Then he stuck his head right down into the slush bobbing around the gash left in the ice. The ice beneath him started cracking and he had to pull back, crawling backwards to a safer spot and shaking some of the icy water off his head before it froze solid. He attached the rope to his harpoon and lobbed it into the water, yelling for Sakku. By then the DPW man had arrived at the shoreline with help, and they were calling to dad to come off the ice and get warm and dry, as it was hopeless. Dad just stayed out there screaming for Sakku, until finally three men formed a line with a rope and walked slowly over the ice to where someone could grab hold of some part of dad's clothing and pull him back to land. It is enough to lose one person. They had to throw a blanket over his head and tie his arms down and stuff him into a van and take him up to the Nursing Station, where they gave him some kind of a shot to calm him down.

They never found any trace of Uncle Sakku, and of course the whole community was sad about what had happened. Kublu said that everyone felt bad and wondered if they should have or could have done more to help him. I think probably no one could help him if he didn't want to save himself.

According to Kublu, Dad had a hard time sleeping afterwards. He would wander around in the night, or sometimes he would thrash and scream in his sleep. One night he ran naked out of the house and down to the inlet, walking out onto the ice in his bare feet. Mom went after him and managed to get him back home, but he fell into a terrible sort of silence and did not seem like himself at all. Kublu said that sometimes mom would have to say something to him three or four times before he would hear her, and even then sometimes he would just lower his eyes and not answer. It took him a while to snap out of it.

My ataatatsiaq Nikmak is a traditional Inuk. Kublu said that while everyone else sat around wringing their hands after Uncle Sakku died, he took action. He hired one of the old shamans to perform some rituals, to make sure his son's spirit would fly off to the other world where it belonged and wouldn't hang around to bother the living. Kublu said that, no matter what you might think, everyone seemed a lot calmer afterwards. I'm not sure if I believe in that stuff or not, but I guess if it can work sometimes, why not.

My sister and brothers and most of my cousins are in their twenties and thirties now—all grown up. Some of them have had kids, but their kids are just babies to me. Picasso's are the oldest of the lot, but they are still too young for me to hang out with, and anyway they are just boys. I guess I kind of fell between the generations, which is another reason Mom worries about me. Now that she has this problem with the breast lump, I think she is even more worried than usual, in spite of the fact that I am fourteen and perfectly able to look after myself when she goes away for treatment. I can even look after Dad, too, when he's not off hunting, and my ataatatsiaq, who is too old to go hunting anymore.

Aiee. I seem to have written and written and written, and I thought I had nothing to say at all.

ALISON 2
Winnipeg, Manitoba
March 14, 1999

Well now I really do have something to worry about and muttering prayers seems to have lost its effectiveness.

I can get by without a breast, but apparently that will not be the end of it, as there were several lymph nodes affected by the cancer. So we did not catch it as early as I dared to hope. I have medical training—of course I know how cancer works. Yet I can't seem to shake the feeling that my body has been invaded by malevolent extraterrestrials.

I have been completely hysterical a few times today. Maybe it is that classic fear of losing my femininity or my womanliness, although Ivaluk assures me he loves me just as much as ever. No, I think it is a sense of panic that I might actually die of this disease.

I don't want to leave Ivaluk, and Ukaliq still needs me, at least for a bit longer, I think. I just plain do not feel ready to die.

When I spoke with Ivaluk on the phone today, he was not cracking his incessant jokes but went all quiet, which is not like him at all. I told him that, if only he had married an Inuit woman, he would not be facing this problem now. He said don't be silly, but it is true. The incidence of breast cancer among Inuit women is remarkably low, while so many of us Caucasian women seem to be vulnerable to it.

I'm frustrated that the outcome lies out of my hands. If only there were a special diet or exercise regime I could follow to guarantee a cure, I would do it. But there is not. I want to rail in fury about this, but it seems all I can do is be as compliant as a lamb, be a good patient, take my pills, go to my appointments, and hope for the best.

I have asked Nancy to pray for me, because I cannot.

UKALIQ 2
Rankin Inlet, NWT
March 15, 1999

Mom is still away in Manitoba, having her surgery or tests or whatever they do in the hospitals down there. I am pretty sure she is going to be okay. I always seem to be out when she calls, and Dad doesn't say much about it. I feel if I keep writing in this diary, it is like a positive connection to her somehow, and she will be okay.

My cousin Mona says I am too traditional. She lives in Montreal now and is going to be an artist, so she wants me to be more "with it." I don't have a problem with modern things, though the drugs that have been showing up here lately scare me half to death. I saw a girl take some pills at a party and she ended up going limp, with no control over her muscles. Not my idea of fun. Maybe I am hopeless, because what I truly enjoy most is working with skins to make all kinds of traditional clothing, especially *tuktuqutit.*

Over the past few summers my Aunt Pitsiark has taught me all about how to select and prepare caribou skins for clothing, and how to prepare sealskin boots that will be 100 percent waterproof. The one thing I do that is different from the really old ways is that I use steel sewing needles. I tried the bone ones once but found them way too brittle and fragile. They are hard to make and break so often, I don't know how women used to sew new clothing for everyone in the family each year using those things.

I would rather work with skins any day than stand in front of a cash register at the Bay, bored stupid, with guys standing around making lame comments to try to win my attention.

Tuktu hairs are unusual—they are hollow like bird bones, so they trap air inside for natural insulation. Without them, we could not have survived in this Arctic climate.

I like the fall hides best. The short fur is so soft you can wear it right next to your skin, while the thick long hair of winter hides is best for the outer layer of clothing. Spring hides are a pain, because they have lots of holes where the warble fly larvae escaped, after driving the poor tuktu crazy, hatching and wriggling below their skin.

I scrape every bit of fat or blood or tissue from my hides, and then lay them out in the sun until they are perfectly dry. Then I soak them and scrape them again and again, until they are nice and soft. I even chew the stubborn spots, the way my ancestors did. Once the skins are clean and soft enough, I can cut and sew them into garments.

Different Inuit groups have different clothing styles, with the front or back flaps cut to different lengths, with or without a decorative fringe, or with different kinds of fur pieced in to make patterns, and different types of fur used to trim the hoods. You could tell which group a stranger belonged to just by glancing at his clothing.

My very favourite thing to make is the atajuq, or child's snowsuit. The way kids play, wrestling and rolling around on the ground, they can easily get snow up between their pants and jackets, so the one-piece atajuq is the answer to that problem. I cut the hood from a caribou head, and leave the ears on for decoration. I also sew the white tail on the butt, just beside the slit that is left open so the child can do its business without having to stop playing and take off the snowsuit. Little kids look adorable in them.

Mona says what I do is not art. I know that! That is why I do it mostly at the Craft Shop, where there are other ladies chatting and working with skins, making all sorts of things. I am not interested in making everyday stuff—wallets and purses and toy stuffed owls. I am more like a tailor with my own private customers, people with wage jobs who pay me good money to make traditional clothing for themselves or their kids. I have been really busy lately, because lots of people plan to wear traditional outfits on April 1.

Because of my sewing experiments, I have a big collection of traditional clothing, mostly made in small sizes. The new Kivalliq Education Department asked me to organize some kids and put on a fashion show of traditional outfits, as part of the Nunavut Day celebrations. I feel excited about that, and a little nervous.

I hope Mom will be home to see it.

IVALUK 2
From: IvalukT@arctic.ca
To: TTunu@nunavut.ca
Subject: News from Home
Date: March 18, 1999

Thomasie: Surpise- Bet you nver in wildest drams thouhgt you'd gett a e-mail message from ths old fart! Alison down south getting some medican attentipn, Ukaliq bugging me do something other than mope arond home. She toook m e to computer lab at shool and kids help me figure out all sort of things. They show me how to "surf net" and discover all kinds hunting fishing plages where I see lots of usful stuff. I evn applied for a charge card so can order myself bullets way cheaper than the Bay and good fishing lures too I never see around here.

I so enter moderm age y brother - - CANa teach old *qimmiq* new tricks) but keybroad is killling me I tinhk wwill go back to paperpen stamps for writingg you in futut ………

try to keep busy and catch up on Council paperwork some til Alison come backhome///////lov ,,,,Ivluuuuk

ALISON 3
Rankin Inlet, Northwest Territories
March 25, 1999

Dear Nancy:

It was so good to get your card, along with the photo of your "kids." I can't believe Roger and Ellen have grown up so fast, that Roger is already attending university and Ellen will be applying soon. They step out into the world so quickly, whether we are ready or not. I regret that I have never been a proper aunt to them, living so far away.

I am back home from my ordeal in Winnipeg. Needless to say, I had hoped I might get away with a lumpectomy, rather than a full mastectomy, but it was not to be. I now look like Arvaluk's stone woman—missing my left breast.

The doctors have recommended a course of radiation treatments, as well as chemotherapy. I am not looking forward to losing my hair, even though it is more grey than red these days. I will have to be away from home for many weeks, and I am not used to that, either. My family grounds me. On my last visit to Winnipeg, I felt like a boat with a broken rudder, drifting toward dangerous waters.

At least the doctors allowed me to come home for a short respite before the treatments begin, and happily this coincides with the Nunavut Day celebrations (I am enclosing some clippings about this big event, in case you have not heard about it in the papers there). I am grateful for that, but soon afterwards I will be packing my bag to go to Winnipeg for several months of therapy.

Ivaluk has no desire to travel south with me. He claims he will be most useful here, keeping an eye on Ukaliq and his father Nikmak, who seems to be growing more fragile by the day. Some moments I resent having to go south by myself, but I know he is right. He will be useful here, and I expect I will be tired a lot and not the best company.

The government offered to put me up in some kind of care facility in Winnipeg for the duration, but fortunately I have an old acquaintance who lives there, a school teacher who used to work in Rankin Inlet and taught all four of our children at some time. Janet retired to Winnipeg a few years ago, and we have kept in touch. She has been planning to take a trip to Asia this spring, and she has invited me to use her apartment while she is gone. So I will have a real home to stay in, rather than an institution, and she won't have to worry about who will pick up the mail and water the plants.

Keep in touch. All for now.

Love,

Alison

UKALIQ 3
Rankin Inlet, NWT
March 31 (Nunavut Eve!), 1999

What a busy week this has been. I'm exhausted. I have tried to at least sort of keep up with my class work, but I also want to take part in all of the fun events that are happening around the community to celebrate the birth of Nunavut, like music and dances and hockey games. This is history in the making, it will only happen once, and I don't want to miss a thing.

On top of that, I've had to rehearse and rehearse to get my "models" ready for the fashion show. Ever try herding eight-year olds? They can turn from cute to a real pain in a split second. And they cry if you yell at them, so tons of diplomacy is required. Even when one of them gets a case of the nerves and wets my best atajuq.

But the fashion show went off today without a hitch. Jancy Tiktok stumbled on the runway (I should have noticed the tail of her garment was dragging and either shortened it or picked a taller kid to wear it), but she didn't fall and the show went on. At the end, just to bring things up to date, I decided to have Jamie Karlingak model a bright red nylon jogging suit with grey inuksut embroidered around the hems and cuffs and *NUNAVUT ROCKS* embroidered across the back. Everybody seemed to enjoy that, too.

I felt so proud, as if all my efforts were completely worth it. Then the crowd in the school gym gave us a standing ovation, and my name was called out for special recognition. My parents and brothers and friends were cheering, and I could see that some people actually had tears in their eyes—that's how much they were moved by the sight of all these cute kids sporting traditional Inuit attire. I don't see how it could have gone any better.

Dad has been knocking around the house these past few weeks. He says he hasn't wanted to go hunting, in case he might get caught in a storm and not get back for the big events planned for tomorrow. But I think he wants to spend every minute he can with mom, before she has to go away to Winnipeg for a couple more months of medical care. He drove me crazy when she was away in Churchill for just over a week, so the next few months should be interesting.

Tomorrow is a community holiday. There is no school and everyone is taking the day off to have fun and enjoy the birth of our new territory. I can't wait to see Missuk and Kavik compete in the traditional games, and they have flown in a rock and roll band from Iqaluit to play for the dance tomorrow evening. I just hope the booze and drugs don't get out of hand and spoil everything. I know some people will use the occasion as an excuse to get loaded. Some kids call me chicken, but I have good reason to be scared of booze. I know where it got my Aunt Kublu and Uncle Sakku.

As for marijuana, which seems to be showing up around more and more, I have an uneasy feeling about it. I know that certain Qablunaat bring it to Rankin Inlet, so I could be wrong (and hope I'm wrong)...but sometimes I suspect that some of those packages Mona sends to Picasso from Montreal might have pot in them. She is an artist, and prides herself on being on the cutting edge and all, and she would certainly have access to drugs living in a place like Montreal. But that would mean that my very own family is involved in this thing that is illegal and can cause addiction. I'd rather not get close enough to find out for sure, and then have to deal with it somehow.

IVALUK 3
Rankin Inlet, Nunavut
April 2, 1999

Dear Thomasie (and Kublu):

I wanted to write to tell you how Nunavut Day went here in Rankin Inlet. It was awfully cold yesterday, even for April. Can't you people in the capital plan better weather for ceremonies as important as the birth day of our Nunavut?

The people started gathering outside the hamlet office about an hour before the new flag is supposed to be raised. Pretty soon they were dancing from one foot to the other and pulling their heads inside their parkas like turtles to try to keep from freezing. The ones who had a hot thermos of tea or coffee were real popular and had lots of new friends. Some had flasks of other sort of antifreeze. Five or ten minutes before the big unveiling people started to get real impatient. The teenagers were still trying to act cool and pretend their noses were not dripping icicles of frozen snot but all the babies start crying at the same time and young kids as well as some adults begin clapping their mitts and stamping their toes and yelling "C'mon, c'mon it's time it's past time! We are freezing out here—*ikii, ikkiialuu!*"

Finally at last they raise up our new flag. That shut everybody up but good. I don't know what everybody was expecting but I guess it was not the white and yellow and red thing they saw. Some people complain the flag is too plain like a child's crayon drawing but I like that it is simple. I thought right away that the white part was for a tundra full of snow with that north star up above it, and everybody saw the inuksuk right away and thought that was a pretty good feature to have there in the middle. But the red and yellow colours had the people stumped. Everyone was quiet for another minute then the jokes start up. "Oh, yeah—the yellow means don't eat yellow snow!" some smarty pants remark. "Hey, maybe that thing in the middle covered with blood predicts the revenge of the inuksut!" some body else yell. Even after someone explained that the red was for Canada and the yellow was for the gold deposits going to make us all rich in the future people still don't seem to feel too fuzzy and warm about our new flag. It still looks too much like blood and pee to some people.

I want to tell you that for me the flag seems perfect. Of course I see myself as that inuksuk in the middle—proud and strong and silent Inuk man (ha). I like the yellow and red colours too because they make me think of my niece and nephew Picasso and Mona Lisa whose middle names are those colours and so to me it is about being surrounded by my family. And then that big white presence on the right side of course is my very own Qablunaaq and guiding star Alison. And the blue in that North Star there is the same colour as her eyes. So I wanted to write and thank you and the people you work with there in the capital for creating this Nunavut flag that has such special meaning just for me.

Love,

ALISON 4
Winnipeg, Manitoba
April 16, 1999

Dearest Ellen:

Thank you very much for the get-well card you sent. It meant a great deal to me. And your letter as well. I'm glad your mum was able to find some of my old letters for you to read. I was not very much older than you are now when I first came to Canada to live in the north. You said you were especially curious to know what ever happened to those children with the unusual names: Radar, Picasso, and Mona Lisa. So I will tell you.

Radar became a bush pilot and was based in Rankin Inlet for a time, working for the same company his father used to work for. It is hard to imagine one could become bored being a bush pilot, but he grew restless and wanted more challenge. He was hired by one of the bigger commercial airlines in Canada, and they trained him to fly passenger jets. Now he flies planes all around the north for First Air. He married a stewardess he met on the job, a Metis girl who grew up near the Mackenzie River, and they now have two small daughters whom we have yet to meet. They live in Yellowknife, about a thousand miles west of here.

Picasso married an Inuit girl and started a family immediately. I should say, he started a family and then got married, as seems to happen frequently here. His wife works as a clerk at the Bay, and Picasso earns his living making ceramic pots at the Craft Shop. Their three boys sometimes help their Uncle Ivaluk feed the dog teams, so we see them lots. Mona Lisa moved to Montreal and took classes at the art school where her mother taught. She has become quite a respectable print maker and has won some grants and awards for her work. She visits occasionally, but I doubt she will ever return to Rankin Inlet to live, as she seems quite settled in Montreal now and enjoys her urban life.

You asked why people would chose to live in a place so remote and so cold. That is hard for me to answer. I could tell you about the beauty of the landscape and the warmth of the people, but words and even pictures can't do it justice. Perhaps some people (like me) are simply bitten by an "Arctic bug" or get a kind of "northern fever." Why else would a bunch of stragglers from all over the world come here, and stay, when others leave at the first opportunity, after a brief northern adventure?

I've been thinking that you might enjoy corresponding with your cousin, my youngest daughter, Ukaliq. She just got an e-mail account. I do not know the first thing about using e-mail, but you probably do, and you might know how to reach her at this odd address: U_Tunu@arctic.ca.

Love,

Aunt Alison

UKALIQ 4
To: EllenHiggins@earthlink.co.uk
From: U_Tunu@arctic.ca
Subject: Hi
Date: April 30, 1999

Ellen—what a fun surprise to hear from you. Of course Mom has talked about her sister Nancy and you and your dad and your brother—the aunt and uncle and cousins I have never met, which is totally weird since most of my relatives live right here and I see them all the time. I guess I never expected to hear anything from you. E-mail is amazing.

Kids at school are completely jealous that I have a cousin and pen pal who lives all the way over in an exotic place like England. I look forward to hearing about your life, your family, and friends, and school, and what you do on the weekends, etc. And I'll do likewise.

Yes, of course winter is cold here, but we have a curling rink that is very popular, and people are crazy about hockey. We have an indoor rink that is booked solid for games and practices all the time. People love to watch sports on TV, too. You would have thought it was a national day of mourning a few weeks ago when Wayne Gretzky, a.k.a. The Great One, played his last hockey game before retiring.

When the sun comes back and days get longer it is fun to go snow camping or Skidooing or ice fishing or cross-country skiing. It's great to get out on the land again.

Summer days are very long, the weather is beautiful, and everyone deserts the town to go out hunting and fishing and camping, to enjoy every ray of sunshine while it lasts. Then it's fall, time to go back to school and play indoor sports and visit with your friends.

Look forward to hearing from you again.

ALISON 5
Winnipeg, Manitoba
April 30, 1999

I don't know what has come over me but I have been in the worst funk these past few weeks. Perhaps I have too much time on my hands, and too much time alone while in a fragile state. Perhaps it is just the drugs and radiation.

I have had time to read the fine print on the Native Land Claims Agreement and it has made me feel utterly strange. As if my adult life has gone unrecognized and is of no value to anyone.

My husband and my children are Inuit. Because of this, they are beneficiaries of the land claims settlement, but I am not—because of my race. I know that my ancestors did not live on this land, and theirs did. But I have loved the north, and married an Inuk, and raised our Inuit children, and I have lived and worked the better part of my life in this place that we now call Nunavut. Yet none of this seems to count for anything.

My husband will have pension benefits through the Nunavut Trust, but I will not. He and my children will be able to get business loans from the trust fund, but I will not. My kids will be able to apply for grants to improve themselves, or to travel throughout the north for various purposes, but I will not—simply because I am a Qablunaaq. Of course I am happy for them, I am, but being left out in the cold personally bothers me.

I don't want to feel this way. I understand that it is the Inuit who have survived on that land for thousands of years, and my ancestors did not. It's not that I feel I am entitled to land or financial compensation or anything along those lines. I would just like to feel that my contribution is not so bloody invisible or lacking acknowledgement of any kind.

It hurts my feelings, though I try not to let it. I have had my knickers in such a knot that I have given some thought to flying "home" to England, rather than "home" to Rankin Inlet. As if I might feel more accepted there, among my own people...though I know this is utter rubbish.

I have been senselessly angry with Ivaluk, and I have been melting into hysteria again, off and on. Ivaluk keeps assuring me that all these emotions are related to my illness. He encouraged me to seek counselling, so I made an appointment to see a therapist the clinic recommended. I hope it helps.

THOMASIE 1
Iqaluit, Nunavut
May 1, 1999

Dear Ivaluk:

Sorry I have not written in a while. Yes, it has been hectic here during these first few months of Nunavut business, but that is not why I haven't written.

I am going to cut to the chase and simply tell you that Kublu and I are in love. I know this might freak you out, but let me remind you that I am your adopted brother, so I am not related to Kublu by blood in any way. I know that she is your daughter, but keep in mind that I was not around Rankin Inlet much when she was growing up, so it is not as if she grew up having me as an important uncle figure in her daily life.

I also know I am quite a bit older than she is, but that does not affect the way we feel about each other. As soon as she moved up here, we suddenly realized how much we have in common, how much alike we are, and how much unlike other people we are. We are both devoted to making Nunavut a big success, and neither of us is interested in having kids. There are plenty of kids around to love, and we don't want to spend the kind of time it takes to raise more of them, when we feel we can be most useful putting our shoulders to the wheel and getting this new territory, our homeland, off the ground and shaping it into something we can all be proud of.

But more important than any of that—we are simply and truly in love. Ever since Kublu moved up here to Iqaluit and we started spending more time together—well, it is as if I have been living my life in black and white and suddenly I can see in full colour.

We gave it a couple of months time, to see if maybe we would come to our senses and things would cool off between us. But they haven't. So I thought it was about time I wrote to tell you about this myself, and to ask for your blessing and permission to marry her, too.

I hope you will understand and accept this and be happy for us.

Love,

Thomasie

ALISON 6
Winnipeg, Manitoba
May 12, 1999

I have been feeling very tired these past few weeks and now I am completely bald. I feel that wearing a wig would be living a lie and hiding something, so instead I have been wearing a simple knit cap, in what I think might be the colours of some African nation or another. I suppose I look either stylish and avante garde, or an utter fool.

I have been to see three different therapists by now, as I am desperate to shake this state of mind I have been in. I feel terrified that I am at some important fork in the road and a wrong turn could ruin what remains of my life.

None of the therapists was any help. I ended up feeling that I should have used the fees they charge to treat myself to a lovely dinner and a glass of good wine. That probably would have calmed me down and cheered me up better than they were able to do.

The first one wanted me to talk about my relationship with my mother. "My mother might as well be dead," I told her. "I hardly have any relationship with her at all."

"That doesn't matter. I sense that she has her hooks in your back. You need to deal with these old issues," she insisted. I refused to talk about my mother. I wanted to focus on my relationship with Ivaluk, and my future, with or without him. But she only wanted to dig deeper into my denial that Mum is the source of my trauma and confusion. After a while, I walked out.

The next one kept asking me how I was *feeling*. Upset, confused, frightened? None of those words were good enough for him. He kept needling me. I'd start to describe the questions that have been on my mind lately. "I don't want to hear what you are *thinking*; I want to know what you are *feeling*. Right here, right now." He was practically nudging the tissue box my way. As if he himself could not use words as tools, use his head to think or dole out sensible advice. He was sure all I needed was a good great cry. Well, I've had enough of those on my own time. That was not what I thought I was paying him for.

The third one listened better than the other two, but as soon as I disclosed the slightest doubts about my relationship and the course I have taken in my life, my ponderings about the way of the future, she came to life and gave me lots of "feedback." She practically had the divorce papers ready. "Just listen to yourself," she said, "you are like a ship straining at its moorings. You are dying to be free of these bonds that tie you down. You are desperate to sail onto some new seas, unfettered. That man is an anchor, weighing you down. Listen to your heart, believe in yourself, and you will know what to do."

I did not know what to do. That's why I sought help. Besides, an anchor is supposed to be a good thing, is it not? I just don't want a ball and chain.

Lately I have sought escape in the television, which has only made matters worse. All the news seems awful—nail bombings, serial killers, military coups, horrific traffic accidents and tunnel fires, and children using assault rifles on one another. I find it all upsetting, so now I want to avoid the news, but it seems impossible. There is always a television on in the hospital clinic, in the doctor's waiting room, in shops, and even in restaurants. Or the person sitting next to you on the bus will have the radio on with some reporter revealing what an utter mess we have made of our lives and this planet.

I have cried and cried. Ivaluk says kind words of love and encouragement to me on the phone, but they don't seem to reach through to me. He asked if he should come to me, but I want him to stay and watch out for Ukaliq and Nikmak. And I feel that I must face these demons by myself, without leaning on him. It is my life, after all.

I have decided that, as soon as I am well enough to travel, I am going to make a trip to England. I want a hug from my Mum and my sister, and I want to meet Nancy's husband and children. What is there to lose? Perhaps a change of scenery will restore my perspective. It will cost a bloody fortune, but I have some money from selling my business. And Winnipeg, while it is by no means half way to Liverpool geographically, is in some ways half way there culturally, or psychically, or something along those lines.

I called Air Canada today and booked a ticket for three weeks hence, and I have written a note to Nancy to let her know that I am coming.

Sometimes I wonder if I didn't flee one rigid and clannish maritime culture, only to attach myself to another. Like the classic male in midlife crisis, who divorces one woman only to marry another who is an awful lot like her.

UKALIQ 5
To: EllenHiggins@earthlink.co.uk
From: U_Tunu@arctic.ca
Subject: News from the North
Date: May 15, 1999

Hi again Cousin.

Just six or eight weeks ago, I was casting about like a *qajaq* without a paddler, wondering what I should do with my life, when the fashion show happened. Now people look at me differently. They treat me as if I am a famous designer, like one trained in Paris or New York.

I've been getting lots of orders to make different things, mostly outfits for kids made from traditional materials. I figured out pretty quickly that it would take me forever to sew the things myself, so now I do the design work and I pay two older ladies in the community to do the sewing, which works fine because they are faster and better than me at sewing, anyway. Dad teases me about being a Rankin Inlet employment centre in my own right, and I know he is proud about that.

My cousin Picasso's kids have been bugging me to compose a rap song for them. They seem to think that because I can create clothing I must be a good songwriter too. Since you live in Liverpool and probably have some musical talent (like your mom), I am hoping you might give me some comments on a piece I put together for them. This is it so far:

> Skin and bone
> Snow and ice
> Rock and stone
> Had no rice
>
> Ice is nice
> Caught some seals
> Not much vice
> Had no wheels

Burned no gas
Made no steel
Had no cash
No movie deal

Snow and bone
Fur and ice
Wood and stone
Sometimes lice

Lived in snow homes
Ate some snow cones
Had no home loans
Sang our poems

Fur and stone
Snow and bone
That's all we had, man
Do you think we were mad men?

Any advice appreciated—I don't think it's ready for MTV yet, eh?

IVALUK 4
Rankin Inlet, Nunavut
May 16, 1999

Dear Thomasie:

Your letter pulled the bearskin rug right out from under me all right. But life seems to be throwing a lot of punches in my way lately.

Yes I was upset at first. My own brother wanting to marry my baby girl?

But then I think a lot about it. I realize you two are different in age but not so different in more important ways. Just like you say you two are a lot alike in many ways. Also I find a way to raise the subject with Ataata and it is water off a duck back to him. He say plenty of this sort of thing happen in the old days and not just with adopted relatives either. There was concern about it but some time it was just the best way to arrange everything and keep every one happy. If he doesn't have any problem with it then neither do I. In fact the more I think about it the more sense it makes in a lot of ways. I can see how you two more than many others might be really happy together and stick together for life like Canadian geese.

So I incline toward giving you permission but I have not talked about this with Alison yet. She is in no shape right now, drugged up and far from home. I will wait for the right time when she is back home here to talk about this with her.

Love you rascal baby stealer,

ALISON 7
Winnipeg, Manitoba
May 22, 1999

Ukaliq tried calling me several times, while I was out at medical appointments or meeting with one of those stupid therapists. When she was not able to reach me, she got help and sent a telegram, which was waiting at the door when I returned. All it said was:

Dad med evac to Churchill. Ukaliq.

I called home and Nikmak answered the phone. He spoke very faintly, and entirely in Inuktitut, and it was not the best connection, so I had difficulty understanding him. Something about Ivaluk being attacked and losing lots of blood. His garbled words seemed to confirm what Ukaliq's note had said, that Ivaluk had been taken away by air ambulance to the hospital in Churchill. I asked him to have Ukaliq or one of my sons call me as soon as possible.

I called the hospital in Churchill, and they confirmed that an Ivaluk Tunu was admitted in critical condition today, but he was not yet out of surgery, so they could not tell me anything more.

I called a travel agent to find out how quickly I can get to Churchill. There are no flights until tomorrow. I am frantic.

ALISON 8
Winnipeg, Manitoba
May 23, 1999

Dear Nancy:

I have been sitting here in southern Manitoba, feeling sorry for myself for having lost a breast to cancer, and I come to learn that my husband has lost a good portion of his left leg in some sort of accident. He is recovering at the hospital in Churchill. I have been trying to get there to be with him, but a series of spring storms have made all flying impossible for the moment. The Churchill airport has been shut down since yesterday and no one knows when it will re-open. It could be hours or days. I would get on the train, except that the tracks between here and there are built over muskeg and swamp, and the trip takes almost three days to complete.

Under the circumstances, I have cancelled my trip to England. I will write again when I learn more.

Love,

Alison

IVALUK 5
Churchill, Manitoba
May 24, 1999

Dear Thomasie:

This is like a riddle: I weigh less than I used to but I have not been on a diet.

I guess my mind has had some kind of bad thoughts lately. How else would I end up getting such a surprise visit from nanuq? Our fight did not go the way I wish but at least I am still here to tell you about it.

I borrowed Picasso's skidoo to go check my trapline. The wind had whipped the ice up into those little points that can slice the dogs' feet too easy. Also, I wanted to go quick because I had not checked the traps in a while and we got a sudden attack of nice weather, so I did not want to waste time to harness dogs and ice the runners of the qamutiik and all that. I just gas up and go.

I collected a bunch of fur from about half the traps and then it got dark so I pitched my tent and banked it up good with snow, rather than make a proper iglu for just one short night. I woke up early to that kind of wind that smells of snow and danger. Whiteout coming I thought so I pack up quick and get going on my way again. Sure enough pretty soon the steady wind is throwing up ice crystals in my face. The sky goes all white and now it is hard to tell what is cloud and what is snow. Then my skidoo takes off over a bump I did not even see. I fly a bit then land the Skidoo like a plane but the qamutiik runners stab headfirst into the ground and yank me to a stop just as the motor dies out. In the barely dawn light I now can see a pair of polar bear cubs playing around tumbling down a bank like the one I just drove over by mistake. I think for a second how much I wish Ukaliq could see these cute cubs and next I get knocked off my feet by about seven hundred pounds of force and fury. If only I had my dogs I think they would raise hell and warn me before that mother bear got close enough to strike.

Next thing I know that nanuq got hold of my leg and is trying to tear a piece off. I was too surprised to feel pain but the sight of my own blood spraying across her black lips and white teeth woke me up. I grabbed my pistol and somehow managed to get the safety off with shaking hands and shot straight into her furry face. My bullet found a way through her nose or mouth into her brain and kill that bear pretty quick. Lucky for me she fell away and not on top of me or I would still be there serving breakfast to bear cubs.

Then I look down and see that part of my leg is dangling off and lay limp next to her bloody head on the snow and blood is gushing fast out from below my knee. I want so bad to pass out and sleep but know that would be the end of me. So I wash my face in snow and crawl to the qamutiik and cut some rope and tarp to tie off that knee and tie up my leg as best I can. I cut the qamutiik loose and left it behind with all my furs and drove the Skidoo as fast as I could back to where I knew there was a mining camp out by Cameron Lake. Lucky for me there were some guys there and their radios were working. Just before my lights went out I heard them call for a helicopter to take me somewhere I can get medical help.

Next thing I know I wake up in the hospital down here at Churchill. I am alive but missing that lower part of my left leg so I guess they could not sew it back on after all. Too bad but these things happen. It hurts like hell but could of been worse. They say I am lucky I was able to get here in time for my surgery when I did.

The hospital nurses have been pretty good to me here, but I am still waiting for my very own best nurse Alison to get here. She's trying but the weather has been crap and lots of flights cancelled the past few days.

The doctor says I will have to walk with crutches for a while but then I can get a fake leg to walk on again. They say the artificial limbs nowadays are just about as good as the original, sometimes better. I don't know. Maybe this slap from a she bear is a big hint that it is time for me to give my hunting and the guiding business over to Missuk. I think maybe it is time to slow down and look at everything with new eyes and fewer legs.

That's all I can write for now.

Take it easy,

ALISON 9
Churchill, Manitoba
May 26, 1999

The Churchill airport shut down for days, just when I was most desperate to get there. I would have hired a helicopter if one had been available, but of course they were not able to fly, either. These moments when Mother Nature takes over—there is nothing to do but be patient. She is reminding us that she is in charge. So many people race around, self-important, expecting the world to revolve around them. All it takes is a flood or a fire, or a major storm, to remind us that we are not in control of everything.

I have sought solace in reading these past few days. I find it can take my mind off the demons that are tormenting me, at least for a while, and every such respite is welcome. I finished the detective novel I was reading and went looking in Janet's shelves for something to tackle next. I was impressed with her collection of books. Instead of the usual array of romance novels I am used to seeing most places I visit, she has lots of serious volumes of English and American and Canadian literature. Somewhere in one of these volumes (Robert Frost perhaps?), I came across a sentence that seemed to spill from the page into my very soul and rang so loud and so true that for a moment I felt like a complete and utter idiot:

> *You can free a train from its tracks, but then it won't go anywhere.*

How simple. How elegant. How obvious. How true. How true for me. Everything seemed to move, click into place, and come back into focus for me. I have built my life with Ivaluk. I have moved a long way along these tracks—raised four children, developed a business, lived and loved, been part of a family and part of a community. Somehow I had fallen into obsessing about all the roads not taken, instead of appreciating the one I have taken and being comfortable with the choices I have made. Of course I could have made different choices, but there is nothing wrong with my life. It is not a bad life at all, and it is my very own life, this life I have built in partnership with my husband.

Yes, I could leave him and leave the north, go back to England, or try something new. But why? Look at the damage such a derailment would wreak on him and our kids and everything we have built up together. And how long would it take to find or build new tracks of some other sort, somewhere else? And what would be the point?

I finally arrived in Churchill around 6 p.m. today and took a taxi directly to the hospital. I found Ivaluk's room with the help of the nursing staff. He was sleeping when I entered the room, and he looked so utterly pathetic against the stark white sheets that I went straight over and kissed him. He seemed very pale. His black eyelashes fluttered above cheeks the colour of new acorns in spite of the hours he spends out in the weather. He was breathing shallowly, the monitors chirping and beeping. There were a variety of tubes and lines channelling fluids in and out of him. At the foot of the bed, I could see the outline of his right lower leg and foot, but the sheets were flat where his left foot should have been.

"Darling Ivaluk I am here," I whispered, grasping his hand firmly.

UKALIQ 6

To: EllenHiggins@earthlink.co.uk
From: UK_Tunu@arctic.ca
Subject: News from the North
Date: June 30, 1999

I have felt a bit like a yoyo lately, with a lot of downs and ups. First there was mom's bout with cancer. Now it seems like she is going to be all right, although I know she still worries it might come back.

Then my dad had his encounter with a polar bear and I guess you could say he "won." He is the only person in Rankin Inlet who was ever attacked by a polar bear and lived to tell about it. But he lost his leg in the process, and he has been different ever since. More mellow and sweet to me sometimes, though he can get grumpy too. And my grandfather Nikmak seems to be going a bit deaf and blind this summer, which makes me worry about him a lot and wonder how much longer he will be with us.

I have come to realize now that mom was right—that I was feeling a bit lonely before, for people my own age. I know that because now I'm not. Having you as a pen pal helps, but then there is Rudy.

Just for fun and to get out a bit, I took a job waitressing in the café at the air terminal. The food is not that great, but people go there for the outing. As usual, there is construction going on. They are making some kind of improvements to the runway this summer. My brother Kavik has been working with the crew out there, and so has a very cute guy named Rudy Anorak, who is from Chesterfield Inlet, north of here. He has an aunt in Rankin Inlet he is staying with for the summer. Rudy is studying Engineering at the University of Manitoba now, so he is just starting the program that my brother finished a couple of years ago.

Rudy paid a lot of attention to me from the start. He would come in for coffee so many times I thought he must spend his whole shift in the Porta-potty. I could tell he liked me. He'd make jokes about how I'd have to change my name when we got married, because Ukaliq Anorak didn't have the right ring to it. When he found out my mom is British, he started calling me "UK" for short, and that caught on and now everyone is doing it.

Rudy is energetic and funny and serious and smart. He has suntanned cheeks with deep dimples in them—which I get to see often because he smiles at me all the time. He always looks flushed, as if he just ran a mile. He has a blue tattoo on the small of his back, a swirly pattern I can't describe—I'd have to draw it for you. There's an intensity in his dark brown eyes that can be spooky sometimes, but mostly it's a beautiful thing to see. We've been hanging out together quite a bit, and I find him lots of fun to be around. Summer is going to be interesting.

IVALUK 6
Rankin Inlet, Nunavut
July 26, 1999

Dear Thomasie:

We are all back home again and doing okay. We all seem to be missing something. Me my leg. Alison her breast. Ataata some of his vision and hearing. He is still singing only not so loud anymore. Ukaliq how ever is full of life. She seems to have all of her parts and has grown so pretty it is scaring me. Ever since that boy Rudy come to town she seems to walk around with a little grin on her face all the time.

If I weren't getting so old I would go work with one of the last shamans around here, learn their wisdom. Then I could do some rituals to make sure that cancer tupilaq stays away from my wife for good. Make every animal fear my name too while I am at it. Maybe then we could both sleep better and worry less about what might happen next.

I think we both realize more than before that life is precious and we should be happy to see each new day. I look at Ataata and think soon he will be gone and then there will be no generation left standing between me and death. Then I think I better make the most of every day while I still have any chances left to become a better man.

Hearing about you and Kublu growing so close was at first like a punch in the stomach that knock the air out of me. But me and Alison have talked about it now and she agrees with me. Yes you are older than our Kublu but not too much older (like you see some politicians and movie stars). Yes in some ways you are her uncle but not by blood so not such a big deal. Yes you have a lot of things in common and seem matched good for a happy life together so we say go ahead and get married.

I hear about so many men and some women who fought like you to work the land claims deal and make Nunavut happen. It seems they are all worn out, many having drug and alcohol problems and broken up marriages. Instead, you and Kublu found each other and give each other happiness and life meaning so you are very lucky that way.

We love you both and hope we see you soon.

UKALIQ 7
To: EllenHiggins@earthlink.co.uk
From: UK_Tunu@arctic.ca
Subject: News from the North
Date: September 2, 1999

I have really enjoyed having you as a pen pal these past few months. Before, when I was keeping a diary, I felt like I was talking to myself in a closet or something. Now I have a new friend, and I am getting to know my own cousin at the same time, but it is also like having a new window onto the world. You tell me stuff about Liverpool that is so strange and foreign to me, and yet it is the world my very own Anaana grew up in. I never wondered much about that place before, but now I am curious to know more about it.

fyi—the Inuit word for window is *igalaaq*, and that is also the name for the new Technology Centre we have up at the high school, which is where I am writing to you from right now. You might be interested in the Inuktitut word for "computer," as well. Obviously, these things were not around in the old days, so there is no traditional word for "computer." The word we created for it is *qaritaujaq*, meaning "something like a brain" or "other brain."

We are all hoping that the rumours about computers failing and systems crashing at Y2K will turn out to be wrong. I think we should be fine here, because all our equipment is practically brand new and state-of-the-art, so it should have been programmed with the Y2K in mind. Still, it would be a drag if, just after we finally get hooked up to the rest of the world electronically, everyone else's computers were to crash. We'd be right back in the dark.

Rudy has gone back to university. I've been trying not to miss him too much. He wanted me to go to Winnipeg with him, and I really wanted to go, but mom and dad said hell no, you are too young for that, you stay right here and finish school, young lady. You know how they can be. I am thinking about taking saxophone lessons and practicing scales in the house so they wish I had gone.

It probably would not have worked out, anyway. Rudy was a dream of a summer boyfriend, but he told me before he left that he isn't sure he wants to live in the north again, unless it is to help build the highway from Manitoba, which has been talked about for years, but which my parents and a lot of others (including maybe me) oppose. I guess Rudy is used to the city now, and he likes a lot of things about living there, though there are some things he does not like, too. I wouldn't mind seeing what city life is all about, but I can't imagine living anywhere but here, where my friends and family are and I am used to everything.

I'm pretty sure Rudy will come back to visit. If not, I guess it wasn't meant to be.

ALISON 10
Rankin Inlet, Nunavut
October 10, 1999

Here I am, over half a century old, and feeling it most days. The cancer has remained in remission, but I do not trust it entirely. I feel I have come to a time in my life when there are many snakes in the grass, and I fear they will only get thicker from here on out.

I've been dreaming about England. I am visited in my sleep by images of brick row homes with riotous gardens, but I also awake with the memory of vivid smells: fish and chip shops, gingkoes in bloom, belching buses. I am not so panicked by these dreams now. I have come to think of them as old memories that have been triggered by the recent traumas I have been through, like mud from the bottom of a pond being stirred up by a passing motor boat. I no longer feel I need to react to these images, as if they are an urgent message from somewhere that I need to run back and redo my life, or revisit old places to retrieve something important I might have left behind.

My life is here, after all. My husband and his family and our children are here. I am still here, and it is where I want to be.

Kublu called yesterday to announce that she and Thomasie will fly down here at Christmas to be married. They would like to stay and visit with us for a few days, then scoot off to Hawaii for a honeymoon week before heading back to Iqaluit. Perhaps when they return from that warm, damp, lush place of tropical splendour, they will have a better understanding of why the White men who first visited this part of the world called it the Barrenlands or the Barren Grounds. When you are used to looking at mountains and palm trees, or vineyards or orchards, the tundra can seem stark indeed, and the climate can seem very harsh and unforgiving. But if you stop comparing it to those other warm and verdant places, and take a closer look at this landscape in its own right, you can see something different—a place of subtle and exquisite beauty, coloured with the most muted palette of whites and greys and blue-greens, with occasional splashes of pink or red from the sun or certain lichens or the northern lights. It is a place that will challenge you physically and mentally and spiritually, and that in itself is something of value to hold in awe. And once you start looking closely, you see that there actually is lots of life on the tundra, from half-ton bears down to tiny bumble bees, including, of course, some remarkable human beings, so it is not "barren" at all, but full of life.

UKALIQ 8

To: EllenHiggins@earthlink.co.uk
From: UK_Tunu@arctic.ca
Subject: **News from the North**
Date: November 5, 1999

Hey, Ellen—you asked what thoughts and hopes I have for the new millennium that is about to begin. That has had me thinking quite a bit. For myself, I hope to find true love and a good career, and I'd like to have some children eventually, but that can wait a while. I want to pursue my fashion design ideas further. My sister, Kublu, gave me a hard time about this at first, but now she is okay with it. She sees that I am different from her and finally accepts that not everyone has to become a high-powered lawyer and a feminist. Actually, she will be pleased to know that I have finished a design for a man's amauti, because I think it would be a great idea if guys carried the babies around on their backs, at least some of the time. Also, now that I have a pretty complete set of traditional costumes, I want to work on designing some more modern clothes that would be good in Nunavut—made from caribou and seal and muskox or polar bear, because those are the raw materials we have to work with here and they provide the most practical and effective protection from the elements—yet more hip or trendy, if you know what I mean. I'm still thinking about whether or not I will ever go south to attend university. I've never loved school the way my sister did. Though I have a feeling it might be important to at least give it a try. Not sure.

As for my family members, I wish good health for all of them, and enough money to get by on, but not so much that they get snooty over it, which I have seen can happen. Now that I think about money, I wouldn't mind having enough of it myself to do a bit of travelling, so I could make a trip to England to visit you.

For my community, and for all of Nunavut, I'd like to see us continue to get along with each other reasonably well, and I'd like to see more economic development happen, so we have less of this Haves vs. Have Nots situation, and so there would be less rivalry over the good jobs, which seem to be too few to go around. Also, I've been thinking that maybe our community needs a better name. I know the Inuit word for this place (Kangiqliniq) is too hard for non-Inuit to pronounce, and it does not sound as pretty to me in Inuktitut as some other places that have taken new Inuit names, like Arviat or Iqaluit. I've been thinking we should have a contest to come up with a new name. If we do, I might enter Nikmavik (after my grandfather, who is an original) or maybe something based on Ivaluk, after my dad, and because his name in Inuktitut is also the word for our traditional thread that is made from caribou sinew, so it seems appropriate for a regional government centre that should be trying to hold things together.

For my country of Canada—and for the world—I want a few little things, like peace and justice and prosperity. And I'd like to see a lot more attention paid to the environment. You would think up here in the Arctic we would be far removed from pollution effects, but that is not the case. Guess where a big gaping hole in the ozone layer has ended up? Right over our heads up here in Nunavut. And the weather seems to be getting wackier each year, with the sea ice not forming properly for polar bear cubbing and the winter sealing season getting shorter all the time. I'm not saying the problems are everyone else's fault, although I do think the traditional Inuit were among the few people on earth who might have truly left "zero footprint," while factories elsewhere were belching great clouds of crap into the air that we all have to breathe. But today we burn oil and gas like everyone else; we drive snowmobiles and cars and heat our homes.

For my science project this year in school, I plan to look into alternative energy. I think some combination of solar and wind energy might be perfect for our town. We don't have much sun here at all in winter, but in summer there is so much you have to tape aluminum foil over your bedroom window to get any sleep. And there is a lot of wind around here most of the time. And we have a tide here too in the Hudson Bay, where ice packs move in and out every year, so maybe there is hope for harnessing some of that energy.

What about you? How do you see your life in the new millennium, and what do you wish for?

NIKMAK 2
Rankin Inlet
December 1, 1999

Aiyaiyayaaa.

Nuliaq—what kind of man have I become? My legs feel as weak as a newborn tuktu calf. Even with my cane they will not carry me out to your grave site one more time, so here I sit in the quiet of the settlement church to talk with you.

Our Ivaluk is home again, and so is Alison. They pay too much attention to the parts they are missing. He a leg, she a breast. These are not nothing, but they are not so important. These pieces of life and bits of flesh come and go like people in and out of an iglu. Like the people in our lives, coming and going and coming again, sometimes missing and sometimes here, then maybe gone again, yet always present somehow.

All these people coming and going, they intertwine and braid together like a rope, stretching from the past into the future. It is that rope I grab onto every day when I get out of bed. I hang onto that rope with every step forward that I take. Along this rope I can see the past stretching behind me and the future stretching out in front of me. And I know that after I am gone I will remain a part of that rope that will be there for the others who will be grabbing onto it and who are also a part of it.

With each small step I take these days, I feel as if I am walking further out onto the sea ice in spring, past where the seals are cubbing. The ice is getting thinner with each passing day and I can see the open water on the horizon now. I know that the day will come when this ice will bear my weight no longer. It will creak and groan and sink, and water will rise up to my ankles, and then to my knees, and then the thin grey layer will cave in and fold up around me, and I will sink slowly into the great bay that has sustained us. There I will meet Nuliajuk and she will let me swim for a while with the many seals and fishes and walruses that surround her. Maybe I will even see Sakku and his Skidoo down there. I will swim and swim like a seal myself until I grow too tired, and then I will ask her to show me the way to meet you again, nuliaq, so our souls can continue on their journey together.

Then we will fly side by side among the stars and swirl amidst the northern lights, until it is time for our souls to be called back to this earth, when our names will be given to newborn babies, and we will see this world once again through new eyes.

Aiyaya-yeah. Aiya.

Taima.

GLOSSARY

aakka – no

aamai – I don't know

aiviq – walrus

ajurnarmat – it can't be helped

amauti - traditional woman's parka

anaana – mother

angajuk – elder sibling (of a male or female)

angakkuq – shaman

ataata – father

ataatatsiaq – grandfather

atajuq – child's one-piece suit, typically made from soft caribou fur

aupaluktuq – red

igalaaq – window

iglu – house

iglurjuaq – modern big house, typically government staff housing

ii – yes

ikki! – how cold it is!

ikkiiraalu – it is very cold

Inuk (s.), Inuit (pl.) – a man or person, the people

inuksuk (s.), inuksut (pl.) – likeness of a person, rocks piled up to resemble a human

Inuktitut — the language spoken by the Inuit, or the way of the Inuit

isumataq – leader (literally, one who thinks)

kamik (s.), kamiit (pl.) – sealskin boots

Kangiqliniq – Rankin Inlet (Inuit name for community)

katuut – drum stick

kinauvit? – what is your name?

naammaktuq – it tastes good (literally, it's good enough)

nagligivagit – I love you

najak – sister (of a male)

najannguaq – nurse

nani nunaqapit? – where do you have land, where are you from?

nanuq – polar bear

natsiq – ringed seal
nukaqtaaq – younger brother by adoption (of a male)
nuliaq – wife
pana – wide knife used for cutting snow blocks
paniga – my daughter
panik – daughter
pijitsirniq – ability to anticipate and serve the needs of someone
Qablunaaq (s.), Qablunaat (pl.) – non-Inuit (term used for most
 Whites or foreigners)
Qablunaatitut – the language or the way of the Qablunaat
qajaq – kayak, or single person watercraft
qamutiik (s.), qamutiit (pl.) – sled made from bone and driftwood,
 usually pulled by dogs
qanuinngittunga – I am not sick
qanuippit? – how are you or are you sick?
qapsinik? – how many?
qapsinik ukiuqaqpit? – how old are you? (literally, how many
 winters have you?)
qaritaujaq – computer (literally, something like a brain)
qujannamiik – thank you
qujannamiimarialuk – thank you very much
quqsuqtuq – yellow
sabgut – long, needle-like instrument used to test snow
siksik – ground squirrel
taima -that's all, that's enough, the end
tukisinngittunga – I don't understand
tuktu – caribou
tuktuqutit -clothing made from caribou skins
tupilaq – malevolent spirit
ugjuq – bearded seal
ujamik – disc number worn around the neck or necklace
ukaliq – Arctic hare
ulu – woman's knife
uqsuq – whale blubber

ACKNOWLEDGEMENTS

I wish to thank the following people:

Bob Williamson, for igniting my passion for the Inuit and Rankin Inlet in the first place.

Tigumiaq and Saimanaakuluk Kappi, for taking me into their home and adopting me as a daughter. Theresa, Margaret, Leonie, Pelagi, Cecile, Madeline, and Caroline Kappi, for accepting me as a sister.

Ray Creery, for having faith and hiring me to be a civil servant in the Northwest Territories, and for being a terrific mentor.

Too many friends and relatives to mention (you know who you are), for reading and commenting on early drafts of the manuscript, providing constant encouragement and astute suggestions that resulted in a much improved book. Special thanks to Linda Morris for multiple reviews and constant nudging, to Mick Mallon for insisting on perfect Inuktitut, and to Richard Howell for providing assistance with Liverpudlian details.

Lynn Freed, for encouraging me to ignore what I had been taught in those writing workshops and just tell the story.

W. Somerset Maugham, for his liberating observation that: "There are three rules for writing a novel. Unfortunately, no one knows what they are."

Last but not least, Deborah Grady, for surviving my obsession to write this novel, supporting its publication, and asking what the next book will be about.

Printed in the United States
133966LV00001B/2/P